G000300717

HUNGRY, THE STARS
AND EVERYTHING

HUNGRY, THE STARS AND EVERYTHING

by Emma Jane Unsworth

Copyright © Emma Jane Unsworth 2011

First published in 2011 by
Hidden Gem Press
28 Hampstead Drive
Whitefield
Manchester
M45 7YA

www.hiddengempress.com
email: hiddengempress@gmail.com

All rights reserved
Unauthorised duplication contravenes existing laws

British Library Cataloguing-in-Publication data
A catalogue record for this book is available from the British Library

Hardback   ISBN 13: 978-0-9568026-0-6

Paperback   ISBN 13: 978-0-9568026-1-3

Printed and bound in the UK by Short Run Press, Exeter

Thanks

To my family: Frank, Lorraine and Lucie Unsworth for their love, support and patience. Also to my grandmothers, Agnes Mackie and Ann Unsworth, and in loving memory of my grandfathers, Bob Mackie and Leonard Unsworth.

To Sherry and Brian Ashworth at The Hidden Gem Press for their belief in this book and especially to Sherry, for being there from the beginning.

To the friends who have read and re-read earlier drafts: Alison Taylor, Nicola Mostyn, Maria Roberts, Sarah Tierney, Jo-Anne Hargreaves, Rebecca Murray, Natalie & James O'Hara (thanks also for the desk, you two), Sue Roberts, Greg Thorpe, Claire Beaumont, Rachel Levy, Chloe Moss, Caroline Hays, Mark Radcliffe, John Niven, Emily Powell, Stuart Maconie and the literary laser-beam that is Ms Katie Popperwell.

To my agent Clare Conville for guidance, friendship and the rum.

To all the friends and editors who have provided encouragement, support and stories, especially: Wayne Clews, Jeni Chan, Emma Collins, Clare & Oliver East, Sarah Thompson, Gavin MacDonald, Gina Garvey, Aoife Woodlock, Bill Broady, Ra Page, Jim Hinks, Nicholas Royle, Luke Bainbridge, David Lloyd, Neil Sowerby, Kevin Gopal, Lianne Steinberg, Jonathan Schofield, Annabel Meggeson, Pete Jobson and Jesca Hoop.

To Mary-Ellen McTague for menu advice and to Joe Anderson for answering my questions about astrophysicists.

To the locations that have provided writing space: Caudale Beck, Kinlochspelve (and the kindness of Pam & Andy Dawes) and the Portico Library, Manchester.

Finally to Guy Garvey, for everything.

To Guy

I was eleven years old when I realised what I wanted most out of life: *more*. This epiphany came at around 3a.m. on Christmas Eve, 1991. I checked my too-tight cartoon wristwatch, a present from my brother (bought by my mother) two Christmases ago, and then I silently made my way downstairs, holding my breath and stepping on the outer edges of the stairs to avoid the creaks.

In the living room, the fake, fairylit tree stood between the open curtains of the front window, and what seemed like a hundred presents were heaped beneath it. I instantly recognised the shape of the gift-wrapped chocolate bar, my father's annual present from my grandmother, and sat down beside it, cross-legged in my pyjamas. I'd made my decision earlier that evening: I was going to eat it.

To put it simply, I was fed up of being good. It felt as though everywhere I went – school, church, even sitting round the dinner table – I was being judged by everyone around me, mostly by teachers and parents, but sometimes by other children, too. It was as though I always had to be on my guard, always watching what I said, how I stood, or used my fork. The scrutiny was almost unbearable.

I jumped at a sudden scuffle from the dining room, and then I remembered the hamsters. The day we broke up for the holidays I had been granted temporary custody of two trembling, gingery hamsters, Mack and Beth, who usually lived in a cage in my form classroom. Because I'd been well behaved, and also because we didn't have a cat at the time, the teacher had allowed me to take the hamsters home to look

1

after them while the school was empty over Christmas. I'd initially put the cage in my bedroom, but two days later, Mack and Beth had been demoted to the dining room because my mother couldn't take the incessant racket in the early hours, what with her nerves. But Mack and Beth's nocturnal bedlam had given me an idea. Unless you had spent a night with the hamsters, you had no idea of the havoc they could wreak – by day they looked so sweet and innocent but then, as night fell, they morphed into little monsters: shredding their beds, breaking their toys, and gnawing at the bars of their cage in a bid to escape. *Aha*, I thought to myself. I had got so bored of smiling through the chores over this particular Christmas that I decided that I would try being bad for a change – very bad indeed.

My father's present was wrapped in gold paper decorated with little white asterisks – the same paper Grandma had used to wrap all of our presents. There was no bow to contend with, just a few mandatory strips of rippled sticky tape. Grandma prided herself on her unfussy approach to Christmas along with her unfussy approach to everything else. Each layer of the present came away like an old skin being shed, until the chocolate lay bare in my hands. I looked at it for a moment, appreciating its size and shape and colour. As I took a bite, the bar snapped, leaving a jagged chocolate claw in my hand.

Children aren't supposed to like dark chocolate. It's one of those bitter things that you are meant to acquire a taste for later in life, like olives and self-pity. But I was different. I enjoyed the taste of wrongness in my mouth, the sheer devilment of what I was doing. After I'd eaten the whole bar I sucked each finger, wiped my mouth and licked the side of my hand where more wet chocolate had gathered. Then I cocked my head to one side while I composed my thoughts. It wasn't as sweet as the chocolate I'd had before, but it was *interesting*. It tasted like metal, dirty water, soil: the makings of a new world.

I stood up by the tree and, as I was batting splinters of chocolate from the legs of my pyjama pants, something caught my attention through the window.

Halfway down the driveway I could see a ghoulish green light spinning up and down. It seemed to gather speed as it dropped, and then, just as it looked as if it would hit the ground, it was pulled sharply upwards. The light would flicker and then it descended again. I strained to see what it was, utterly mesmerised.

It had been snowing on and off a lot throughout that December, so as the green light dropped low, the white, powdery ground glowed peppermint, and then as it whipped up again, the light momentarily illuminated the outline of a figure: the bottom corner of a trouser leg, a cat's eye cufflink, a jacket tail.

I could see that the figure was that of a young man and the light beside him was coming from a glow-in-the-dark yo-yo. As the steady stream of light from the yo-yo continued to rise and fall, I saw more details: a pinstripe suit, a stiff white shirt, a hat with a band of ribbon round it, a tie with a knot that looked too wide. The man was dressed like one of the Rat Pack singers my grandmother had been cursing that very evening. *Womanising gangsters*, she'd said, as Frank Sinatra, Dean Martin and Perry Como had larked about on the swing music showcase I'd insisted on watching, *look at their evil little shark eyes*. This man was dressed like those singers but he didn't look like a womanising gangster to me – he looked suave and sophisticated, like someone I would want to know. And then I noticed something else. Where the man's shirt cuffs ended, I saw flashes of red skin, burnt and sore-looking, like my mother's fingers when she picked them round the nails. I looked up to his face and saw it was heart shaped with sharp cheekbones, and his lips were impishly lopsided. Finally, either side of his trilby hat, two red horns protruded, their rude silhouettes spiking thornily against the moonlit sky.

I blinked, and he was still standing there. I blinked a second time, and when I saw him there still, I felt a wide smile spread slowly across my face. There he was, for real, and as gorgeous as anything. There – among the constellations of the tree lights reflected in the windowpane, the monstrous privets, the looming rhododendrons, the dark, the night, the great beyond – the devil himself was leaning against my mother's freshly waxed Austin Maestro, playing with a yo-yo on a string.

I stayed still and quiet until finally he looked up and we locked eyes, and I felt a strange feeling in my stomach, as if my guts were yawning open. I didn't want to look away but when I felt my right palm prickle I unclenched my hand to see the birthmark there, pink and straggly as a lace of raspberry liquorice, stretching from the base of my middle finger to the bottom of my palm. I had been teased about the birthmark at school and had scratched it until it had bled, trying to remove it, desperate to be the same as everybody else. My grandmother hadn't helped. The one and only time I'd let her read my palm she had recoiled, exclaiming: *Look at that monstrosity, right over your lifeline! I can't imagine that's a good omen.* Now the birthmark glowed like a crack in a hot coal. I looked up again and felt the voltage shoot between my eyes and his, and I realised I was totally unafraid. More than that, I was *interested*. He waved at me and tipped his hat.

'Pleased to meet you,' I whispered, and the sound of my voice fluttered around the quiet room.

I chose to forget all the times my grandmother had told me that the devil was involved in terrible things: the details, the deep blue sea, rock 'n' roll. I stood there, thunderstruck in my pyjamas, and I felt my mouth stretch into a wide grin.

4

Then, in a puff of thick grey smoke, he disappeared.

I ran to the window and pressed my palm against the icy pane, straining to see him on the street, at the corner, anywhere, but he had disappeared without a trace, and the world opened up again into a dull, excluding place. I ran out of the room to the front door and turned the key in the lock as quickly as I could, but when I opened the door all I was greeted by was a blast of snow-scented air. I felt bereft, as though something tempting had been offered to me and then snatched away. I lingered, hoping that he would reappear, and then as I looked down I saw the yo-yo lying, lifeless, on the doorstep. I bent down and picked it up, passing it between my hands, loving its coolness and roundness. I looked up one last time into the hollow night, and then I closed the door and made my way up to bed.

The next morning, as my family sat round the tree, I kept quiet about what had happened the night before.

'I'm sure I put it just *here*,' said my grandmother, rooting through the presents under the tree.

'Never mind, love,' said my grandfather. 'I'm sure we'll all be eating enough sweets over the next few days!'

My grandmother, who was never impressed by my grandfather's optimism, stopped hunting and turned to face me. I occupied myself with my stocking, which was stuffed with satsumas and walnuts, and tried to disguise the fact that my cheeks were flushing red.

'That's very odd,' my grandmother said, and I knew she was still looking at me, 'very odd indeed.'

I widened my eyes and said nothing, because my grandmother had an uncanny knack of seeing right through me. Sometimes I felt she knew me so well that it was as though she had stolen a part of me. She had grown up where the air was damp, in a town to the north called Burnley, and had started working at a cotton mill when she was just thirteen.

I can see her now, bellowing over the rattling spools in that over-enunciated Lancashire way of talking, lip-reading her co-workers' stories over the thundering looms. She read the other girls' palms in the toilets on her lunch breaks, telling them what to do with their lives, and so rumours flew around the mill that she was a witch – rumours she did nothing to quash. At times like this, the best thing to do was to avoid eye contact with Grandma so I continued to pretend to be engrossed with a walnut. After a few seconds she turned her attention back to her own presents, and nothing more was said about the missing chocolate.

When I'd finished opening my presents – a flash camera, a palette of eye shadow, a cassette tape – I got up to kiss my parents to say thank you, but I felt a distinct lack of excitement about Christmas. I looked out and saw the empty space on the driveway where the devil had stood the night before and a pang of loss shot through my stomach. It felt like hunger but not for food, and I didn't know what the hunger was for, but I knew that whatever it was, I wanted more. As I kissed my mother on the cheek she grabbed hold of my wrist and raised it high for everyone in the room to see.

'What we should have got you was a new watch,' she said, prodding the bulging skin around the thin black strap.

She had a strange look on her face, a look of easy triumph, and I didn't like it, so I tilted my chin and said: 'What I *really* wanted was a glow-in-the-dark yo-yo.'

'What?' my mother snapped, and I could tell immediately that I was onto something. I thought of the yo-yo secreted in my jewellery box under the loose floorboard in my room, and I grinned inwardly.

'A glow-in-the-dark yo-yo,' I said, shooting her a sly glance as I walked over to my father and kissed him on the forehead. 'I put it on my list, remember?'

'You're an ungrateful girl...' my mother began. Then she turned to my father. 'I told you to bury it in the park.'

My father looked down at his slippers. My grandmother smirked. I wondered what more would be said.

'You buried a *yo-yo*?' said my seven-year-old brother, a smear of caramel across his chin. He had been steadily working his way through a selection box.

'It was radioactive, Benjamin,' said my mother. 'There was a warning in the paper. They advised people to bury them.'

My brother shrugged and carried on eating.

My mother unwrapped her dressing gown to reveal her flame-retardant nightdress and then wrapped the gown around herself again, only tighter. 'Fancy bringing that up when you've got so many other presents. I hope you're not planning on ruining Christmas, Helen.'

I blinked but I didn't say anything. As it turned out, I did ruin Christmas.

As we sat round the tinsel-strewn table in the dining room I watched the TV out of the corner of my eye. Marlon Brando was stalking around New Orleans in *A Streetcar Named Desire*. I thought he looked cool in his tight white t-shirt, but I still couldn't get the devil out of my mind. *If only I could make him come back*, I thought to myself as I watched my grandmother sway in her seat and then straighten up as my father put another vermouth on the coaster next to her plate. My grandmother nodded and her grey perm crackled against her paper hat.

'God's drink, that,' she slurred. 'Nice and sweet.'

'Do you want another drink with your dinner, love?' my father called to my mother in the kitchen.

'Gin and slimline!' my mother shouted back, her voice barely audible above the rumble of the cooker hood.

All my mother ever drank was gin and slimline tonic. *Practically zero calories*, she would say proudly.

When she marched in a few minutes later carrying the turkey, she was red-faced and sweating. She plonked the thick foil platter down on the table and the turkey bounced a few times before rattling to a standstill.

'Who wants to carve?' said my mother, snatching her drink from my father's hand and collapsing into a chair. She drank half the gin and tonic in one gulp.

'I will!' said my grandmother.

But before she could reach for the knife, one of the hamsters scampered out from its ratty den and began to sip water from the bottle attached to the side of the cage, the ball-bearing rattling against its hard little teeth.

'I THOUGHT I TOLD YOU TO MOVE THOSE FILTHY LITTLE CREATURES OUT OF THE ROOM BEFORE DINNER!' my mother blasted.

'Alright, alright,' I said, walking over to the cage and picking it up, feeling the tiny weight of the hamster travel from one side of the cage to the other as it ran back across the plastic base on its little tip-tapping paws. As I carried the cage into the lounge and placed it beside the TV, I whispered through the bars: 'I only wish I could join you in *there...*'

There was silence back in the dining room. My father was over by the hulking Welsh dresser, pretending that he was busy making drinks. I watched him drop four ice cubes into a glass, take two out, and then put one back in again – anything to avoid getting involved in a conversation. I looked round at the rest of my family: at my mother who was staring, vexed, at the wall, at my grandmother who was hiccupping, at my grandfather humming to himself, and finally at my brother, who was leering like a gargoyle at the burnt turkey.

'Looks a bit dry, that turkey,' my grandmother continued. Liquid swooshed out of her glass as she swung her hand in the direction of the platter. 'Still, a sharp enough knife should get through it.'

I felt my mother's stare intensify until it was almost burning a hole in the wall. My father opened a drawer of the Welsh dresser. I knew if he had been smaller, he would have crawled inside it.

'I'm starving,' said my brother, oblivious to the tension in the room.

'Someone needs to carve the bleeding turkey then,' said my mother.

'I said I'd do it didn't I,' said my grandmother, leaping up and grabbing the carving knife. My mother didn't move. *Please come back*, I appealed to my devil, in my head.

My grandmother plunged the carving fork into the turkey and hacked off one of its legs, hurling it over onto my mother's plate where it landed with a clatter.

'Thank you, Emily,' said my mother, her lips tight and bloodless. *She won't be able to eat any of that*, I thought. *It's all skin and fat.*

'Pass your mother the gravy, Ben,' said my grandmother, in full matriarchal flow, before resuming her attack on the blackened bird.

My mother shook her head at Ben and waved the gravy boat away.

'Breast, Jonathan?' my grandmother said to my father.

'Er, yes – yes please,' muttered my father, still by the dresser, fumbling with the corkscrew as he tried to open a bottle of red wine.

Please, I said again, loud as I could in my head, and quick as a flash the devil appeared in the leaded glass door of the dresser. He was wearing a t-shirt and a leather jacket, and smoking a cigarette – inside the house! I felt a searing heat travel along my birthmark. I looked around at my family but it was clear that I was the only one who could see him. He smiled as he exhaled smoke into the back of my grandmother's hair – and then it happened. The carving knife slipped across the hard turkey skin and sliced straight into the top of my grandmother's other hand as she clutched the handle of the fork. Within seconds, blood was seeping out around the blade and dripping down onto the table.

My grandmother didn't scream or cry, she just looked at her hand and calmly said: 'Well, I've made a right pig's ear out of *that*.'

Just as quickly as he'd appeared, my devil disappeared – not in a puff of smoke, but in a barely detectable flick of red glitter.

My grandmother's hand was bleeding badly and had now saturated a plate-sized patch of holly-patterned paper tablecloth. My grandfather was standing up, shaking his hands and saying: *Emily, you shouldn't have had so much to drink!* My mother, who always came into her own in times of actual crisis, jumped up to fetch a tea towel from the kitchen, which she wrapped in a tourniquet around the injured hand.

'Jonathan, car keys! Helen, the candles!' my mother yelled, before dashing to the cupboard under the stairs to yank our coats off their hooks.

I sat in the back seat of the car on the way to the hospital, repeating the word *Thanks* in my head, over and over. At last, I thought, I had found an ally, someone I could be truly honest with about my feelings – and he would come whenever I called. I discreetly uncurled my palm and looked at my birthmark; that unsightly brand I'd always hated so much, I'd always seen it as a mark of difference, now I saw it as a mark of distinction. It *was* a lifeline, after all.

Vintage champagne

I turn the polished brass doorknob and the freshly painted door, its glass panel warped with age, opens with a little jingle. I shake my umbrella as I step inside, wishing I had a proper raincoat. How have I managed to live in Manchester so long and never buy a proper raincoat?

'Here, let me take that for you, madam,' says a smartly dressed man with slick dark hair. 'Welcome to Bethel.' His voice is heavily accented. A maître d' with a French accent. Perfect.

'Thank you.'

'May I take your jacket, too?'

'Yes, please.'

I shrug it off and hand it to him, along with the umbrella. He hangs the jacket on a hat stand next to the door and places the umbrella on the floor beneath it.

'Do you have a reservation?'

'I do.'

'What name is it, please?'

'Charlotte.' It is a lie that I am used to telling.

He walks over to a wooden lectern and runs his finger down the left hand side of a large open book.

I look around and my first impression is that the décor is slightly incongruous. The red leather booths are too erotic for a converted chapel; they look out of place among the chunky wooden tables and fat, creamy church candles. However, the details I've come to expect from an ambitious establishment are all in evidence: the white table linen is starched and ironed, the napkins are rolled up like snail-backs, the silverware has

11

been polished so thoroughly that I imagine I'd be able to see my face in every spoon. Abstract artwork is splashed across the walls, and on the long sideboards velvety red flowers laze in wide vases, the glass so thin that it is almost invisible. To the left, the optics and bottles of the bar twinkle behind a bartender straining a cocktail into a glass. In the far right corner of the room, the porthole window in the kitchen door is misted with condensation. As I stare, hoping for a glimpse of the chef, a waitress emerges. I turn my attention back to the maître d' in time to see him tap the book and raise his eyebrows.

'Ah, yes, here we are. Table for one?'

'That's right.'

He looks me up and down. In restaurants, lone diners are generally regarded with suspicion: they're either sociopaths or, worse, Michelin inspectors. I don't flinch. I stare right back into his eyes. His pupils flicker with distant candlelight.

'Would you care for a complimentary glass of champagne while you look at the menu?' he asks.

'How do you mean, complimentary?'

I'm always on my guard for preferential treatment. I like to remain as discreet as I possibly can, which is why I usually bring along a companion when I'm reviewing. I don't use a notepad and I refuse to have my photo printed in the paper. I've been in a few sticky situations where I've had a "complimentary" bottle of wine forced onto me, which I felt I couldn't drink. One time a manager overheard my dining companion using my real name, he put two and two together and refused to let me pay the bill. I had to hide a wad of cash inside a used napkin. (I called shortly after I left to warn them before they washed it.) It's crucial that the experience I assess is the average experience – the one any diner could expect, warts and all.

'The champagne is how we like to welcome our guests,' says the maître d'. 'It's company policy,' he adds, when I look unconvinced.

'In that case, yes please.'

The maître d' nods to the bartender and picks up a menu. 'Please.' He gestures to a white, wrought iron bistro table by the window. I walk over and take a seat. He hands me a single page: the day's menu. The menu is printed in looping black font on thick cream card. There is a small à la carte section and a tasting menu: £90 for eleven courses with wine. Such a short menu suggests confidence, arrogance even – it says: *I know what you want, even if you don't know that you want it yet.* It's a bold move and, almost in response, I roll up my sleeves.

'Is the head chef cooking tonight?' I ask when the maître d' returns with my champagne.

'Of course.'

'Can you please tell me his or her name?'

I'm pleased with myself for slipping the question in so seamlessly, but then the phone on the front desk springs to life with an old, rattling ring and the maître d' rushes over to answer it.

'Excuse me,' he mouths and then loudly down the phone, he says: 'Good evening. Bethel.'

I reach for the champagne but then I hear my own phone start to ring. I pull it out of my bag to see that it is Keith, my editor.

'Hello?' The restaurant is so quiet that I feel the need to whisper.

'Helen?' Keith's voice is posh and punchy.

'Keith?' I say, as though I haven't just read his name on the screen before accepting the call.

'Yes, it's me. Did my name not come up? I'm calling from my mobile.'

'Well,' I say, 'I'm shy.'

'Shyness is a form of vanity, Helen.'

This is the way Keith and I talk to each other. You couldn't really call it a conversation; it's more like firing rockets into the air.

I see the lines of champagne bubbles streaming up from the bottom of the flute and I feel suddenly impatient. 'What do you want, Keith?'

'Are you at Bethel yet?'

'I've just arrived.'

'Any word on the mystery chef?'

'Give me a chance, would you?'

'He's got to have a history.'

'Or she,' I counter.

'Radical.'

I'm still staring at the champagne. 'Is that it?'

'Yes,' says Keith, but I can tell that it isn't.

'Did you take a friend in the end?'

'No.' I think of Pete at home on the sofa with his plate on his lap, and I feel slightly guilty. 'I came alone.'

I hear an intake of breath at the other end of the line. 'That's just a waste of good company,' Keith says, and then he takes another breath. 'I can jump in a taxi... be there in thirty–'

'No, Keith,' I interrupt. 'I'd like to fly solo, if you don't mind. I could do with the thinking time.'

I hear him take a sip of something and I realise that he has probably been drunk since lunchtime, as usual.

'I understand,' he says, trying hard to sound casual. 'Well, Helen, you know I'm here...'

'I do,' I said. 'I'll have copy to you by eleven tomorrow. Bye, Keith.'

I hang up the phone and push it deep into my bag.

I look at the glass of champagne. The flute is cool and slender, frosted, beckoning. 'Come on, then,' I think. 'Impress me.' I pick up the glass by the stem and take a sip. It's good. I take another sip. It's *really* good. I draw back from the glass and hold it up to the light. Elegant and intense with a long finish, I think, surely vintage, and very expensive. This can't be the free stuff; they must have made a mistake when pouring it – there has been some kind of unfortunate bottle-switch behind the bar, but in this instance I am not honest enough to question it. I drink greedily before anyone notices, tipping the flute steadily, closing my eyes.

* * *

'*Champagne* is a drink for *winners*.'

I turned to look at Pete.

'I think you might be right,' I said, smiling at him and raising an eyebrow.

We clinked our glasses and took clumsy sips of champagne.

'Game over, Cupid,' said Pete and I laughed.

It was our five-year anniversary. We had celebrated the occasion with a bottle of bubbly and a new thirty-seven inch TV. Pete cooked a three-course meal and we sat up late together, watching TV and giggling about the fact we were drinking champagne on our own sofa at home. It felt just like an anniversary should feel: nostalgic, reassuring and slightly silly. I felt full of contentment and full of love for Pete.

I took another sip of champagne and sank back into the sofa. We were watching a programme about Jocelyn Bell Burnell, the British scientist who discovered pulsars back in 1967. Pulsars are dying stars, suns of the past, dense with age and gravity. They emit a powerful beam of radiation as they rotate, which to a static observer appears as a flash, like the lamp of an abandoned lighthouse. No one even knew that pulsars existed until Bell Burnell spotted a sequence of equally spaced peaks on the chart-recorder papers of the radio telescope she was helping to construct at Cambridge. The peaks on the graph seemed to amount to a pulse. *Things don't pulse in space*, thought Bell Burnell.

'Smart lady,' said Pete, draining his glass and feeling around on the floor for the bottle.

'I think she's my new hero,' I said, picking the bottle up from next to my foot and handing it over to him without looking away from the TV. I was transfixed.

We had eaten our dinner on our laps, which was unusual for us but we were so excited about the new TV that the dining room had seemed dull by comparison. We watched back-to-back documentaries, shouting *More!* each time one ended. By the time we got to Bell Burnell, I sensed that we would definitely have to call it a night – not just because of the time, but because nothing was ever going to better her story. We had hit an emotional apogee.

'Brilliant,' I said, 'just brilliant.'

'Mm.'

Pete helped himself to another peanut from the bowl on the marble-topped side table. I motioned for him to pass the bowl of nuts and shovelled a handful into my mouth without looking away from the screen. A peanut fell down the front of my scoop-necked top and I ignored it.

Bell Burnell changed the shape of modern science when she discovered pulsars. At first she couldn't believe her own eyes when she saw the data. What could pulse in that way, at exactly the same frequency? Extra-terrestrial communication seemed the most likely explanation, and how *unlikely* was *that*? But there it was. *Pulse pulse pulse pulse pulse*: a beating heart at the back of beyond. Not only did Bell Burnell's fellow students not believe her, they didn't want to. Her thesis supervisors excluded her from meetings and discussed destroying the data because they didn't want to risk it getting into the news. What if the pulses were signals from an overcrowded alien planet seeking to invade? Even if the data did compute, which it didn't, it could shake the world. So what did Bell Burnell do? She found another pulsar, on the other side of the universe.

'Brave lady,' said Pete.

I rubbed my thumbs against the balls of his feet through his slippersocks, which were flopped across my lap. I suppose in a way I was telling him to be quiet. It was one of those coded actions that couples do when they have been together a long time and know each other well. Similarly, Pete could touch me gently on the shoulder at a party and I would know that he was telling me to calm down, to not drink so fast. Or I could curl my toes around his in bed and he would know that I was telling him that I loved him.

If we assume we've arrived, we stop searching, said Bell Burnell, her glasses reflecting the camera light and twinkling for a split-second.

'Is that a famous quote?' said Pete.

I rubbed his feet harder.

'Ouch,' he said, 'too hard.'

'Sorry, I'm just interested in *this*.' I nodded at the TV.

'Sorry.'

'It's okay.'

Pete started to edge up off the sofa.

'Where are you going?' I said, hoping he wasn't going to move into my line of sight.

'To get us both a glass of water. We're probably dehydrated after all that booze.'

'Want me to pause it?'

'It's okay, I'll catch up.'

'No, I'll pause it. This is amazing, you don't want to miss it.'

As I pressed pause the image of a radio-telescope, bleached white in bright sunlight, was frozen on the screen.

'Great,' said Pete.

'Here,' I said, 'I'll bring these through.' I picked up the empty mugs and plates from the floor and followed him into the kitchen.

The hall was bright and minimal, like the rest of the house – a three-bedroomed semi in a leafy southern suburb of Manchester. We had bought the house four years ago from a couple in their sixties whose children had grown up and moved away. The couple were looking to move somewhere smaller and more manageable. On our second viewing I knew that Pete was thinking the same thing I was: we'll be in exactly the same position in thirty years. So we offered the asking price and they accepted.

Our kitchen was modern but comfortable, with just enough farmhouse touches to not look twee. Out of all the rooms in the house, the kitchen felt like the part that was most alive: warm, moving and visibly growing. Pete picked up a new gadget whenever he ventured into town and for his birthday he asked everyone for vouchers to buy expensive knives and pans. I had scoured the racks and rails of charity shops and car boot sales and had amassed a classy yet eclectic collection of retro crockery.

For once though we hadn't cleaned up after dinner. Pots and utensils littered the work surface, surrounded by blobs of sauce and soapy shavings of lemon rind. Usually we loaded the dishwasher immediately after dessert, but that night we had given ourselves the excuse that we were celebrating. Pete had made chicken tagine with preserved lemons, which had left its traces in the air of the kitchen with a faint tang of stewed citrus. That day Pete had headed straight home after the lunch shift and had started making the tagine from scratch, first slicing onions into translucent half-moons, then hacking chicken quarters in half with a cleaver. The other chefs Pete worked with said they could never be bothered to cook properly for themselves at home – they ate microwave meals and packets of ready-made pasta. I knew that Pete cooked for me as a way of pleasing me, even though I sometimes said that I liked things more than I did because I was so grateful for everything he did, and because sometimes I felt guilty for not doing more of the cooking.

'You're a team,' my friend Kate always reassured me. 'It's give-and-take. You do give too, you know, Helen.'

The truth was I hated cooking and was much happier with my side of the bargain: shopping and laundry. Meanwhile, despite the fact it was also his trade, Pete relished his role as domestic demigod. He could open a clamshell and fillet a fish, pluck a pheasant and debone a rabbit, he made his own pastry and stock, and then he froze the surplus for rainy days. He strained, pared, whisked, emulsified, whipped and deglazed. He grew his own tomatoes in plastic sacks of compost by the back door and kept a miniature hedgerow of fragrant herbs in a trough on the kitchen windowsill. We threw very little away because he had such a creative way with leftovers.

'He's a *feeder*,' Kate always joked, but "feeder" struck me as an unkind term. It turned something like love into something like hate.

Pete rinsed the cast iron tagine base and slid it into the bottom of the dishwasher.

'Shall we clear all this now then?' I asked, following his lead and picking up a plate, but hoping he would say no so that I could get back to the documentary.

'I suppose we should... still, if we've left it this long, it won't hurt to leave it until tomorrow.'

Tomorrow was Sunday. We usually took a drive out somewhere in the countryside in the afternoon. We could clear up in the morning and still have time to read the papers.

'I was hoping you'd say that.'

I put the plate back down on the pile. Pete set the tap running and I opened the cupboard and took out two tumblers.

Pete reached into the freezer for the ice and then I held the glasses out while he filled them, firstly with ice and then with water.

Once we were settled back on the sofa I pressed play on the remote control and the documentary continued.

It took Bell Burnell's superiors a long time to accept that she had discovered a new type of star, and even then she was denied the Nobel Prize, which was instead claimed by two of the very professors who had wanted to burn her data.

'It's because she was a woman,' said Pete, who like me considered himself a feminist.

'It's not just that,' I said, swallowing a slug of water. 'That's the way it works in research. The supervisors get the grants, so they get the credit regardless of who makes the discovery.' Pete looked at me curiously. 'And people *fear change*,of course,' I said quickly. 'Having your mind blown is a messy business.'

There was a pause and I sensed Pete's tidy mind flitting back to the state of the work surfaces.

'Maybe we *should* clean up tonight,' he said.

'Maybe we should. What do you think?'

'I don't know. What do *you* think?'

'I think I'm probably too tired to think about it right now.'

Monochrome end credits rolled up the TV. I scrutinised the remote, found the right button and the screen went to black. A tiny red standby light glowed on the base panel.

'Bedtime?' I said.

Pete finished his glass of water and smacked his lips.

'Yep.'

I stood up and dimmed the living room lights. Pete gathered his phone and wallet from the arm of the sofa where he always lined them up. I picked up my glass of water and followed him out into the hall. He went up the stairs ahead of me and turned on the landing light when he reached the top. I stopped by the front door. Balancing my glass of water in one hand, I locked the door and pulled out the keys. The keys would sit on my bedside table all night, just as Pete's wallet would sit on his.

Then for some reason I turned off the hall lights before I walked up the stairs, even though it was quite dark without them. I don't know why I did it. It wasn't exactly a sensible thing to do and I instantly almost tripped. But I kept my head up and my eyes forward, my free hand grasping along the rail to my right, the keys jangling in my pocket as I lurched uncertainly up each step. I headed towards the dim bedroom lamplight, a creeping sulphurous orange along the floor of the top hall, where it was escaping from beneath the bedroom door.

Spam fritterati

The champagne must have gone to my head. I'm feeling woozy and slightly sick. As though he can read my mind, the maître d' returns and deposits a dish of little beige-coloured sticks on the glass surface of the wrought iron bistro table.

'What are these?' I ask.

'Spam fritterati.'

'Cute.'

He coughs and widens his eyes. 'Are you ready to order, madam?'

'I'll take the taster menu, please. And a jug of tap water.'

The maître d' smiles, nods briskly and then glides away. I look up to the rafters in the roof, sloping down over either side of the room like a gigantic rib cage. Inside, the remnants of the converted chapel are harder to spot than they are from the outside. I stood outside Bethel for ten minutes before I made my entrance, sizing up the new restaurant from the other side of the Bridgewater Canal. The restaurant's wide, pointed windows and arched doorway created a centre point of calm on the Castlefield waterfront, amongst the cluttered warehouses and squat, florid office blocks. In fact, the more I looked at it, the more Bethel looked so out of place that it was as if it had fallen from the sky.

I look down at the dish of nibbles on the table. I'm not particularly hungry, but I know that food will calm me down. It will balance my blood sugar. The fat molecules will absorb the toxins of the champagne. The nibbles are golden brown, blistered with heat. I pick one up and toss it casually into my mouth. The batter is dry and crunchy – twice-fried if I'm not mistaken. The meat inside is pink and soft, salty, melting.

* * *

'Posh prison' was my grandmother's nickname for the grammar school I attended, but I knew instinctively that this was only because she was jealous. She was a smart woman who felt as though her intelligence had been wasted with mere millwork and motherhood. *You're a very lucky girl*, my grandmother said every time I told her how much I hated school, and I detected more than a shade of envy in this.

The school uniform was blue and grey – the colours of depression. I was on a scholarship as my father was only a deputy manager at a packaging factory, which meant that my blazer was second-hand. I tried to ignore the comments from the older girls as I walked to and from assembly, but there was no respite from the competitiveness – hordes of clever girls jostling for position created a tense environment potent with bullish ambition. I tried my best to be self-contained but it was hard work, harder than the lessons.

'Who's your favourite, Helen?' said Kimmy Lennox, the hardest girl in the year, prodding her meal of Spam fritters, chips and beans around her plate. Spam was on the menu at school at least once a week and the other girls hated it, but not me. My mother disliked cooking so much that meals at home were pretty diabolical so I looked forward to everything in the canteen – even the stuff that everybody else detested. My love of school dinners was yet another thing that isolated me from the other pupils but I had stopped caring because I had a new best friend. The devil and I were becoming thick as thieves. I summoned him regularly, always feeling my palm prickle just before he arrived and the pang in my stomach when he went away again.

I was eating lunch with the netball team. Well, when I say 'with', I mean we were sitting at the same long marble-effect plastic table. I was reading *Wuthering Heights*, holding the floppy library book open between the cruet set and a water jug. Even though I was only twelve I was thickening at the hips and thighs into a precocious pear shape. I wore large, NHS-issue blue-rimmed glasses to go with my unconditioned mousy hair, which was usually petrified with static. I looked up from my book and glanced over to see that the netball team had spread a teen magazine with a double-paged poster of a new boy band between their trays of untouched food.

'So who do you like, then?' said Kimmy. The other girls smirked. I knew it was some kind of test but really I didn't have a clue about the band. Fresh-faced boys did nothing for me.

'The cute one,' I ventured.

'There isn't a cute one,' sneered Kimmy.

'The funny one then.'

'Nope.'

'The *tall* one?'

I heard one of Kimmy's minions whisper audibly in her ear: 'She can't *afford* magazines, that's why she doesn't have a favourite...'

I felt anger stir in the pit of my stomach. They knew I wasn't interested in pop stars or footballers. All they knew about me was that I covered my textbooks with Anaglypta wallpaper and coloured in the scuffs on my shoes with black marker pen. *Shall I call him here now, and damn you all?* I thought to myself, toying with my fork.

'Look, there's Mr Jackson!' Kimmy shouted, standing up. 'Let's go and make him blush!' Skirts whirling, the netball team abandoned the table and ran towards the Design & Technology teacher, who had his head down and was attempting to exit the canteen as quickly as possible.

Later that afternoon I sat in double Geography, skimming a rollerball over my fingernails so that it looked as if I was wearing black nail polish. My desk was next to the window and I often found myself staring out towards the motorway, where cars and lorries glinted like shiny beetles, and rows of tall grey Y-shaped streetlights split into two against the sky, like birds drawn by a child.

My form teacher, Mrs Robertson, set impossible challenges and hurled condemning threats at us about our future: *You will run a chip shop for a living if you're not careful, missy* – that kind of thing. I hated her with every fibre of my being. On this particular afternoon her chosen torture was to grant us just thirty seconds to locate Cape Cod on a map of the USA. I put down the rollerball and began to panic. The map ran across ten pages in the textbook so without a decent grasp of the layout of North America, I knew that my chances of success were limited. I couldn't help but think the task was biased in favour of the better-travelled girls. So, I cheated.

I had the good luck to be seated next to Claire Pilkington – who as well as being pixie-cute had a mother who taught in the kindergarten and a father who worked in offshore banking. Claire had been everywhere. After every half-term she boasted about hot holidays abroad in five-star villas, often with a resident cook. She told of barbecues packed with top-and-tailed sardines, of drilling holes into giant green coconuts, of tomatoes shaped like plums, of chicken-on-a-stick with peanut sauce. I was enthralled by her tales. One time, on holiday in Cyprus, she said she'd seen a pelican eat a pigeon on Paphos harbour. She could see the pigeon's wings fluttering through the pelican's thin neck skin as it swallowed. Claire had been so traumatised by this that whenever a pigeon came in the playground she covered her eyes and screamed. 'That'll make it worse,' I'd say. 'Only memories in there.' But I was jealous of her exotic experiences, even the traumatic ones.

Claire confidently flicked through her geography book and held her finger victoriously over the correct section of coastline. I leaned back in my chair, slid my gaze down to where her palm was concealing the page number, waited for her hand to shift...

'Helen Burns!'

I widened my eyes and said nothing.

'Come up here!'

I obeyed.

'You were looking at Claire's page then!'

'I wasn't,' I lied. I felt slightly sick.

'She was,' said Claire, her hands clasped together like she was a child in a choir.

'I wasn't, Mrs Robertson,' I lied again. 'I really wasn't.' I felt desperate but Mrs Robertson's disapproval of me was absolute.

'Come up here and find it! Find it here in this book!' she screeched.

I scrabbled at the atlas on her massive desk, knowing I was done for. There was nothing I recognised, nothing I knew. Green and yellow expanses of land, blue oceans, dots and place-names – all of them random and faraway. I could see them morphing into the undeniable shape of a shop, a chip shop: *Helen's Plaice*...

There's nothing else for it, I thought. And then I found I was thinking the same words over and over again. *Help me*. I scanned and scanned the atlas, frantically turning the pages, repeating the words, telling myself that he'd come, he would, he always did – and then, just as I was starting to lose all hope, I felt the birthmark on my left palm crackle into action. I didn't dare turn my hand over to look but I knew instinctively that I was getting closer to the answer in the book. *Warmer, warmer.* The soles of my shoes began to get hot too and my feet began to sweat in my socks. I rubbed my slimy toes together. Within a few seconds it felt as though the floorboards beneath me were on fire. Then, like new blood, the heat began to power up the veins in my legs, warming my stomach, prickling my neck hairs, until it reached my cheeks in a violent flush. I felt more confident. I looked up at Mrs Robertson and saw that her eyes were filled with hate and disbelief. But then I looked over to the window by my desk. There, among the hopscotch squares and the nestless trees, the bitty tarmac and the rusty railings, stood my beloved devil – brooding and sexy, staring at me. Above him the sky swirled purple with storm clouds.

I looked around the room but the eyes of the other girls were all firmly focused on me, their expressions a mixture of pity and exhilaration. I looked back to the book, turned another page, and that's when I saw it, in the top right-hand corner, Cape Cod, the black letters snuggling into the spine of the atlas.

'There!' I said, pointing triumphantly.

Mrs Robertson readjusted her bifocals and looked at the page as though it was a very bright light. She sucked in her cheeks and let them out again with a clicking sound. There was a reverential hush among the class.

'Pipe down, girls,' Mrs Robertson said, although everyone was completely silent.

But she hadn't finished with me yet. When it was time to go home Mrs Robertson pulled me to one side by the shoulder of my jumper.

'Show me your hands,' she said.

I hesitantly uncurled my palms and looked at her face desperately. Surely she couldn't have figured out my secret? On my left palm, the red streak of my birthmark glared out accusingly, like a line of red pen across a page.

'The other side,' ordered Mrs Robertson, and I flipped my hands over to reveal four fingernails scruffily painted black.

'You know nail polish is forbidden at this school,' said Mrs Robertson.

Kimmy Lennox walked past snickering with another girl. I didn't say anything but gave Mrs Robertson a mutinous look.

'Come with me please,' said Mrs Robertson and I followed her to the classroom that the teachers used for detention. She left the room for a minute, and returned carrying a large book and a stack of lined paper. She put these down on the desk in front of me. The book was *Paradise Lost* by Milton. I'd never heard of it.

'Do you have a pen?' she said.

I sheepishly pulled the black rollerball out of my pencil case.

'I want you to copy out this book onto this paper,' said Mrs Robertson, tapping the book as she said the words.

'What, *all* of it?'

'As much as you can, until home time.'

But copying out the book had quite the opposite effect to what Mrs Robertson had intended. At first I struggled with the difficult language – the letters sat there, mute and freaky-looking, the e's with little famished faces, the f's like snakes dangling from branches. I didn't feel as though I could relate to the book at all. Still, I diligently copied line after line, until even my own handwriting looked alien to me. And then, a group of words jumped out at me, clean off the page. *The mind is its own place, and in itself can make a heaven of hell, a hell of heaven*. I thought I understood what Milton might be getting at.

Later that same year I was shopping in Manchester city centre with my mother and brother. Back Pool Fold was a tiny street cutting between the buildings that made up the town hall annex. Legend had it that the devil had been sighted there back in 1863, in late December, when a small crowd of horrified onlookers had watched, slack-jawed, as – ever the cavalier spirit – he had casually walked along the sides of the buildings, branding the snow with coal-coloured hoofprints. As I looked up at the buildings I wondered why he had chosen this particular spot. Was it this feeling that I had sometimes, that yawning yearning feeling, that sense of deja-vu? Was that what had lured him to Back Pool Fold – the unshakeable, compelling, incomprehensible, *gutting* hunch that he'd been there before?

'I need to withdraw some money from the building society,' said my mother, hugging her faux fur coat around her waist. Her boot heels clicked on the pavement as she stepped from foot to foot.

'I want to come too,' said Ben. 'I want to lindo.'

'Li*m*bo,' I said. He meant dance underneath the belt barriers that snaked the queue into parallel lines.

'Are you okay to wait with all this shopping, Helen?' my mother asked.

I ignored her for a couple of seconds. Things had been stilted between us for six days, since she shouted at me for eating two chocolate mini rolls after tea. She called me a *greedy little pig* and I called her a *tight bitch* before storming to my room. Since then I had been civil with her but I hadn't eaten a thing just to show her that unlike her I could eat what I wanted when I wanted.

'Helen?'

'Yes,' I said, 'I've got my book.'

I reached into my bag and pulled out the book I was reading, Byron's *Don Juan*. I located my leather bookmark within its frail pages.

'Fine,' my mother said, and as I glanced up I saw her eyeing the book suspiciously. She found my compulsion to read threatening because, unless you took into account the *Weight*

Watchers Handbook, literature was a world she knew nothing about. It was practically another planet to her – cold, distant and somehow rude, like Uranus. 'There's a bit of a queue but we shouldn't be long.'

I watched her and my brother walk away and then I slotted my canvas shoes through the handles of two carriers so that the plastic slits encircled my ankles. I looked at the contents of the bags: California tan pop socks, twisted paper bags of boiled sweets, a plasticky wedge of Edam cheese, and a crusty French stick. My stomach rumbled at the sight of the bread and cheese. *No*, I said to myself. *Not yet. I'm going to show her.* I rubbed my stomach to quieten it and went back to my book.

It was a busy time of year and whenever I looked up from reading I could see that my mother and Ben had barely inched up the queue in the building society. After about ten minutes or so my head started to feel light and cold, and soon I had a splitting headache. I closed my book and managed to catch my mother's eye through the window of the building society.

'I don't feel well,' I mouthed, pressing my palm to my forehead.

My mother held up a splayed hand. 'Five minutes.'

But the headache grew rapidly worse and within another few minutes I felt so dizzy that I had to sit down on the pavement. I looked again to my mother, who rolled her eyes and turned her back on me. It was clear she thought that I was just being dramatic.

'Ow,' I said, holding my throbbing head in my right hand. 'Help.'

I felt the birthmark in the core of my palm pulse once, twice, three times, and then crackle with heat, and then when I looked back towards the window of the building society I saw a familiar image in the glass pane. There – among the slide-down stairwells and the smoke-scarred brickwork, the rusting iron railings and the dusty pigeons, the rain, the clouds, the weighty gloom of a city once dedicated to industry and now just full of shops – my devil stepped out onto the street. As he moved towards me I saw that he was trailing two animals, a monkey and a leopard, and that he was dressed in a frilly white shirt that gaped open to reveal his chest, although it looked as though he had hurt one of his hooves. He was limping, dragging his right foot along behind him.

'Hello,' I said, still holding my head, trying to ignore the pain.

He turned around to the leopard and then pointed towards me, and the animal prowled round to my side and lay at my head. I lay down, resting my head on its soft warm fur that felt as soft as my mother's fur coat. Then I blacked out.

When I came round, I was alone in a hospital bed. I could hear the distant sound of the song 'Santa Claus is Comin' to Town' and could smell reconstituted meat and disinfectant. I was aware of a low, dull pain on the top of my hand and looked down to see a needle pushed under the skin and connected to a shiny plastic tube that was hooked up to a drip at the side of the bed. A nurse walked towards me and smiled.

'Hello,' she said. 'You're not very well, Helen, and you're in hospital, but you're going to be alright.'

'Where's my mum?'

'She's been here for the past few hours but she needed to take your brother home. I'll give her a ring to let her know you're awake.'

She checked the drip and then she poured me a glass of water. The song continued faintly in the background.

He's making a list and checking it twice, he's gonna find out who's naughty and nice...

'My hand hurts.'

'It shouldn't hurt too much.' The nurse inspected the needle and then stroked my arm reassuringly. 'We had to put that in to give you some water and vitamins. You were very

31

dehydrated, Helen. Do you know what dehydrated means?' I nodded. 'What did you have to eat this morning?'

'Nothing.'

'No breakfast?'

'No.'

'Why not?'

'I'm on a diet.'

I couldn't tell her the truth. *I'm punishing my mother.* The nurse gave me a grim smile.

'When did this diet start?'

'A week ago.'

The nurse brought the glass of water to my lips and I took a little sip. The water felt cold as it trickled down my dry throat. 'Just little sips,' said the nurse as she placed the glass on the bedside table.

'I'm hungry.'

'I'm not surprised. I'll get you some crushed ice to start. Then in an hour or so you can have some soup.'

'Thank you.'

The nurse tucked the bedclothes around me. When she had finished I looked down at the sheet over my stomach and saw how flat my body looked against the bed, as though I was barely there. The nurse stroked my forehead.

'When you're feeling a bit better there are some doctors who would like to have a little chat with you, just to check that you understand how to be healthy. You're not in any trouble but you can't put yourself on a diet again, Helen. It's very dangerous.'

'Will I be well enough to go home for Christmas?'

'Hopefully.'

'It doesn't matter if I'm not,' I said, and she smiled at me uncertainly. 'I mean, I don't mind, either way.'

I slipped in and out of consciousness all through that night, unsure of what was real and what wasn't. Sometimes another child would cry out and I was dimly aware of a nurse rushing to their side to see to them. One time I awoke and the silent air around me felt loud and oppressive. I looked up behind me, through the bars of the hospital bedhead, and saw the sky outside, riddled with stars, and sensed the primal, unsettled feeling like a previously unfulfilled space, deep inside. The feeling slowly grew, spreading as high as my throat and as low as my knees, and then my birthmark began to burn – hotter than ever before. Just when I thought I might faint again with the intensity of the heat, I spotted something flicker over in the far corner of the ward, in the rectangular mirror above the small cloakroom sink.

First the tips of two horns rippled the mirror's surface, like raindrops on a puddle, and then an angular red head began to emerge. Next, his sinewy body slithered through the glass, shoulders wriggling, hips twisting, knees fisting like chicken knuckles. Finally, his long, forked tail was whipped out by the weight of his body, leaving the mirror to settle again to its natural state. And there, among the plastic curtains and the beds on wheels, the buzzing strip-lights and the bleached bed linen, the bags of saline, the untouched grapes, the get well cards and the crossword compendiums, stood Satan, Lucifer, Beelzebub, Old Nick, Mephistopheles – call him what you want. He looked at me and licked his lips.

He was still wearing the ruffled white shirt, open to his navel-less stomach, although this time he was alone with no animals in tow. He walked up to the side of the bed and leant down, and I realised he was going to kiss me. His lips were hot and sweet, like the rim of a mug of hot chocolate.

'Stay here with me,' I whispered, so as not to wake the other children or alert the nurses. 'I won't feel so alone if you are here.'

And so he sat in the high-backed green chair at the bottom of my bed and stayed there all through the night. I slipped in and out of sleep, and whenever I came round, I looked for him, and he was still there, his spindly legs crossed, his triangular chin resting on his thumb. He stayed until my mother arrived the next morning, and then he returned the night after, after she'd gone, and the night after that, and the night after that, until it was time for me to go home.

I came out of that hospital a *much* older girl.

Back at school, Mrs Robertson never did quite forgive me for finding Cape Cod. In the February of the following year, when I was thirteen, I made a Ouija board by the back fence of the playground. I'd seen how to do it in the film *Witchboard*, and the other girls were very keen when I suggested it as a game. I wrote the letters of the alphabet and the numbers between one and ten on pieces of plain A4 paper and laid them in a circle on the frosty ground, with a big YES at the top and a big NO at the bottom. I also added, of my own invention, a NOT SURE on the left and a NOT TELLING on the right. Well, I thought, dead people were people all the same, and I imagined they had the same doubts and secrets. We'd just got going when a deafening bellow halted activity across the dimensions.

'GIIIIIIIIIIIIIIRRRRRRRRRRRRLSSS!'

I rolled my eyes and spun around. Mrs Robertson was limbering across the playground in our direction. A couple of girls made a dash for it, one of them losing a mitten in the confusion. I watched the mitten land on the piece of paper saying NOT SURE.

'W-w-what's this?' Mrs Robertson shouted when she reached the rest of us. I imagined I'd never heard a 'W' before I met Mrs Robertson. The other girls looked at me. I widened my eyes and said nothing.

'We've been talking about you in the staffroom, Helen Burns,' Mrs Robertson went on. 'How you've changed recently, how you've gone all cocky...'

'We're contacting the dead,' I interrupted, meeting her bifocals with a knowing stare. 'Any requests?'

'Helen Burns!' she shrieked, shaking her hands, but there was a waiver in her voice and I knew I was onto something. What she had said was true. I *had* changed in the past few months. I felt powerful and in control. I smiled.

'Well, I never!' she said, looking beaten. There was nothing more she could say. She was utterly exasperated with me and I almost – almost – felt sorry for her. I sensed my palm waiting to prickle, the fire bristle in my fingertips, the lightning surge behind my eyes, poised and ready to strike. I knew I could reduce her to ashes with just a word. She didn't say anything more, just turned around and walked away. The other girls turned to look at me, and I saw something new in their eyes – a kind of wired shine. I saw it again when Kimmy Lennox said *Hello* to me, for the first time, in assembly that afternoon.

From that point on, I was treated with respect at school. I didn't get picked on for having holes in my tights or not knowing the dance routine to the latest Madonna song. In fact the other girls kept out of my way. I knew that they were all just playing at love, nurturing their little infatuations as they had once nurtured cress plants or sea monkeys. I, on the other hand, was plumbing depths so deep that I hadn't found the bottom yet, nor did I expect to.

As it turned out, Mrs Robertson died the very next year, the sixth of the decade, on the sixth of June, after a mysterious fall.

'Helen, come and look at this,' said my mother. I walked over to the dining table where she was sitting and reading the paper with a cup of black coffee. 'Isn't it sad.' She passed me the page of newspaper.

GRAMMAR SCHOOL TEACHER IN FATAL FALL

'Didn't she teach you last year?' said my mother.

'Well, it was more that; she *had it in for me*,' I said.

'It's very sad.'

I looked down at the newspaper and saw Mrs Robertson's face muddy with badly set newsprint, and I felt nothing at all. I said: 'Mum, I think in death Mrs Robertson has managed to teach me much more even than in life: that all of us, at any time, are only a banana skin away from our fiery fate.'

'Don't you think it's odd though that she died falling *up* the stairs?'

As the months passed I fell deeper in love with the devil. I longed to spend time alone in my bedroom and excused myself straight after dinner and sometimes for whole days at weekends, telling my parents that I wanted to read a book or do my homework, when in fact all I wanted to do was sit on my bed and stare at the long mirror on the wardrobe, willing him to walk through it. I felt as though I had my own secret kingdom there among the nailed-up necklaces, the fruit-flavoured lip-glosses, and the dog-eared scientific posters – and nobody came close to guessing what I was really up to, except perhaps for my grandmother.

'What's this?' she said gleefully, waltzing into the dining room brandishing a piece of paper. It was the Sunday before my thirteenth birthday. She had excused herself from the table to go to the toilet and while she was upstairs she had been snooping round my room. I recognised the scrap of pink notepaper in her hand – I'd left it inside a book on my desk earlier that day.

'Give me that!' I said, getting to my feet, my blood rising. My grandmother straightened her back and cleared her throat.

'*With you down here how could I crave aught higher? You make me feel far more than heaven or fire,*' she scoffed, her arm flailing up and down in excitement.

'What is that?' said my mother.

I thought quickly. 'It's Shakespeare.'

'Good girl.'

'Gah,' said my grandmother, screwing up the note and throwing it down onto my plate.

Selection of homemade breads

I see that the bowl of nibbles is empty, and I hope I haven't ruined my appetite. The maître d' walks over from the bar and I look up and smile when he reaches me.

'Nikita will show you to your table,' he says, beckoning to an orange-haired girl hovering behind me. She leads me through the restaurant to a booth in the corner, where a bronze candelabra casts a smooth light over a silver cruet set. I ease myself down onto the leather seat.

'Would you like something else to drink before your meal?' asks the waitress.

I think for a moment about what I would like to drink; what I would like to taste. Normally I order a jug of tap water on autopilot, but tonight everything has been so pleasant that I'm tempted to choose something more interesting.

'I'll have a vodka-tonic, please.'

Vodka-tonic is my favourite. It looks so pure and it is anything but.

It's still early – just after half six – so there are only a couple of other diners examining and chewing their food. Occasionally one of them emits a little gasp of delight. Bethel feels like a place of quiet rapture. On the table by the cruet set is a basket of different breads, beside a dish of butter and a larger dish of marinated olives. The miniature loaves of bread are colourfully studded with nuts, seeds, olives and sun-dried tomatoes. There are certain things you expect in a good restaurant and homemade bread is one of them. It's something of a litmus test, even. The bread should be something like the service:

graceful and non-intrusive, a loveable sidekick rather than a star of the show.

I choose a loaf with pieces of walnut protruding from its curves. As I break the bread in two, the smell is warm, comforting, homely. I hold each half in my hands wondering which to bite.

* * *

'Give us this day our daily bread...' chanted the congregation of Prestwich C of E Church.

'Helen,' hissed the minister's daughter, Meredith Fairweather, standing next to me in the row of worshippers. 'I think that boy over there is looking at you.'

I looked up to see a boy peering at me through a pair of binoculars from the far side of the church. After a minute or so he let the binoculars rest on his chest while he scribbled something down in a notepad. He was wearing a white shirt, a waistcoat and a red tie.

'I think you're right, Meredith,' I whispered back.

I admitted to myself that I was intrigued. I adjusted my pose, angling my head so that my cheekbones and chin were favourably lit by the church's yellowing, fly-filled striplights. I was thirteen and had recently discovered contact lenses and hair conditioner. I saw the boy raise his binoculars again and I smiled a small, pouty smile without looking directly at him and then I continued reciting the prayer.

'And lead us not into temptation...'

On Grandma's orders Ben and I had been going to the church for a couple of months. She had already come dangerously close to discovering that I was in love with the devil, and church seemed as good a way as any of throwing her off the scent. It wasn't just the note she had found, or even her psychic powers – things had come to a head during

39

my grandfather's funeral when she had caught me winking at a stained glass window depicting a scene from the Book of Revelations.

'Your problem, dear,' she whispered in my ear on the way home, 'is that you want to feel special.'

I couldn't take her too seriously. She had gravy on her collar.

'Keep your enemies closer,' I said, tapping my nose.

But I didn't trust her to keep her suspicions to herself and the last thing I wanted was my entire family knowing my secret. When Grandma told my parents that "those kids are running wild" and suggested that we join the local Sunday School, it felt more like a dare than a punishment. Much to her surprise I immediately agreed to the plan.

After the main service, I looked for the boy as I followed the other younger members of the congregation into the room where Sunday School was held. The room was a lot like an amateur gymnasium, with wet-look varnished floors, high windows divided into little squares, and acoustics so bad that even the Word of God had difficulty making it from one end of the hall to the other. Meredith's mother Patricia (no one was allowed to call her Pat, except maybe Jesus) organised the Sunday School. She had long grey hair and dangly earrings in the shapes of crosses. I saw that the boy with binoculars had come along too, following a little way behind, pocketing his notepad. He sat in the back right-hand corner as Meredith and I took our seats down at the front.

'So!' said Patricia brightly. 'The big question for this week is: why do you come to Sunday School?'

Keen to impress my new fan, I raised an arm and solemnly declared: 'To find out God's will and fulfil it wholeheartedly.'

It was a quote from *The Sound of Music*, my favourite film. Fraulein Maria's doomed bid for purity. For some reason it seemed like an appropriate thing to say but immediately I caught a confused glance exchanged between Patricia and her husband, Ron, who sat to one side and played the guitar for hymns. The room was very still and quiet. Somewhere, a clock gently tutted.

After a while, one of the other children audibly exhaled and Patricia said: 'What, you don't come to Sunday School because you *like it*?'

I widened my eyes and said nothing. I looked away, at the drawings of Bible scenes that had been tacked to the walls, and I saw the corners curling where the Blu-tac had come unstuck. I looked from image to image – from saints smug with sadness, to impossibly tall angels.

Who was the only one smiling with his teeth?

I looked at Meredith, who was making a discreet apologetic face at her mother. I looked at the boy on the back row, who was now furiously writing in his notepad. Patricia asked the question again and hands shot up all around me.

When Sunday School was over the boy followed me down a side street to my mother's blue Austin Maestro hatchback, which was chuffing out toxic black fumes by the kerb. I ignored him until I had almost reached the car and then I spoke to my mother through the open car window.

'Excuse me a moment,' I said, raising my finger as though I was about to take an important phone call. My mother looked miffed. Then I turned to face the boy. 'Why are you following me?'

'I want to cast you in my movie,' the boy replied.

'What's the part?' I said, trying to sound unimpressed, when in fact I was incredibly flattered.

'Tragic heroine,' he said.

His face was flawless and tight, like an unripe piece of fruit. 'I'll do it.'

'Helen!' yelled my mother. 'Come on, will you! I've got a piece of beef in the microwave!'

I rolled my eyes.

'My name's Roger Dunn,' said the boy quickly.

'Helen Burns,' I said. 'See you next week then,' and I winked at him as I climbed into the car.

A week passed without a visit from the devil but I didn't really notice – I was far too busy thinking about Roger Dunn and the movie I was going to star in. *I can pull off a tragic heroine*, I thought to myself, and I practised my best "wretched" face in my bedroom mirror.

When next Sunday finally rolled around I felt thoroughly excited about the prospect of going to church. I sat at the dining table in my scarf, bashing in the head of my too-hard-boiled egg. It was so cold outside that my father had to boil the kettle twice to melt the thick crust of ice on the windscreen of his car.

'I'm surprised our John found the kettle without a map,' my grandmother said, piously drinking a cup of tea with her pinkie finger extended.

My mother was viciously buttering toast on the work surface and began to butter more viciously still.

'I'll have a piece of that if you don't mind,' my grandmother said. 'Unless it's for you, love?' My mother never ate bread and my grandmother knew it.

My mother hacked the toast into thick strips. 'No no, it's not for me, it's for the kids. But I can do another one, Emily, if you give me a minute.'

'Can I have my toast whole so that I can make a sandwich with the egg?' I said. My family all turned to look at me as though I had just sprouted horns. 'Please,' I added.

My mother slammed a sloppily buttered piece of toast down in front of me. I scooped the egg out of the shell and draped it across the toast, then sprinkled salt ceremoniously over the egg, throwing my hand back over my head with a little flourish when I had finished, just like I had seen them do on the TV. Ben watched me, his own soldiers blunt and vanquished on his plate. I loosened my shoulders and then I folded the piece of toast in half and took a bite. 'Oh my god,' I said, looking at Ben, my mouth full. 'It's a taste sensation.'

'I don't know where she gets these phrases from,' said my mother.

'Grammar school,' said my grandmother. 'They whip the big words into them.'

When I arrived at church Roger was standing with Meredith by the gate. He was wearing a yellow tie beneath a broad grin. Meredith was wearing a pair of snow boots and had a thunderous face on her.

'*This* boy says he's sitting with you in church today,' she said, jerking her head towards Roger.

'That's right,' I said, smiling at Roger.

'Fine,' said Meredith, and turned on her heel.

But Roger and I didn't go into church – we picked our way across the icy pavements to the nearby park and sat thigh-to-thigh on a wrought iron bench.

'Have you ever French-kissed a girl?' I said, cutting to the chase.

'No,' he said and looked away, a rash of embarrassment spreading up his neck from his shirt collar.

'This is what we do with our tongues,' I said, and I wiggled my index fingers around each other. Roger looked petrified.

'I'll show you,' I said to him, glancing around.

After I had kissed Roger I pulled back and saw that his eyes were closed. When he eventually opened them he looked as though he had just woken up from a very long sleep.

'Helen, will you be my girlfriend?'

Maybe it is important to try this for a while, I thought. *See what comes out in the wash.*

A few months later, when I turned fifteen, I lost my virginity to Roger. It was one of the most disappointing moments of my life, especially considering I had taken great pains to build up the sexual tension between us, applying strawberry lip balm to my puckered mouth with my index finger while Roger declaimed his grand plans to be a film director just like Stanley Kubrick. He introduced me to all kinds of new tastes such as houmous and guacamole, anchovies and artichokes, which his mother bought from the delicatessen. It was nothing like the food we had at home. But then, later, when we rolled around on his creaky single bed, I realised with dismay that the hard pang of the first-time was the most that Roger was capable of making me feel. His hands were clammy and cold, like two fat little dead fish. We tried again and again, hiding the empty condom packets in video cases, but too often I found myself studying the dust on the light bulb during his amateurish fumblings and after a few more weeks I broke it off. *I'm too young for a proper relationship*, I told him, when almost the exact opposite was true: I felt as though I was too advanced for a schoolboy, even one with ambition. Roger declared himself heartbroken and, even though I didn't believe him, out of respect I stopped going to church.

Then one day he just turned up at the house.

'Roger!' said my mother as she opened the front door to reveal him standing there with a bouquet of petrol station carnations in his hand. The cellophane wrapping was spotted with pale pink hearts. I stood at the top of the stairs, hoping to hide, but to my mortification my mother hugged Roger and called out my name. I knew that she was still proud of the fact that I had had a boyfriend for a while, even though she knew that I wasn't really happy. She must have hoped that it might have moved me one step closer to leaving home. I on the other hand was unmoved by Roger's sudden appearance. I descended the stairs and told him to *Go Home*.

'How dare he turn up like that, at our house!' I said, hoping that my mother would understand the way I felt. Roger scurried away sobbing, his tail between his legs. I knew that was being cruel to be kind, but I didn't love Roger and despite what he had said about being heartbroken, I knew that he hadn't really known me – except in the loosest biblical sense.

'I thought Roger was a *nice boy*,' said my mother as she closed the door, lost in her own world – no doubt a world where I was married off and living in Australia.

'You're desperate to get rid of me, aren't you?' I said, still fuming.

'It's not that,' continued my mother. 'It's just that you give up so easily, Helen.'

By then I was as tall as her so I stared directly into her eyes – those startled, barely defined, dishwater-blue eyes that I myself had inherited – and I saw disappointment surfacing, and I couldn't stand it.

'Well, you never go to church for anything other than a funeral,' I snapped. 'At least I've been experimenting.'

'I'm talking about giving Roger another chance.'

I thought of all the times she had thrown plates of food across the dining room at my father, usually after my grandmother's visits, the bright shards of porcelain spraying up from the skirting board like fireworks. If there was spiritual grandeur to be found in this life I realised that my mother, like me, was still searching for it.

I followed her into the kitchen, where a lumpy mass of mashed potato substitute was soaking in a plastic measuring jug. My father came in from his shed at the bottom of the garden and kicked the back door open, which was swollen from the cold and damp weather. 'Oh!' said my mother, jumping. It was put-on fright, we all knew it, but my father responded in character, saying: 'Just me, love, just me', as my brother bounded in wearing his battered old Goofy baseball cap and the kettle did a low drum roll at the end of its boil. And there it was, right in front of me: domesticity

ise, like drizzle – just something going on in the
't was everything I didn't want out of life. And
absolute certainty that my mother was never
g to advise me to hold out for the lightning bolt of true
love. It was something I was going to have to pursue myself
– with a little help from the devil of course.

* * *

'Happy birthday!'

As I woke to the sound of Pete's voice I realised that I was
lying on top of the bedclothes, wearing only my bra. The sheets
were cold and damp beneath my thighs. It slowly dawned on
me that we had had sex – a rare occurrence. We hadn't had
sex for a fortnight, not since the night of our anniversary, but
the fact that Pete and I didn't have a lot of sex wasn't ever
an issue. Our relationship was about much more than that –it
was about companionship, trust and mutual respect.

'You fell asleep!' Pete said.

I squinted in the half light. He was standing with a
breakfast tray in the doorway of the room.

'Sorry,' I said.

He carried the tray across the room and rested it precar-
iously on the end of the bed. I heaved myself upright and
swung my feet round onto the floor.

'Where are you going?' he said.

'Nature calls!' I staggered into the bathroom.

I caught sight of myself in the mirror as I passed and
noticed that I had bluish bags under my eyes. I hadn't slept
properly since the night of our anniversary.

As I sat on the toilet I noticed the Pete-sized footprints
on the duckboard and the gobs of foam on the glass shower
door. Pete always showered immediately after sex. I found

this oddly endearing, like the way he only bought white toilet paper and washed his hands every time he used the loo.

Back in the bedroom Pete was already re-making the bed. As I stood behind him I saw that his buttocks were taut in his boxers, his hair sideswept from the shower. I tipped my head to one side and watched him. Wet swipes of thin brown hair were combed across the thin skin of his temples.

'Sorry,' I said again, even though I wasn't sure what I was apologising for.

'It's okay. Why don't you get back into bed?'

I snuggled under the duvet and surveyed the offerings before me: homemade bagels, cream cheese, orange juice. Pete sat on the end of the bed and smiled at me. I smiled back. The pale blue voile curtains billowed at the open window and a single white feather escaped from the duvet and floated calmly to the carpet.

'Do you want your present?' Pete said.

'Yes please, angel.'

Pete stood up and walked over to the Victorian pine chest of drawers. I tensed and then relaxed as he opened the top drawer, *his* drawer – his regimented socks and underwear drawer, to be precise – and pulled out a large white envelope and a paper bag with cord handles. He placed these on the bed next to the tray of food.

'First things first,' he said, grasping the bottle of champagne by the neck and wiggling the metal hood from the cork. He tried unsuccessfully to remove the cork – once, twice, three times – and then he knocked over the open carton of orange juice.

'Want me to do that?' I said, watching the orange juice swill into the carpet's deep, expensive pile.

'Okay,' he said, relinquishing the bottle, 'although I'm not sure it's the right thing for you to open your own birthday champagne.'

'Don't worry,' I said, 'I'm not superstitious.'

I twisted and grunted and pulled at the bottle until the cork finally came free with a repressed pop and hiss. Pete held out two wine glasses. As I poured fizz into the first glass Pete watched the champagne froth and settle. His face always expressed exactly what he was feeling inside: anticipation, excitement, adoration. It was an open and honest face – a face full of the moment only.

I lay down on my side, resting my glass of champagne on the duvet, and looked down at myself as I slowly breathed in and out. I saw how the latitudes of my body, my woman's curves, undulated against the creased sheets. *Here they all are*, I thought, looking down at myself, *my twenty-nine years*. If this had been Pompeii in AD 79, when Vesuvius erupted, a deposit of scalding ash would have suddenly engulfed me, fossilising me forever. How would archaeologists of the future have labelled the grey cast of me, frozen in this moment? What would have been my distinguishing features, what would have been written on the information card in the museum display? Maybe just something like *Girl in a good place*. Yes, that would do for me.

Pete nudged the stiff paper bag closer to me and coughed nervously. I raised a comedy eyebrow and reached for the cord handles at the top of the bag. Pete laughed once, a forced little laugh that reminded me of my mother's, and I pulled the bag towards me and peeked inside. A grey box with a bow around it nestled ominously at the bottom. Whatever the present was, it was small.

Almost instinctively my stomach knotted with fear. *Perhaps it's a pair of earrings, or a pair of cufflinks. I've always wanted a pair of cufflinks.* I took a deep breath to allay the sickness creeping up towards my throat. Not many things came in small boxes.

'That's a big bag for a small present,' I said and I heard how quiet and timid my own voice sounded in the still room. 'Shouldn't I open my card first?' I said, putting the bag down and looking up at Pete, anything to delay what I knew then was inevitable. 'You know,' I blundered on, 'to be polite?'

Pete didn't say anything. His expression was tense, anticipatory – similar to mine, though I suspected for different reasons. But I didn't want to read his face, I was too busy buffering my own emotions, trying to get my head up to speed with my heart.

'Open the box,' he whispered and I knew that there was no way of delaying it any longer. Liquid terror surged through me.

I love Pete, I said to myself. I thought of all the years I had steadily grown to love him, more and more, every day. I thought of the many ways he made me love myself more. I thought about how happy my family were, to think of me with someone like Pete. I thought about how nice our home was, how dependable our friends were, how happy I looked when I looked in the mirror.

'Pour me some more of that, would you?' I said, gesturing to the champagne, and then I removed the little grey box from the bag and laboriously tugged the ribbon out of its bow. Prising open the box was just as painful and just as slow. And then the box was open. I stared inside and, from its position in a slot in white card, a straight band of silver stared back.

'I thought you'd prefer something plain,' Pete said quickly.

I didn't know what to say. I felt a tight, airless shock, as though I'd fallen out of a tree and my breath had been knocked out of me.

I had thought about marrying Pete so many times before that morning. I had fantasised about his proposal. I had planned our wedding day, on a bright morning in a smart registry office, with ten or twelve of our closest friends and family present, all jiggling excitedly into the nearest pub afterwards and everyone shouting *Mrs Duce!* at me whenever they could. I had conjured up our children's faces and their names, even their favourite flavours of ice cream. I had thought about the end of my life as a widow, the long, lonely days of missing Pete in the home we had shared, and not being able to throw out any of his clothes. But now that this vision had become my reality, I didn't know what to do.

Pete didn't say anything. He just looked at me, trying to work out how I was feeling. I couldn't meet his eyes. The silence was unbearable.

'So?' Pete said after a while.

I still didn't know what to say.

'It's a nice ring,' I said, to fill the silence.

'I bought it from that little jewellers in St Ann's Square,' Pete said. 'You know, the one we always walk past when we go to the fish market.'

'I know it. In the Assurance Building.'

'That's right. They were really nice in there. I told them all about you.'

'That's nice.'

'So... are you going to put it on?'

I tentatively touched the ring with my index finger. It felt cold and hard.

'I don't know,' I said.

Pete reeled backwards a little, as though I had punched him lightly in the chest.

'You *don't know*?'

I looked up and saw that he was scrutinising my face, unsure as to whether I was joking.

'You're kidding, right?' he said.

'I don't know.'

'You don't know whether you're kidding or you don't know whether you want to marry me?'

He looked crestfallen and I found it incredibly hard to see that look on his face. I had only seen it twice before: once when he had lost the first job he loved at a famous gastropub, and then again when his mother had died the previous year.

'I feel very... confused.' It was all I could manage.

I couldn't look at the ring any longer so I closed the little grey box and dropped it back into the bag.

I looked at the untouched tray of food and I felt sick and guilty.

'You know, I'm not sure I could eat anything,' I said.

'Never mind that,' said Pete. He looked as though he was about to cry.

'I'm sorry, Pete. I don't know–'

'I didn't get you another present,' Pete interjected, either to cut me off or to save me the discomfort of speaking, I didn't know which.

'You made me bagels,' I said. 'That's a lot of work. The boiling, the baking...'

'I enjoyed it.'

We sat in silence for another few minutes. My body felt heavy on the bed.

'I might try and get some more sleep,' I said.

I lay back down and closed my eyes, but really I think I just wanted Pete to leave me alone so that I could digest what had happened.

'No problemo,' said Pete, standing up.

I heard him pick up the tray and make his way to the door. I sensed him loitering in the doorway for a long time, the wooden frame surrounding him, like somebody expecting an earthquake.

Hours later when I woke up again, this time in the mid-afternoon, Pete was sitting on the end of the bed. The shape of him startled me and I covered my body as though he was a stranger. I felt a dull, aching awareness that something bad had happened. Then I remembered: it was my birthday and Pete had proposed to me.

'It's two o'clock,' he said. 'Want me to get your computer so you can finish your work before everyone arrives?'

I thought for a moment. Of course, the review.

'Yes please,' I said and then I thought I would rather get up and finish the review downstairs, not in this bed full of raw memories from the morning. But Pete didn't need telling twice. I got the feeling that he had been waiting a long time for me to wake up. He bounded out of the room, galumphed down the stairs and returned with my laptop in his hands.

God preserve this man, I thought, as I opened the laptop. The computer screen came to life, and my half-written review of the Thai Banana – deadline Sunday lunchtime for Monday's first edition – appeared. The last word I had written was 'tasty'. I grimaced.

'What's up?' Pete asked.

'The last word I've written is 'tasty'.'

Pete made a pantomime concentration face – the face of someone trying to remember an actor's name they never knew in the first place.

'Why don't you just delete it and write another word instead?' he said.

I looked at him and I saw that he was still worried.

'That's what I'll do,' I said, holding down the delete key until the five letters had disappeared. 'Shan't be long.'

'I'll put the kettle on,' he said, backing out of the room.

I watched the shape of him recede down the magnolia-hued upstairs hall. The temptation was to call him back for a hug or a kiss, it would have been so easy to do that, to get that instant gratification – but something stopped me. I tapped the mouse twice to open the thesaurus application and shook all thoughts of the proposal from my mind.

After I'd submitted my review I took a quick shower, pulled on a sleeveless grey dress and headed downstairs. Pete was in the kitchen, preparing vegetables. I wriggled my bottom onto a high stool at the breakfast bar.

'Morning,' I said. It was a timid joke but it was the best I could muster. I was still in self-defence mode, my hatches battened down as though I'd just weathered a huge storm. It was unfortunate that our friends were coming round shortly for what was meant to be a happy occasion. We were going to have to skirt over it now as best we could, at least for a few hours.

Pete placed a bone china cup on a seagrass coaster in front of me. He poured Assam tea from the Japanese-style pot into the bone china cup. I picked up a bamboo-effect teaspoon. I had discovered that details were important when making a home – adjectives were everything. I tried to summon the comfort that the details of my life usually gave me.

'Thanks,' I said.

'You're welcome.'

He smiled at me but I detected a twinkle of irritation in his voice. It wasn't much, though – it wasn't anything like anger. It was – what was the word? – *cross*. That was it, Pete was cross. Not angry. Never irate. In five years I had never heard him so much as raise his voice.

'Look,' I said, 'about earlier.' It felt too weird to not acknowledge what had happened in some way.

'We don't need to talk about it,' he said, so quickly that I knew it was the beginning of a prepared speech. I looked into my teacup and waited for him to say more. 'Take some time to think about it,' he continued. 'You know I want to be with you forever whether we're married or not.'

'You see, that's just it,' I said. I felt as though I had the power to make everything alright if I chose my words carefully. 'I thought we were *happy* as we were.'

'We are,' Pete said, turning to look at me, and I realised it was another question without a question mark.

'We are,' echoed our three-year-old African Grey parrot, Adrian, from his perch on the back of a chair. We both turned to look at him and Adrian began to peck at his tail feathers.

Pete's best friend Mike, who worked as an animal welfare officer, had found Adrian when he was investigating an abandoned flat. The flat was in a tower block in a poor part of the inner city. The stairways were full of needles and piss-stink, and Mike didn't really expected to find anything alive by the time he reached the ninth floor, but one of the shut-in elderly neighbours had reported hearing screeching sounds from a flat and thought a bird might be being abused. Mike broke in to find a filthy front room full of rotting cardboard boxes and a flickering television. In the corner was a cage, and in the cage was Adrian. He hadn't had food or water for a week, he'd plucked out most of his neck feathers with his claws, and his companion lay dead in the sawdust next to him. All he'd had for company was a Quentin Tarantino DVD stuck on the menu screen. Mike claimed that as he opened the cage door, Adrian shuffled towards him and croaked a gentle *Motherfucker* before collapsing into his arms. When Mike put the call out for a new home for the parrot, Pete asked me whether I'd mind if we took him in, he was such a sucker for a stray. Of course I agreed. To compensate for the bizarre horrors he had experienced, we gave Adrian the most sensible name we could think of.

'What's up, mate?' said Pete.

Adrian stopped preening himself and squawked. I sipped my tea and relaxed a little. We made a fine little family, the three of us, there in our small but sophisticated home, among the stripped wooden floors and the framed pop art prints, the retro-look digital radio, the tastefully selected rack of European and New World wines, the chrome juicer, the designer toaster, the vintage lampshades and the high-speed broadband. Everything was functional and in its place, and there was some sort of beauty in that.

'Can you tell I used skimmed milk in the tea?' said Pete.

I tried a mouthful and gagged. 'Why did you do that?' I said.

'Well, it's obviously healthier–' he began.

'It's thin as piss,' I said without thinking.

'Pardon me?' said Pete.

I looked up, realising what I'd said. I never made negative comments about Pete's cooking and over something such as milk it seemed ridiculous. I didn't even swear in front of him that often. Pete looked shocked.

'It's fine,' I added quickly, taking another sip and swallowing. 'Mmm.'

Pete turned his attention back to the cooking. He shook the lidded pan to rough up the par-boiled potatoes, then he tipped the potatoes into a pre-heated baking tray, slicking them around in the spitting olive oil.

'I love you,' he said as he basted the potatoes with a large stainless steel spoon.

The roasting tin creaked as it cooled on the hob.

'Are you talking to me or the potatoes?' I said, trying to crack another joke even though inside I was feeling taut and brittle.

Pete put the roasting tin back in the oven and patted the oven door with his oven glove.

'All of you,' he said.

'I want to eat you,' I said, looking at his face, trying to make him laugh, but when he didn't respond the silence was oppressive again. Adrian sat beside me, stepping from foot to foot, the way he did when he was feeling indecisive. He wasn't really helping so when I finished the teapot of tea I opened a bottle of red wine, even though it had only just gone four. Pete didn't say anything and I wasn't sure whether the disapproval I could feel came from him or myself; I suspected it came from myself. As I sipped at the wine I reminded myself that nothing had changed. I was in the house I owned with the man I trusted, enjoying a glass of red wine and swinging my feet in my slipper-socks. Tomorrow morning I would get up at 7.15am and take a shower and eat a bowl of cereal and drink a glass of fresh orange juice and pick an outfit and a pair of shoes and comb my hair and brush my teeth and put on some lipstick and pick up my bag and head out of the door to catch the bus and it would be another week in my life. My *good* life.

'Well,' said Pete as he scattered sliced almonds over an earthenware dish of apple crumble. 'I suppose I should get changed.'

'I'll set the table,' I said, slithering down off the stool.

As I put my glass back down on the table, the base of the glass caught the edge of the bone china saucer and a high little chime rang out. It was only a small thing, a minor detail, but the chime told me that I'd had sufficient wine to affect my spatial awareness.

'I'm not drunk,' I protested.

'Just take it easy,' said Pete. 'You want to enjoy your birthday, don't you?'

He lifted his pinny over his head and took a glass out of the cupboard, then poured himself a glass of wine.

'To us anyway,' he said, raising the glass in my direction.

'To us,' I said. 'Any way.'

By the time our friends arrived a few hours later, I had got so drunk that I had decided to hide in the toilet.

'Helen!' Pete shouted from the hallway just after the doorbell rang.

I pulled up my knickers and rolled down my dress.

'Just a sec!'

My voice sounded a lot better than I expected it to – I wasn't slurring even though I knew that I'd had a lot of wine. In the kitchen the smell of cooking, along with the tension between me and Pete, was making me feel sick so I thought I'd escape somewhere cool and quite for a few minutes before everyone arrived. The toilet seemed a logical choice. I washed my hands and then made my way down the stairs, fixing my face with a bright smile as I turned the corner in the staircase. Mike and Jenny were taking their coats off in the hall. Through the window by the door I saw their beat-up Volkswagen collapsed in the driveway.

'I thought you'd fallen down the loo,' Pete said suspiciously. He looked flustered. A tea towel was draped over one of his arms.

'We've brought pink wine,' Jenny said, brandishing a garish, gold-embossed bottle. Mike looked at her with mock disapproval. Fortunately Kate and James arrived before Mike and Jenny had the chance to take it any further.

'Happy birthday!' said Kate and she kissed me on the lips. Kate always went for the lips. She was confident like that – a proper woman.

I met Kate and James six years ago in the local park. Kate had fallen down a hillside and broken her leg and James hadn't wanted to leave her alone while he went to get help, so I sat with her while he went to call 999 at the Farm Centre, and we had a conversation that turned my life around. I loved Kate from that point on. She said everything like she meant it. She changed the temperature of rooms. Many a time I'd sat cross-legged with her, clutching a glass of something, spilling my guts. A few years back she and James ran off to Las Vegas to get married in one of those tacky little chapels. No one even knew they were engaged. I enjoyed picturing the scene: there it was, true love, surrounded by vending machines and neon cowboys – one in the eye for religion or what.

The five of us sat in the garden while Pete finished preparing the starter. I'd moved onto white wine – something Kate brought – a watery, deceptively strong pinot grigio. I'd lost count of the number of glasses I'd had in total but with every mouthful I was feeling more relaxed. Kate was sitting on the grass, scrunching her toes into the foam bases of her flip-flops. She glanced at me and I smiled and looked away but then I sensed that I had looked away too quickly so I looked back. She was still staring at me and I felt my cheeks redden so I tried another smile but it was as though I suddenly wasn't in control of my mouth – as though my face was contorting into what I thought a smile should look like. I drew each corner of my mouth up, pressed my teeth together, bared them. It felt horribly unnatural.

'Have you had a nice birthday, then?' asked Kate.

'Lovely, thanks,' I said, trying to sound convincing.

I knew that if I stopped concentrating on just acting normal for even a moment I would come loose and unravel before them all, right there on the grass. I'd end up telling them all about the proposal and my refusal, and where would that leave the party?

'I'd better see if Pete needs any help,' I said, getting up, deliberately holding my half-empty glass, and myself, straight.

In the corner of my eye I saw the pale oval of Kate's face turning with me as I made my way to the house.

The kitchen was cool and smelled of lemons. Pete was standing over the chopping board, wrenching apart lobster tails.

'Hi,' he said, looking at me and smiling.

'Hi.'

'Hi,' said Adrian from the back of a chair, his beady eyes on the lobster meat.

'Do you think we should put Adrian upstairs?' I said. 'You know how much Jenny hates him.'

'Whatever you think.' Pete stirred a bowl of white sauce and then dipped the tip of a teaspoon in and brought the spoon up to his lips, tasting the sauce with a quick little suck before dropping the spoon in the sink. He went through a lot of spoons when he was cooking – a lot of spoons and a lot of dishcloths.

Pete placed chunks of lobster into the six hurricane glasses lined up on the work surface, repeating exactly the same action for each glass. One, two, three, four, five and six. Through the sides of the glasses, ragged ribbons of lettuce were jumbled artfully with spiral-shaped pea shoots. Then he worked his hands into a pair of rubber gloves and began to finely chop a red chilli.

I took a bottle of wine from the rack and pulled open the utensils drawer. I scrabbled around for the corkscrew.

'Don't you think you've had enough?' said Pete, scraping the pieces of chilli into the bowl of sauce and peeling off his rubber gloves.

I stopped and looked at him. 'What do you mean?'

'I mean, maybe wait until after you've had something to eat?' he said, faltering.

He looked away and began to spoon sauce over each lobster cocktail, one after the other, until all six were done. I gripped the neck of the bottle and aimed the point of the corkscrew's coil at the centre of the cork before twisting angrily once, twice, three times, and yanking hard. The cork came out of the bottle with a defiant little pop. Pete let out a long sigh. Then he shrugged, shook his head and put the empty sauce bowl into the dishwasher. He unwrapped the cellophane from a head of broccoli and rinsed the bobbly green mass under the tap. When the broccoli was clean Pete broke it into florets, ready for the steamer.

'You can call everyone in if you want,' he said. 'I'm just about good to go here.'

I downed my glass of wine and poured myself another.

I sat silently at the dining table, looking around at the faces of my friends, trying to find somewhere safe to stare where no one would stare back, even though it was my birthday and I was supposed to be the centre of attention. Mike tucked his napkin into the collar of his shirt and held up his knife and fork expectantly. Jenny poured everyone a glass of sparkling pink wine. Kate looked at me whenever she could, and I looked away whenever our eyes met.

'Shall I do some bread and butter?' said Pete.

'Let me,' I said, getting up and edging past him into the kitchen, glad of a chance to escape Kate's gaze and away from all the food, which was still making me feel queasy. Adrian hopped after me and Jenny ducked dramatically even though he was nowhere near her.

'Is he *clean*?' I heard her say as I reached the navy blue enamel bread bin.

I slid the uneven half-loaf of home-baked bread onto the breadboard. After I had buttered seven pieces I tossed one of them towards Adrian. He hopped onto the work surface and gobbled up the bread, and I didn't shoo him off. I placed the remaining six slices onto a plate and carried it through to the dining room. I carried myself like a bowl of hot water. When I got back to my seat Pete stood up and pushed my chair under the table behind me as I sat down. I was hoping that they would have started without me but they had waited, of course they had.

'First, a toast!' declared Mike and we all held our flutes of wine aloft. 'To Helen, one year closer to the big 3-0!'

We all clinked glasses. Jenny's bright pink lipstick scalloped the rim of her glass. I pronged the smallest piece of lobster onto my fork and carried it up to my mouth.

'How would you rate this then, Helen?' said Mike. I looked at him and quickly shook my head. I was afraid to swallow because of how loud the sound would be. I took a sip of wine and held the wine and lobster in my mouth for as long as possible. When I did swallow I felt as though the noise of my throat was deafening, the action exaggerated and grotesque. 'I wouldn't,' I said when my mouth was empty.

'Go on,' said Mike impatiently. 'If you had to. Four stars?'

'Helen doesn't rate my food,' said Pete.

'I don't talk shop at home,' I clarified.

Mike went back to his lobster. I poured myself another glass of wine.

'Reviewed anywhere good lately, Helen?' asked Jenny.

'We went to a nice Thai place on Friday,' said Pete.

'It was okay,' I said.

'It was delicious,' said Pete, without looking at me.

'It was okay,' I said again. 'Three stars. Six-and-a-half out of ten.'

'I can't remember the last time you gave a restaurant anything other than three stars,' said Pete. It was almost a criticism in itself.

'That's because I'm consistently underwhelmed.'

'I was reading about a new place opening in Castlefield,' James cut in. 'It's already tipped for a Michelin star. Some kind of religious name...'

'Bethel,' I said. 'I've heard about it.'

Pete shifted uncomfortably in his seat. 'Who's the head chef?'

'Well this is the thing,' said James. 'Nobody knows. It seems they've come from nowhere.'

'No head chef comes from nowhere,' said Pete. 'More likely they've poisoned someone or run up a load of debts.'

'You'll have to see if you can review it, Helen,' said Mike. 'See if you can kick that three-star habit of yours.'

'Yes,' said Pete. 'I could come with you.'

'Oh I daresay my editor will pull rank on that one,' I said. 'I never get the best gigs.'

Kate put down her cutlery. She had left a tiny bit of food, as she always did: a few strips of lettuce and a little pool of sauce. Kate had a healthy relationship with food. She never overate or dieted – she had her fill and then she stopped. It was one of the many things I admired about her.

'I'm just nipping out for a cigarette,' she said. 'Excuse me.'

I watched her leave the room.

'I quite fancy one myself,' I said, hoping that no one would notice how I had merely picked at my starter.

Pete sat up straight. He looked tense. 'I thought you'd given up?' he said.

'It's my birthday!'

I picked up my wine glass and walked through the kitchen, closing the back door behind me so that Adrian didn't escape. Kate was standing under the apple tree, looking up at the leaves and serenely smoking.

'Can I bum a snout?' I said.

'I thought you'd quit.'

'I have.'

'Then it'll taste even better,' Kate said, shaking a Camel out of the light blue carton in my direction. I put the cigarette into my mouth. Kate lit it with a steady hand, then put her lighter back in her pocket. 'So come on,' she said. 'What's got your goat?'

As I exhaled the smoke into the air I felt a weight slip away. 'Pete proposed.'

'When?'

'This morning.'

'Ah.'

I took another toke on the cigarette. It tasted hot and smoky and wrong. I blew smoke up into the tree and watched the hazy indigo plumes swirl among the leaves.

'I haven't said yes yet.'

'Do you think you will?'

'I don't know.'

I looked at Kate and she squinted back at me, as though I was a pane of frosted glass and she was trying to see through me, to the other side.

'I'll leave you some of these, if you like,' she said, skimming over the question, rattling the fag packet.

'It's okay,' I said. 'I've got some hidden in the house.'

She threw the cigarette end onto the ground, twisted her shoe over it, and then bent down to pick up the extinguished dimp. Then she looked at me and smiled. 'You're a dark horse, Helen Burns.' I smiled back, my lips rigidly curved around the orange filter tip.

Later, when everyone had left, I crept into the dining room while Pete loaded the dirty plates and glasses into the dishwasher. Adrian was asleep, his cage covered with a bright flowery throw. I crouched by the sideboard and opened the left-hand cupboard. From the kitchen came the sounds of metal on pot, of pot on metal, of glass on glass. I got onto my hands and knees and reached inside the cupboard, right towards the back, beyond the takeaway menus and the emergency birthday cards. I fished around blindly until my fingers tightened around my cigarettes. I dragged my clenched fist back through the cupboard's debris. I opened the box to see that around half the pack remained, an aquamarine Clipper nestling to one side. I closed the cupboard and made my way to the front door. I quietly stepped outside the house and closed the door gently behind me.

It was dark outside. I lit a cigarette and my eyes followed the smoke upwards, towards the night sky. The constellations were clearly visible, each point of light a small tunnel-end of hope. I looked for the Plough, the constellation I always recognised first, and its seven constituent stars shone back reassuringly. I saw Orion, Ursa Major, the Seven Sisters. Mercury lay low on the northwest horizon. A shooting star streaked across the sky in a fast, thin blaze of glory. Meteors. I'd always had a thing for meteors. Another one fell, followed by another, and then another. I tugged on the cigarette and wondered what the shooting star might mean. *Of course*, it was August, which meant that the annual meteor shower known as the Perseids was due.

Don't think about him whatever you do, I told myself. *You'll just get upset.* But the alcohol was high in my blood, and I was too weak to resist the thoughts I normally censored. Above me, the meteors were now falling in fast succession, like bright rain, and the more I looked up the more I realised that memories were waiting in every corner of the sky, ready to flare up and remind me of things I had worked hard to forget. I smoked and swayed and stared until eventually my mind buckled and a fragment seared through.

He would stand behind me more often than not, kissing my ears as he spoke in that soft low night-time voice he reserved for me and astronomy.

Right now we're passing through the tail of a comet. Those meteors you see are specks of space dust burning up in the atmosphere. It's a fatal encounter but also a glorious one, and fatal encounters are generally glorious...

I pressed my palm against the porch wall to steady myself. He would say things like that all the time, just casually, as though they were normal things to say. I lapped them up because being taught often felt to me the same as being fed. The trouble was, I had ended up trusting him. I finished my cigarette and stamped out the butt on the driveway.

'Are you properly smoking again, then?' I heard Pete's voice from the hall. 'Helen?' he said when I didn't answer. 'Are you coming to bed?'

'No,' I said and then, remembering my manners, I turned around and opened the door. 'Not just yet, love.'

He nodded and I smiled and then, without kissing me, he turned and walked up the stairs. I closed the door to and then turned to face the front garden. I looked at the immaculately manicured diamond of lawn, the moonlit gravel gathered carefully around each pruned little plant, and I knew that right then, at that precise moment in time, I felt completely detached from the details of my life. Maybe it was the wine, maybe it was the memory, but I felt my soul rising against the garden, the house, everything in it, and most of all Pete's proposal. *No*, I told myself because I knew I had to resist. *Think of the alternative.*

I looked down at my shoes on the ground and found the sight of them oddly comforting. *This is who I am now*, I told myself, *I am down here, with my feet on the ground*. Then, as my eyes slid upwards, something caught my attention over in a patch of gravel by the fence. It looked like a strange mark of some kind. I dropped my cigarette and walked over to get a closer look. I stood above the patch of gravel and then I crouched low, my heart pounding in my chest. I reached out to touch it, the irrefutable shape of a cloven hoof imprinted in the stones. I felt sober with shock and yet somehow not as cold as before.

When I woke up the next morning I was lying on the dining room table, my prostate body loosely covered with a tartan picnic rug. Pete was standing by my feet, dressed for work, jangling his keys in his trouser pocket.

'What time is it?' I asked, rubbing my eyes. The pale walls of the dining room were bathed in acid light.

'Eight o'clock.'

'Shit.'

'Why don't you phone in sick?'

'Monday edit meeting,' I said, pressing a palm to my forehead. I sat up and rubbed the middle of my spine. 'How did I get here, on the table? I didn't say it accusingly, more in bewilderment, but Pete pounced on me.

'I'll tell you how you got there,' he said curtly. 'Three bottles of wine and no food is how you got there.'

'Oh,' I said, hearing the lonely syllable dissipate slowly into the air.

'I'm laced to the gills, cupcake,' said Adrian suddenly, from the corner of the room.

It was the kind of thing I hadn't said for a long time.

Marinated olives

The tablecloth is covered with crumbs from the mess I have made by eating three of the miniature loaves of bread. I could easily finish the entire basket but I tell myself that I had better stop. I won't have any room left for my meal, and it's going to be good – I know that already. I haven't felt such eager anticipation about food for a long time, despite the fact that I have eaten in four Michelin-starred restaurants over the course of the last few years. On each occasion, Pete took me as part of a weekend break for my birthday after selecting a location from the travel supplements in the weekend papers. In Ludlow I ate the most luscious greens I have ever tasted – curly kale sautéed in bone marrow. In Edinburgh I tried things I'd only ever read about in books – jellied quail, mock turtle soup. In Cornwall I ordered an unlikely pairing of oysters with chorizo sausage. Each time I was impressed but I wasn't blown away.

Bethel, I can tell, is something else entirely. Not that it's perfect, of course, it can't be. Even three stars, the highest accolade awarded in the *Michelin Guide*, only ever denotes 'exceptional cuisine – worth a special journey' – not perfection, whatever the head chef might say. So I start to try and pick fault with the place. Where is my waitress with my vodka-tonic, for a start? My mouth is dry from the bread and I don't have a drink – that's an oversight. A teething problem perhaps, it often happens, even in the best places. I decide I'll deduct a point for such lackadaisical service. I look around and then I see her, walking towards me, smiling. She produces a table scraper from her vinyl belt – a continental touch – and drags it across the littered cloth, scooping the breadcrumbs into her hand.

'Thank you,' I say.

'Welcome.'

I look over to the bar and see the bartender topping up my vodka-tonic with a little bottle of mixer. She adds a stirrer and gives it a single stir. Another squeeze of lemon and a swift wipe of the wedge around the rim.

I look down to the table and see how inviting the dish of olives looks. The glossy little fruits are piled into a tumbledown pyramid, draped with a few marinated garlic cloves and strands of char-grilled sweet pepper.

I take a large green olive, put it into my mouth whole and push it down onto my molars. I bite down to the stone, roll the olive across my tongue and then bite down on the other side. The olive is crisp and plump, laden with thick oil. The first taste in the mouth is garlic. Not Greek, I decide. Too subtle. I bounce the olive around my mouth, detaching the fruit's flesh with my tongue, until only the rough, savaged stone remains. Italian, I conclude. Young. I spit the stone into my hand and transfer it to the little pot beside the dish. There is no dignified way of eating a stoned olive, however hard you try.

* * *

When I first met Pete I hadn't exhaled properly for six months.

We were outside the Odeon Cinema on Oxford Road in Manchester. I'd left my friends, and for me this meant box-fresh friends, a few months in the making, by the pic 'n' mix while I stepped outside to smoke a cigarette.

It was a windy day in early September and the sun was starting to bare its winter teeth. I was painfully thin, chain-smoking my way through every waking hour in staccato huffy gasps – and oh those *hours*. I couldn't bear to count them any other way than with cigarettes. Sometimes it felt as though the only way I could regulate my breathing was by smoking. My face had the ghoulish green pearl-sheen of a dead oyster and my hair sat like a long-empty nest on my head. The wind did it no extra favours. I was fussing over my hair in the half-reflection of the cinema's dirty, poster-covered windows when I noticed a boy looking at me. I say *boy* because that's what I took him for.

'You've got popcorn on your skirt,' he said, pointing. I didn't look down.

'Stop looking at my skirt, you rapist.' I'd had a pre-cinema cider or two.

'I wasn't looking at your skirt. I was looking at the popcorn,' he insisted. He was brown-haired and brown-eyed, in brown cords and a brown tank top with red piping round the hem.

'Don't get metaphysical on me,' I said but when he offered to buy me a coke I thought *what the hell.*

Over cokes, Pete told me that he was a sous-chef at a gastropub but that he was getting a promotion to head chef soon, when the current head chef bought his own place. It all sounded very wholesome – just what I needed. I told him I was a restroom cricket.

'A *what*?'

'A restaurant critic.'

'Oh. Ha ha.'

We exchanged phone numbers and went to watch our respective movies.

I had no expectations when I met him the following week at an average Italian restaurant – although I had combed my hair. We stood outside and he watched me smoke a cigarette, and then we went in. As we sat down at the table I noticed there was a spiky brown olive stone on the corner of the gingham cloth.

'Ugh,' I said, and I looked around briefly before flicking the stone onto the floor with the menu.

Pete watched the olive stone roll under the next table and then he said: 'You keep sending me question marks in the early hours.'

'Excuse me?' I said, putting down the menu and tucking my hair behind my ear.

'Text messages,' he continued. 'Consisting of just a question mark. All week.'

'Really?' I said, genuinely shocked. 'It must be a fault on my phone.'

He looked unconvinced. By the time we ordered dessert, however, I had him charmed. I'd told him all my best stories, shaping them to fit, according to the look on his face, the darts of his eyes – because that's what you do, isn't it? You say: *Here is a story from my past that gives you an insight into my present character*. It's a cheap trick. We ordered tiramisu and crème brûlée, and I was finishing the story about Ben as a three-year-old insisting on eating the bones from a Chinese takeaway. 'He was yelling, "But I want to eat the *bones*!"' And we were all looking at the pile of glistening, gnawed grey strips in the foil tray, thinking there was nothing that could be appealing about them except to the contrary mind of a child. But he kept yelling "I want to eat the *bones*!" until eventually my father caved in and passed him a handful of bones, and Ben put them into his mouth, and immediately went "Aagh!" and spat them out down his front.'

Pete was laughing uncontrollably. The desserts arrived. The waiter didn't ask whose was whose, and gave us each the wrong one. We swapped.

'Thanks,' I said.

'Thanks,' said Pete, wiping a tear from his eye.

'*Prego*,' said the waiter, who wasn't Italian.

'Don't you love that about kids though,' I said, 'that kind of irrationality?'

I saw Pete was looking at me with an expression of sublime concentration. It's a very specific look, that look. It's the way you only want to be looked at when you're feeling that way too, when your heartbeat is in time with the rhythm of the room, and the world and the entire universe around you seem to be beating in time, too. That feeling of being part of the biggest, greatest thing. I saw the gratitude in Pete's eyes, and I knew then that he had fallen for me. Little did he know that my heart was in the deep-freeze. When you see someone looking at you like that and you're not feeling the same way you have two options: run or lie. So, I lied. I led him to believe that I was in the same place as him, that I was ready, that I was open-hearted. I think I wanted to be.

'I can't remember how I got onto that,' I continued, cracking through the rink of caramelised sugar on my crème brûlée, but I did know, it was a charming story and it was my way of saying: *I'm tolerant and easygoing, and I like children. I come from a nice, normal family. And I'm the most normal one of the lot.*

'What's that?' said Pete, nodding at my left hand as I brought a spoonful of crème brûlée up to my lips. 'Have you hurt yourself?'

'Oh it's nothing, just a birthmark,' I said, protectively curling my hand tighter around the spoon. 'No one's perfect, are they?'

Pete tried a spoonful of his tiramisu. 'Mm,' he said. It was a moment before he looked at me again, and when he did I smiled as warmly as I could, and he couldn't hold my gaze. And I thought, *I've got you.* This was instantly followed by, *Do I want you?* And the answer in my head was: *Yes, yes, you'll do, for a while.*

Pete and I quickly bonded over movies and food – easy ways of being around each other. We both loved pesto, Parma ham,

The Godfather, Jaws. He said he was happier. I ate more and drank less. My cheeks filled out and my eyes were brighter. I started to look almost healthy again. And there was the odd time when I knew we were on the same wavelength, and the more times like that that came along, the more I relaxed, until that feeling of relaxation was almost a constant.

And there were times when I knew that we were on the same wavelength. We'd been dating a few months when I woke up in the early morning and I didn't know where I was or who Pete was. I knew there was a presence in the bed next to me so I turned over slowly and saw Pete and I felt something like relief, and then respect, and then envy. Even when he was asleep, Pete was smiling. A mind at peace. So unlike mine. He must have sensed my stare because he woke up and moved towards me for a kiss.

'I've been dreaming about seafood in jam jars,' he murmured.

'Alien,' I said. We'd watched the film a few nights previously, with a pizza and two Peronis.

'That's right,' he said. And I breathed out all the way.

* * *

Occasionally my mother and I went to the supermarket together because Pete and I didn't have a car, but whenever I could I went with Kate at the weekend instead. Going with Kate made for a much pleasanter experience – my mother saw the supermarket as a place of sin and temptation: Sodom and Gomorrah with a freezer section. When I had the strength I accompanied her for moral support because I knew how stressful she found it. Still, I could have done without a shopping trip the day after my birthday when I was battling with my emotions, not to mention a raging hangover. I had just got in from a difficult day at work when the phone rang at 6pm and I was caught off-guard.

'Hello?'

'Helen, you sound terrible.'

'It was my birthday yesterday.'

'I know that. I've still got the stretch marks to prove it.'

'Yes well, I had a little too much wine.'

'There are eighty-five calories in a glass of wine.'

I didn't respond to this. I had stopped indulging my mother's obsession with the calorific value of food. When she realised I wasn't going to engage with her comment, she continued.

'I'm calling to see if you want to come to the supermarket with me this evening.'

She sounded desperate. I imagined the kitchen cupboards at my parents' house bare apart from a jar of instant coffee; my father coming home from work with an empty stomach and a head full of worry; my mother wringing her hands about having to defrost a ten-year-old pie left over from the days when Ben still lived with them.

'Let me just check with Pete to see if we can eat late.'

When she pulled up in the car I walked out clutching my Bags for Life, my purse and a shopping list. As I opened the car door I saw Pete standing at the porch, flapping a white tea towel.

'Dry olives! Sorry, I've just remembered!'

'Okay, I'll add them!' I shouted back, and Pete waved us off with the tea towel, which I noticed was covered in reddish stains. We were having vegetable chilli for tea and he had been reducing a spicy tomato sauce since four.

'Dry olives?' my mother remarked as I fastened my seatbelt. '*Dry* olives?' Like they were foreign words.

I clicked the biro in my hand and wrote DRY OLIVES on the list Pete had given me, just beneath ALBACORE TUNA CHUNKS – IN JAR!!! Then I clicked the pen again and sat hunched in my tracksuit bottoms and my trainers and my hoodie. In my mother's company I always seemed to regress slightly.

'You look pale,' my mother said, shunting the steering wheel through her small hands, which she kept perfectly opposite each other on the wheel – it was always quarter to three when my mother was driving. 'Have you lost weight?'

'I don't think so. It's probably just the hangover.'

'Last time I saw you, you looked as though you'd put a bit on around your chin. I brought you some clippings on jaw exercises and a few other things in case you were interested.' She nodded and jerked her thumb towards the back of the car.

I turned around to see a weathered carrier bag on the back seat. The bag was bulging with torn-out magazine clippings and from one protruding page I read the headline: *Jennifer Aniston's Secret: A 150-Calorie Lunch.*

'Thanks, Mum.'

She snapped on the indicator. 'Your metabolism slows down when you hit thirty, you know.'

'I'm only just twenty-nine.'

The indicator clicked off as we rounded the corner.

'Mine slowed down at twenty-seven. I had to start taking pills.'

I turned to look at her. She kept her eyes on the road ahead.

'Mum, I know the supermarket makes you nervous, but I'm going to get out of the car if you don't stop this.'

'I just don't want you to end up miserable, or fat.'

'Seriously, Mum. Stop it.'

She flicked up the lever to wash the windscreen and the slim wiper blades yelped back and forth in front of us, four times. I used the time to take a deep breath.

'I spoke to Ben this morning,' she said when we stopped at a red light.

My brother lived in Brighton with his partner, Ricky.

'What's he up to?'

'He's buying a house. He's going to call you to talk about it.'

'About what?'

'Buying a house.'

'What do I know about it?'

'You've bought one. And you're his big sister.'

I sighed. The clutch pedal creaked as my mother shifted up the gears.

'He said he had a dream that you were pregnant. I said I thought you might be.'

I turned to look at her.

'I'm not pregnant.'

My mother kept her eyes on the road. 'You should start yoga if you're even thinking about getting pregnant. Or swimming. Swimming would be fine.'

'I'm pretty sure I'm barren, Mother. Too many Margaritas in my formative years.'

'Oh, *Helen*.'

I wondered how many times my mother had said those words in that very tone. I wondered whether, in her strange parallel universe, I exasperated her as much as she exasperated me.

'And anyway we've got Adrian,' I added.

'Lovely,' said my mother. 'A great big greedy bird, riddled with fleas.'

Adrian and my mother had never taken to each other. She was convinced that he could smell the cat on her. I knew it had more to do with the fact that Adrian didn't like my mother's nervy-twitchiness. He preferred the steadiness of my father – his careful rituals; his resigned, sullen tread.

'The African Grey is considered the most intelligent of all birds,' I said. 'You should hear how many words Adrian knows now. As he gets older, he'll become wilful and destructive – just like a real child.'

'You got *that* bit right.'

75

The truth was I loved Adrian but I knew I had only really agreed to keep him because Pete wanted children and I wasn't sure about them yet.

'How's Dad?'

'Working.'

'On a Monday night?'

'You know what he's like.'

I did know what my father was like: gutless, browbeaten, always wanting to be out of the house. The most interesting thing he had ever done was when Ben had come out in his first year at university. My brother's sexuality had hardly been news to me – I had threatened enough of the bully boys at the bus stop who shouted 'puff' at him – but otherwise I wasn't interested in Ben's sex life, just as he wasn't interested in mine.

The day Ben came out, it was a foggy Sunday afternoon and he led us through Loughborough to a student pub where you could get a beer and a burger for £2.50.

'I've had some counselling about the fact that I was in denial for a long time,' Ben said, and I could hear in his softened consonants that he'd already employed a spot of Dutch courage.

'Do you think we're COMPLETE FUCKING MORONS?' my father had shouted, but whether he'd known it or not, the words out of Ben's mouth *were* real news to him – particularly the word 'counselling' – as though by their very utterance they became real things in the real world – before that, Ben's sexuality had been the great unspoken. But my father *swearing*? That was bigger news. Ben and I looked at each other, scandalised.

'*Jonathan!*' said my mother, looking around the pub to see who might have heard. But it was too late. For once in his life, my father had stolen somebody else's thunder.

Inside the supermarket my mother and I filled our trolleys side by side. I crossed items off Pete's list (goat's cheese, baby spinach, dried rigatoni, sparkling water, stewing lamb) while my mother stocked up on her usuals (crumpets, crackers, Weight Watchers pizza-for-one, frozen sweetcorn, tinned curry). I watched my mother theatrically heaving the small trolley round the corners of the aisles and knew what she was thinking: its growing weight would be gradually packed inside her over the course of the following week.

When we reached the household goods I pulled a twelve-pack of recycled toilet roll off the shelf into the trolley.

'Doesn't it revolt you buying *that* after all that food?' my mother said. Her brow was furrowed and there were beads of sweat along her hairline.

'Do you mean because it's recycled?' I replied, rugby-tackling a double pack of kitchen roll. 'You know it's not actually recycled toilet paper, right?

'No, I mean –' she lowered her voice '– the *before and after.*'

'Before and after?'

'You eat something, then, *you know.*' She pressed her hand to her stomach and looked suddenly anguished.

'Well,' I said, picking up a roll of pedal bin liners, 'life does go on, mother. Would you pass me some of those disinfectant wipes? No, the lemon ones.'

But as we queued at the checkout I realised that I wasn't sure that life went on: sometimes it stopped when you realised that you were never going to get what you really wanted, and carrying on regardless after that was all just part of growing up.

My mother read the splashes on the covers of the magazines as she transferred her shopping onto the conveyor belt.

'Have you got anything in the paper this week?' she asked.

'There's a review of a new Thai restaurant,' I said.

'Any good?'

'It's not going to set the world on fire.'

My mother carefully laid a bottle of skimmed milk onto the juddering belt. 'Did you say nice things?'

'I always say nice things.'

We both knew that this was a lie.

'Well, I hope you're not going to get any more death threats.'

'They don't scare me.'

'They scare me – and your father. I tell people you get death threats and they ask me whether you work for the police. And I have to say no, a newspaper.'

'It was just the one, and the editor told me it was nothing to be afraid of. He knew the owner, you see. They were golfing buddies. That's the only reason we ever reviewed his shitty little restaurant.'

My mother grabbed a couple of magazines and slammed them onto the conveyor belt. I could tell that she was annoyed at herself for her own lack of willpower – she had succumbed to an impulse buy. 'If someone's trying to set up a new business then you should be supportive,' she said, taking it out on me.

'The point is, positive comments have no meaning without negative ones. If I say everything's good then no one will take me seriously.'

'But what if everything *is* good?'

'It isn't, Mum. Ever.'

'You can be very mean in your reviews, you know, Helen.'

I looked at her and saw that she was cradling a two-litre bottle of diet cola. I reached over the conveyor belt for a plastic divider.

'Pete asked me to marry him yesterday,' I said, sliding the divider behind her shopping on the belt.

My mother almost dropped the bottle of cola. The checkout girl paused for a moment before continuing to scan the items through the till.

'Would you like any help with your packing?'

'No thank you,' said my mother. 'I'll be there in just a minute.' She shoved her shopping along to make room for the bottle and placed it onto the belt and then she turned to face me. In the background, the till resumed its regular pulse: *blip, blip, blip, blip.* 'Congratulations,' my mother said uncertainly.

She moved forward to hug me, but I held her shoulders and said: 'No, Mum. I'm not sure congratulations are in order. I didn't say yes.'

My mother stepped back. 'Oh, *Helen*,' she said. 'I thought you were *happy*.'

'Well, that's it. I was. I mean, I *am*. Anyway, I'm sorry. I feel like I'm disappointing everyone at the moment.'

As we loaded the shopping into the boot of the car my mother sang a fast, high-pitched tune to herself, mechanically lifting and depositing bags, then spinning around neatly, like a little robot. When the handle snapped on one of my overloaded bags my mother sprang into action and chased the jar of dry olives across the car park.

'Thanks, Mum,' I said when she returned.

'Come on now, let's get on with it,' she said, handing me the jar. She tied a swift knot in the broken handle of the bag and slung it in the boot with the rest. I twisted open the jar of olives and popped one into my mouth. It had a consistency like tar.

Back at home I snuck upstairs while Pete unpacked the shopping. I crept into the bedroom and locked the door behind me. I looked across the room and saw that Pete had tidied the gift bag containing my engagement ring into the corner, by the laundry box, as though it was in disgrace. I made my way over to the chest of drawers and pulled open the bottom drawer. *My* drawer. I scraped aside the old knickers and bras, the ones I never wore, the ones that were there purely for camouflage.

There, secreted at the back of the drawer like buried treasure, was my old red leather jewellery box. I pulled the box out of the drawer and sat it on my lap. I carefully lifted open the lid and removed the layers of jewellery – bracelets, earrings, necklaces and brooches – until I could see the bottom of the box and the faint square outline of the tiny trapdoor concealing the secret compartment. I pressed the corner of the trapdoor and the compartment sprang open. Stowed away within the compartment was a diamond ring lying in its little resting place. It felt like another lifetime, that engagement. I didn't know why I'd kept that ring except to remind myself that my former life couldn't touch me any more, that it didn't matter. As I moved to replace the lid of the secret compartment, the ring gave me a dusty wink – once, twice – like a newborn star.

* * *

When you fall in love, I mean *really fall in love*, time reduces down to nothing. It's as though everything you've come from has been leading to that point. The chaos, the floating – all the randomness of your previous existence – suddenly it all makes sense because you see how it has brought you to a new beginning. Your very own Big Bang.

I was twenty-one years old and on my way home from visiting my university friend Ruth, who had moved to London. Ruth and I had spent two days reassuring each other that we wouldn't lose touch and I was exhausted, not to mention unconvinced. I finally broke away shortly after nine and rushed to Euston to catch the last train. I had a job interview the next day at a café in Manchester. I thought waitressing work would suit me: the short skirts, the simple questions, the daydreaming time.

There was a delay on the Northern Line so I abandoned the tube at Warren Street and ran the last half-mile. It was warm for February but I didn't think much of it until the sky cracked open above me and an epic storm began. Wind whipped around the buildings and rain lashed the paving slabs. I kept running towards the station, using a newspaper supplement as an umbrella. When I reached Euston I hoofed down the concourse just as the guards were closing the barrier and jumped, skidding, bedraggled, onto the train.

The train was busy and people stared without smiling even though I started to giggle at the thought of how I must look – like a wet rag slung across a very dry, neat room. The sliding glass doors hesitantly opened into each new carriage and I walked and walked, shedding drops of water, until I eventually reached a carriage that had some empty seats.

I walked halfway down the carriage and placed my bag on a table where a lone woman was sleeping, her head resting against the windowpane. I binned the sopping newspaper and peeled off my coat. The ends of my hair were dripping so I scrabbled in my bag for a bobble and roughly scraped my sodden locks into a ponytail. I threw my coat and bag onto the overhead shelf and then I threw myself into the empty double seat opposite the sleeping woman. The train began to pick up speed. In the window I watched my reflection flick endlessly over translucent images of bricks and cables.

'Buck up,' I whispered to the bare moon of my face, suspended there in the darkened window, and then I felt that old yawning feeling inside, like a door opening onto an empty room.

That's when I saw him.

Across the carriage, at a table, alone, his body hunched, his blond head angled downwards, vivid as life in the glass. There – among the bright velour and the wipe-clean plastic, the stubby coat hooks and the dog-eared magazines, the buzzing strip lights and the creaking metal joints, the fast food and dreary conversations of the other passengers – Luke Edward Smithy.

He was reading a book and after he had read each page, he tore it out, then, while he was reading the next page, he screwed the torn-out page into a ball and tossed it across the table. He did it so swiftly that it made only the slightest of sounds. A pile was forming on the seat opposite. He was a fast reader. It was methodical, rhythmical, beautiful – his left hand holding the book, his right hand ripping and balling – the action repeated perfectly, framed by the rectangle of the window, like a piece of film on a loop. I wanted to know which book he was reading, I wanted to know where he had come from and where he was going, and I wanted to know every last detail. I felt so many desires writhing with me – but all I could do was stare and stare. Suddenly, he stopped reading, downed the contents of a plastic cup on the table, and looked slowly across the carriage where his eyes met mine in the reflection of the glass. The rhythm of the wheels hitting the cracks in the tracks quickened and within a beat my heart was up to speed. I held his gaze and felt a deep, dark energy ripple between us.

'Hello.'

I turned to look at him in the reality of the carriage.

'Hello,' I replied.

'Winter warmer?' He held up his plastic cup and tipped it from side to side.

'Sounds good.'

He reached inside his jacket and pulled out a bottle of single malt whisky.

'It *is* good,' he said, filling the cup. I picked up my bag and coat and moved across the carriage, pushing the pile of screwed up pages over onto the seat by the window.

'I don't know about you,' he said, handing me the cup of whisky, 'but I have a *voracious appetite* for literature.'

I downed the whisky, trying to think of something to say back to him, but I was enjoying looking at him so much that I didn't really want to distract myself with mere words. He had a pointed nose and a dimpled chin, eyes the colour of the North Sea. A houndstooth check scarf, fraying at each end, was knotted twice round his neck. I hadn't seen anyone so interesting in a long time.

'What is it you're devouring?' I asked.

'A tale of passion and redemption.'

I picked up the broken book and turned it over to look at the cover. *Jane Eyre*. Depleted of over half of its pages, it hung limply in my fingers, like a dead bird.

'You're not going to make many friends doing that,' I said. '*Jane Eyre* is everybody's favourite book.'

'Friendship is for cowards.'

'I know exactly what you mean,' I said. 'I've just spent two days lying to someone I'm probably never going to see again.'

'Liars are some of my favourite people,' he said, pouring two more whiskies. 'And manipulators, too. I've got a real soft spot for manipulators.'

I was intrigued by the bold way he spoke and could tell he had read a lot – if you could call it reading. There was an animal insouciance to him, the way he tossed his head and barked, but I detected a nobility in him too – an abstract reckoning, a kind of holiness but not in the way of goodness so much as in the way of *separateness*. I felt things magnetising inside of me. I sat there, my face tight from the air conditioning, my lips sticking as they slid across the plastic cup. Until that point I'd thought I'd known everything – the way people often do when they're just out of university. I thought I even understood the intricacy of dying adult platonic relationships, perhaps the most complicated thing of all. But this was new and exciting. It was out of my hands.

With each shot, each smile, each crackling flash of contact, I could feel my insides drying out and unfurling. Up to my mouth went the cup of whisky, along came the spark in his eye – a spoke of bright yellow shooting through indeterminable hazel-green – back tipped my head, my teeth numb, my eyes rolling, as the whisky streaked down my throat, burned a path to my stomach, and then – sweet holy Jesus – up, up, up, in luxurious licks and flickers, went my heart.

I had a fleeting vision of the two of us naked in a blank high-rise apartment, the city lights pale in the window as our hips banged together like chips of flint, and all this time I was praying for my body not to betray me – not to twitch or squirm or let out any kind of sound.

We matched each other shot for shot all the way to Crewe. Then he stood up, put on his coat and said: 'Come to Liverpool and see the water.'

'I can't,' I said. 'I have a job interview in the morning.'

'Where?'

'Manchester.'

'But that's not where I live.'

'So what are you doing on a *train* to Manchester?'

'Meeting *you*.'

He leaned in towards me, his hands flat on the table. His pupils dilated as he encroached on me and the light between us was gradually blocked out. I felt as if he was weighing up my height and my width and depth. Like he was taking me in all over. Like he was *starving*.

'You're one of those people with no appreciation of personal space, aren't you?' I said.

'What's your name?' he said, moving closer still.

'Helen,' I said, offering my hand for a handshake.

'Luke,' he said, taking my hand – but instead of shaking it he took it into his other hand, opened it and bent the palm flat. 'What's this?' he said, tracing the shape of my birthmark with his finger.

'That's my naughty streak.'

'I love it,' he said and he took my palm up to his lips.

Tap water

The waitress brings over a pink metallic jug the colour of crushed raspberries and places it in front of me along with a glass filled with ice.

'Your water, madam.'

'Cheers.'

The jug reminds of those we used at school. It could even be an original from that era; it looks as though it has a couple of dents and scratches on it. A retro water jug in a new restaurant strikes me as odd. The jug has definitely seen better days, and it is a quirky addition to the otherwise smooth and pristine Bethel. I wonder whether it constitutes a 'statement piece', a talking point. The problem is that I don't have anyone here with me to talk to about the water jug. I can't say, what do you make of *that*? All of a sudden I miss Pete. But then, what would Pete make of the water jug? Would he have anything interesting to say about it? Still, I find myself longing for his physical company – his hand on my arm, the reassuring sound of his voice. I remind myself that I should be able to entertain myself with my thoughts. And besides, dining alone is underrated – there is such pleasure to be had in eating what you want and how you want, and allowing yourself to be completely immersed in the experience.

I realise that I am thirsty. My throat is dry and garlicky from the bread and olives. I lift the jug and hold it over my glass, tipping it only ever so slightly as it is full to the brim. The ice cubes react by swirling and tinkling as water pours over them.

I put the jug back down and take a sip from the glass of water. It tastes plain and pure, like Pete's love. Drinking a glass of water feels like the right thing to be doing at this moment in time. It is sensible to balance rich food and alcohol with something hydrating. Then I detect an aftertaste of chemicals, of something synthetic. As the cold stream plunges into my stomach I long for something stronger to drink.

* * *

When I heard the phone ring I turned on the lamp – a silly, semi-conscious action of the half-stirred brain. It took me a moment to realise that the sound was in actual fact coming from my mobile phone, which was buzzing and flashing across the bedside table. I picked the phone up and it vibrated in my hand. Pete groaned and rolled over next to me, flopping his arm across my stomach.

I brought the phone up to my face and looked at it. *Withheld number.* 3am. Who on earth was it? I pressed the green key. 'Hello? Hello?'

But there was no answer, just the far-off crackle of static.

There was a time when I loved early morning phone calls – the dawn chorus of thwarted lovers – but I had grown out of it. Nowadays it was far more likely to be just bad news: a failed organ inside one of my parents or a boating accident involving Ben.

My palm was warm from the heat of the handset. 'Hello?' I said again to the dead line.

'Hello,' repeated Pete, coddling me in the crook of his arm, still half-asleep.

'Shh,' I said. 'It's okay. My phone rang but there's no one there. Go back to sleep.'

It was the second time I had woken him up that night. The first time had been an hour earlier when I had come upstairs from the dining room after finding myself lying on the table again. This time my shirt had been pulled open at the buttons, my skirt hiked up around my waist, the flesh revealed, appealingly in places, as though my body was a meal that had been served up to a lascivious guest, but there was nobody there.

Pete opened a rheumy brown eye.

'Turn your phone off at night please,' he said, rolling over in the other direction. 'And I think you should make a doctor's appointment tomorrow.'

'What for?'

'For the sleepwalking. And the drinking.'

'I'm sure it's just a phase. Stress or something.'

'What are you stressed about?'

'I don't know. Nothing.'

Part of me knew that Pete was right, that I hadn't been myself since the weekend, but I didn't want to think about it late at night when everything always seemed worse. I still hadn't given him an answer to his proposal and he hadn't asked again, either.

'Your water's by the bed,' Pete said.

I reached for the pint glass, which Pete had filled for me as usual before we came upstairs. I couldn't remember Pete ever having asked whether I wanted water every night for bed, it was just something that he had started doing. It was sensible enough, I supposed – but I also thought that maybe, given the choice, I would rather have had sugar-free orange squash – at least that tasted of something.

I leaned over and put down the empty glass, then I groped for the flex and traced it along to the slider switch. The bedside lamp went out with a glassy ping. I lay there listening to the occasional sigh of tyres on the main road outside and when I heard Pete start to snore gently I knew that I was alone again in the dark. The screensaver of my mobile phone – soon to blink out to its own sleep mode – was the room's only source of light. It was a photo of Pete with a hairy pink raspberry poking out of his mouth. 'An audio-visual joke', he'd called it. Pete felt so fragile and mortal as his hard little body rose and fell next to mine. I had the sudden urge to put my arms around him but something stopped me.

As my eyes became used to the dark I began to pick out certain objects in the room. I knew that it was because my eyes were tired but familiar objects began to distort into unrecognisable shapes. The hooks on the back of the door became beckoning fingers. A cardigan folded across the back of a chair mutated into a set of disembodied antlers. Then the Virgin Mary herself showed up by the wardrobe, right in the place where my hooded terry-towelling bathrobe had been.

I pressed the red key on my mobile until the screen flashed out to black and then I dropped the phone down beside the bed where I heard it tumble onto the carpet. I told myself that I was being silly, that my palm was only warm from holding the phone, and that it would cool down again and I would be able to get to sleep. I lay there for a while, slowing my breathing, calming myself and willing unconsciousness by focusing on the night sounds of the house: the distant hum of the American-style fridge-freezer in the kitchen, the draught clicking the brass letterbox in the hall. And then, as it became apparent that nothing was going to happen after all, the phone wasn't going to ring again and I really was completely alone in the dark, another feeling began to creep in – something softer and more lasting than fear. I allowed myself to name it just before I drifted off. *Disappointment.* I felt a sudden, old feeling of insufficiency – as though my plate had been snatched away before I had finished eating.

Vodka & tonic

The maître d' places a paper coaster on the tablecloth, swiftly followed by a glass of gleefully fizzing vodka-tonic.

'Sorry for the delay, madam,' he says. 'The tonic wasn't quite cold enough so we put it in the freezer for a minute to get that extra few degrees' chill.'

'Thank you.'

Attention to detail – I like it, although I'm not sure whether he has just told me an elaborate truth or an elaborate lie. This vodka-tonic has taken so long that I thought they might have forgotten my drink order. He nods briskly, as though he is refusing to take me as anything other than earnest. I open my mouth to speak, but then the doorbell jingles as two more customers come in.

'Excuse me a moment,' he says and walks over to greet them.

Curiouser and curiouser. It isn't uncommon for someone with an unsavoury past to attempt to disguise his or her identity when they set up a new business, and this could be the case at Bethel. The head chef could have fled their previous establishment leaving a trail of salmonella or debts – that *would* be a scoop for Keith. I'm suddenly struck by another thought: if I've reviewed the chef *really* badly at their previous establishment, he or she might recognise me and poison my food, spit in it, or worse. My mother was right: *I should have been nicer*.

I bring the vodka-tonic up to my lips and take a sip. I can tell instantly that it is expertly made. Thin lemon wedges are muddled with ice at the bottom of the glass. There is just the right number of ice cubes and they are exactly the right size, meaning they will melt at the right pace and make my drink cool but not watery. The vodka is a double measure. The lemon swiped around the rim has left tiny ellipses of fresh lemon fruit that burst into sourness on my lips. I look over to the bar. The bartender looks at me and nods her head. I raise my glass and nod back. *Pride*. That's what this place is full of. I bring the glass back up to my lips and knock back a long draught.

* * *

As I stared at my face in the greasy mirror of the underground ladies' toilets I wondered what could have possessed me to go out drinking with Keith. I bared my teeth and saw that the gaps between them were getting bigger. Was I too old to get a brace now? What else was I too old for, at twenty-nine? Pigtails? Dungarees? Messing around? I saw that my lips looked to be getting thinner, too, so I licked and plumped them, and then scrunched my face into a grimace, which only served to show me where my wrinkles were deepening. I felt a heaviness in my chest and knew that all that would help was another drink, even though another drink with Keith was probably a bad idea.

It was Keith who first employed me as restaurant critic on the newspaper, six years ago when I was temping as a secretary to the editor. I sent an email round the office about discount gym membership and referred to the Living Well Health Club as the *Living Hell Wealth Club* – a moment of badness. The next thing I knew, a six-foot lusty fawn god had manifested on the other side of my computer screen, grinning an admiring grin.

'If you don't have plans after work I know where you can get a formidable amount of free wine,' he said, putting his foot up on the dustbin and flexing his leg in a show of macho prowess, his balls straining against the crotch of his trousers. I could tell he'd had a mainly liquid lunch.

'That sounds right up my boulevard,' I said, and saw the heads turn around the office. I felt a puff of pride, followed by a surge of giddiness.

Keith took me to a newly opened wine bar, which he declared 'Full of tossers, as per' at the top of voice as we walked in. Even though Keith was drunk and rude the PR looked after us extremely well and I realised that Keith was a bit of a big deal in such circles. We drank champagne, Chablis, Viognier – each fresh glass appearing as we finished the last. Keith stroked his patchy goatee and laughed at everything I said.

'You seem like a capable girl, Helen,' he said, his breath a warm, fermented current in my face.

'I bait my own hook, Keith, if you know what I mean,' I replied.

I don't think I was entirely sure what I meant but I think Keith thought it was a come-on because he kissed me on the cheek. 'I'm looking for a new reviewer.'

'What happened to the old one?' I said. I could feel his wet spittle drying on my skin.

'A dreadful accident involving mussels in a landlocked Irish pub.'

'Ah.'

'Think you've got the stamina?'

I said: 'I know what you're talking about. *The merlot was particularly robust*. That kind of shite.'

'I mean food,' said Keith, chugging back his vodka-tonic and beckoning the PR girl for another. I saw that the whites of his eyes were bloodshot around the bluish halos of his contact lenses.

'I'm not the world's greatest eater of food, Keith,' I said. At the time I was averaging half a meal a day: a few crackers with cheese, seven cups of tea, a bite of an apple.

'But you do *eat*?' said Keith. 'And you have done all your life. Best of all, you've got your wits about you.'

'Barely.'

'Well, have a bash. If you're crap, I'll sack you.'

'Fair enough.'

'I'll let you in on my bulletproof reviewing technique,' Keith began, falling silent as he waited for the PR girl to take away our empty glasses and replace them with two Cointreaus on ice. Then, leaning in towards me, a thick tongue of orange liqueur fumes rolling out of his mouth, he whispered: 'Whenever I leave a place, I ask myself three questions. One: How do I feel? Two: Where did that transport me to? And three: What did I enjoy the most?' He sat back with a wonky grin. 'Never fails.'

I'd tried to follow Keith's advice ever since.

I heard a toilet flush behind me and I quickly pressed the soap dispenser so that I didn't just look like someone who had been gawping at herself in the mirror for several minutes. The soap came out in a frothy little white pat, as though someone had spat on my hand. I ran the cold water and rinsed my hands. The hand dryer was broken so I rubbed my hands on my thick tights as I ascended the stairs to the bar. I was wearing denim hotpants that day – or rather I hacked off a pair of jeans mid-thigh with the serrated kitchen scissors after Pete had left the house. I didn't know why but I'd had a mad urge. As the day had worn on that urge hadn't dissipated and I was still brimming with a desire to do *something* although I didn't know what, but mostly to stop resisting the feelings that had been bubbling up inside of me.

Back out in the poster-covered bar Keith was reclining on a ripped banquette, his long, slender body bending to the shape of the furniture, his hands behind his head. He looked as though he was sunbathing in the dark.

'I took the liberty of getting you a double,' he said when I got within earshot.

'Are you grooming me?' I said, sliding onto the opposite banquette.

'For what?'

'Iniquity.'

'Iniquity's too good for you.'

We had started drinking at 4pm, straight after the Thursday edit meeting. I was quiet in the meeting. I was still carting around round the mixture of guilt and anger that Pete's proposal had provoked in me the previous week, so when Keith asked me how I felt about more of my reviews going online, I make an *Oh no* face and then I said *Fine*. I couldn't stop staring at the things on Keith's desk; the details of his daily working life: a map-of-the-world mousemat, a mug from a museum, blue pens, grey pencils. I was enamoured with their simplicity, their appropriateness, in comparison to the glut of gadgets and gizmos at home. After the meeting Keith asked me if I wanted to talk about whatever it was that was bothering me. *No*, I said, *but I wouldn't mind drinking about it*.

The next thing I knew it was 8pm and we were slamming shorts in a live music dive in the city's Northern Quarter. A table for two was booked for 8.30pm at an upmarket pub round the corner, where a maverick local chef was cooking a gourmet dinner for thirty select diners – mostly media and PR types. Keith's wife had been taken ill – some kind of gastric flu – so he asked me to accompany him to the restaurant. I was thinking that it would be fun reviewing a meal with Keith; an education. The other reason why I wanted to stay out upset me when I thought about it: it was because I didn't really want to go home.

'What's on the menu tonight, then?' I asked, swiping up my vodka-tonic. Keith brought his hands down from his head and put them on his bony knees. He was one-part old school hack, two-parts excited child.

'In French cooking it's a type of ballotine,' he said energetically. 'In America it's known as a Turducken. In Britain we call it a 'multi-bird roast'.

'Oh Jesus.'

'Best of all,' Keith said with a glint in his eye, 'the chef has shot everything himself.'

I knocked back a third of my vodka-tonic.

'Don't you think that sometimes food reviewing can be a little too, I don't know, *epicurean*?'

'If by that you mean hedonistic, then yes, I do. But do you know what, every now and then, human beings should be able to just say *Fuckit*.'

I downed another third of my drink.

'I think it's possible to relish food just that little bit too much. Like the walrus in the Lewis Carroll story, burping after he's lured all those baby oysters into the pot.'

'You don't actually mean *epicurean*,' said Keith. 'Epicurus advocated moderation. It's a common misconception. You mustn't be embarrassed about getting it wrong.'

'I'm not embarrassed,' I said but I knew I was blushing – I couldn't help it; it turned me on a bit when Keith corrected me. I hated to admit it but I was enjoying the attention of an impressive man – especially one who, in his mid-forties, somehow had the metabolism of an adolescent Olympian.

'Have you seen the film *Harold and Maude*?' Keith asked.

'Many times.'

'Where Maude says: *It's best not to be too moral, you cheat yourself out of too much life...*' Keith straightened his glasses. 'Maude is my philosopher of choice.'

I sat back and ruminated in the light of this comment. I knew that Keith was, in a roundabout way, declaring his intentions. I was the current coy mistress and he was trying to seduce me – not necessarily into bed but to admit that I admired him for his brightness and his brain. It was the way it had always been with us, but I was careful as always not to let things get out of hand.

'Anyway,' said Keith, 'it won't be *that* many birds inside each other, just two or three. FYI, the record is seventeen at a royal feast in nineteeth-century France.'

'Seventeen?' I finished my drink. 'What was the last bird?'

'A garden warbler. Stuffed with a single olive.'

'That's sick.'

'I think eating that roast would have been very similar to talking to you.'

'How do you mean?' I asked. *Flatter me*, the proud part of me thought. *Say something that makes me feel adored and defined.* Keith belched but I didn't recoil.

'You're a Russian doll, Helen Burns.' Keith was staring at me like I was food. 'And I'm about three layers in.'

'I should warn you I'm hollow in the middle.'

Just then my mobile rang. I pulled it out of my bag to see that it was Pete. I hadn't told him I was going anywhere after work. There it was again, that feeling in my guts – the thing I was trying to put my finger on – how something motivated by greed can only ever result in carelessness, in waste. I dropped the call and then I turned off the phone with one long, meaningful depression of my thumb. Keith took a swig of his whisky-coke and then held the half-full glass out towards me. I shook my head.

'I forgot,' Keith said. 'She doesn't drink whisky.'

He took the glass to his lips and downed the rest of the drink himself. I pressed another button on my phone to check that it was definitely off and then I stuffed the phone deep into my bag.

'He'll be wondering where you are.' Keith's empty glass landed on the table with a jarring crack.

'Let him wonder.'

The next day I woke up alone again, but this time I wasn't on the dining table – I was in an expensive hotel room. The duvet had been folded over me and someone had taken the hairgrips out of my hair and removed my boots – otherwise I was fully dressed in yesterday's clothes. I sat up and looked out of the window and began to piece together the scene.

When I was in my late teens, running wild, whenever I found myself emerging from a random flat or house the morning after a party, I looked for the red aircraft warning lights on the tops of the tallest buildings in the city. They told me exactly where I was and they helped me find my way home – it was simple triangulation – the same way that the stars once guided lost sailors.

That Friday through the hotel window I could see two masts either side of a wall of grey squared glass. A heartless, hopeless landscape of walls and floors and windows – people locked into pinched, meaningless, electrically lit spaces. I stood up and staggered to the window. Once I had located the spire of the cathedral I knew that everything would fall into place. From the cathedral spire the two red lights were at one o'clock and nine. Therefore I was west of Piccadilly, north of Ardwick, east of Ancoats. I was in the newly built Metro Inn, to be precise.

I stumbled into the bathroom, my head pounding with poisoned blood. It was without a doubt the biggest hangover I had ever had. *I really am getting old*, I thought. *I can't recover like I used to*. As I rinsed my wrists under the cold tap I noticed that the lid had been twisted off the hotel-issue toothpaste and the plastic-wrapped toothbrush had been ripped open and left in the soap drainer on the sink. So Keith had brushed his teeth. There was something painfully endearing about that fact. I looked down at my fully clothed body and moved from foot to foot, and then ground my hips round and round, like I was hula-hooping. No, we definitely hadn't had sex.

The phone on the bedside table emitted a shrill ring. I walked slowly out of the bathroom, holding myself up with my hand on the wall, wondering whether they had ibuprofen on the room service menu. I picked up the phone.

'Hello?'

'Have you put all your layers back on, Russian doll?'

'I'm pretty sure I didn't take any off.'

'No, you were a picture of decorum. I just made the last tram.'

There was a long pause during which the room seemed to bulge around me. I brought my cool bloodless fingers up to my forehead and rubbed my temples.

'I was thinking,' Keith went on, 'why don't you review the new place in Castlefield for me? The so-called saviour of Mancunian fine dining.'

'What's this?' I said, my nerves bristling, 'your conscience commissioning me?'

'I appeased my conscience when I paid for the room. Come on, Helen. Manchester's bare as a dolphin's fanny when it comes to real contenders so you should be biting my hand off. Go on. Say *Fuckit*.'

'*Fuckit*,' I said and hung up the phone.

I left the hotel like a criminal, avoiding eye contact with the reception staff and praying that I wouldn't bump into anyone I knew. I sidled along the wall towards the revolving doors, past the suited and booted security man who nodded a businesslike good morning.

On the bus ride home I remembered that I had a doctor's appointment. The surgery was at the bottom of our street.

Dr Khawam was an Iraqi national with a perfect side parting, a perversely optimistic outlook and a very northern talent for randomness. Whenever I went to see him, he told me how sunny he thought Manchester was.

'I've bought a convertible Mercedes!' he said when I walked in.

I closed the door behind me.

'A *convertible*?'

'Mediterranean feeling in Manchester, warm people, warm city! What's the problem?'

'I've not really been sleeping too well.'

Dr Khawam pressed the cool metal disc of his stethoscope on my chest. 'Deep breath. Okay, fine.' He sat back down at his desk. 'Any headaches, back pain?'

'No,' I said, instinctively touching my head and then my back, as if to double check.

'Any recent bereavement, jet lag?'

'No,' I shook my head firmly.

'How much caffeine and alcohol do you take each day?'

As I answered this question I was careful not to cough or scratch my nose or allow my body to perform any of those other telltale signs of a liar in action. 'Not much. A few cups of tea. The odd glass of wine. With dinner. The occasional vodka.'

'What about exercise?'

'No.' I add a comedy *Can't you tell?* look.

'Medication?'

'Just the contraceptive pill.'

'And how is your diet?'

I looked at Dr Khawam's kind face, his precise hairdo, his shipshape filing cabinets. I liked him so much I could only half-lie to him. 'On the wane.'

'And you're how old now?'

'Twenty-nine. Just.'

'You feeling anxious about something? Worried? Anything at work, or at home?'

I pursed my lips and squinted, pretending to think.

'There is a crooked doc in Davyhulme pointing fingers,' said Dr Khawam suddenly. 'He thinks I'm afraid. Hey! I met Saddam! I look into the eyes of evil and I say, once I'm out of here, I fear nothing. So here I am. He,' he jerked his thumb in the direction of Davyhulme, 'mistakes my patience for naivety and then tries to destroy me. Big mistake.'

I laughed, albeit nervously, but Dr Khawam was on a roll.

'Do you think you still see food as a pleasure?' he asked. 'In your work? Sometimes my wife says when I touch her she feels like an autopsy cadaver! Ha! I say, I'm a pathological lover, but I'm no pathologist!'

'I know I *want* to see food as a pleasure.'

Dr Khawam interlinked his fingers and smiled. 'Keep a diary over the next week,' he said. 'When you wake up, how many times, etcetera. Make sure you eat plenty of fruit and vegetables. Drink more water.'

'I was hoping for some drugs,' I said shyly, but at least this was truthful. I really did want some drugs. I wanted something that would give my mind a rest, stop me remembering, stop me wondering.

'Try herbal ones. Over the counter. We're treating the cause, not the symptoms. Diet. Anxiety. These are things that need to be addressed. Come back next week and we'll maybe arrange tests. Make sure you check the Mercedes on the way out!'

When I arrived home, Pete was shelling peas in the kitchen-diner, slapping around in open-toed Moroccan leather slippers.

'Where the *hell* have you been?' he said in a low, dangerous voice.

'The doctor's,' I said, pretending to look as though I was interested in what he was making.

'What, all night?'

'I was out with some people from work and we got carried away,' I said. 'I'm sorry. I would have called but my phone died.'

He wiped his hands on his pinny and turned to look at me. I felt his gaze travel along my cheeks, my neckline, down my chest, as though he was looking for evidence of some kind. His eyes lingered on my hotpants.

'So where did you stay?'

'A hotel. Alone.'

'Bullshit.'

I opened my mouth and closed it again. Pete turned back to his peas.

'Why aren't you in work, anyway?' I said.

'I'd arranged a long weekend. I was going to take you somewhere. The coast, or a country house hotel. A nice dinner. You know, like we do sometimes.'

'I'm sorry.'

He smiled a wry smile, to no one. 'You're sorry a lot lately.'

'What are you cooking?' I said, putting down my bag and moving towards him.

'Pies. So what did the doctor say?'

'He wants me to keep a diary. Sleeping, eating, you know, the basics.'

Pete didn't reply. He split open a peapod and slid his thumbs down each butterflied side – pit-pat-pat – peas fell into the plastic bowl. I shrugged off my jacket.

Pete stopped shelling peas and said in that low, dangerous voice again: 'I tore the house apart this morning, Helen. I went through all your clothes, your books, your photos. I felt sick to my stomach while I was doing it.'

I felt that horrible feeling, like falling and disintegrating, the same sensation I had felt when I had seen the ring box sitting in the bottom of the bag.

'And what did you find?' I said croakily, my throat constricting. I wondered whether it was too early to have a drink.

'Absolutely nothing,' Pete said and a heavy breath escaped his mouth either side of the words. '

I breathed a long, subtle breath of relief.

'I didn't really know what I was looking for.'

'I'm really sorry I didn't call last night,' I said. 'I got... carried away.'

'That's what I was afraid of.'

'I didn't get *that* carried away.'

'It's not like you to not call.'

'I got drunk, that's all.'

'None of this is like you, Helen. I don't know what's going on.'

'I'm sorry.'

Pete picked up another peapod, pressed it firmly on the spine, and then dropped it again.

'Don't you think it's *odd* that you don't have any photos or anything from the years just before you met me?' he said. 'It only just struck me today, but I've heard you talk about school and your family, and then it's fast-forward to me and you. It's like there's this big black hole in the middle of your life.' He picked up the peapod.

'That period of my life is just a time I'd rather forget, that's all.'

He looked panic-stricken and I felt the urge to reassure him.

'Look, it's nothing *that* bad,' I said. 'It's silly, really. And I don't think it's relevant to dredge it up – or healthy, for that matter.'

'But it's part of who you are.'

'Well you don't know me any less for not knowing about it,' I said, standing straight in front of him, holding out my palms, the birthmark on the left looking cool and innocent. 'This is me. This is who I am.'

Pete didn't look convinced. He smiled a smile that was a slice in his face, a slit in latex.

'Who was he?' he said. I ignored him. 'Come on,' he said. 'A rock star? A married man? Who?'

'Don't be ridiculous,' I said, but I couldn't meet his eye.

When dinner was ready we sat with trays on our knees in the lounge. I couldn't swallow a thing. I chopped it all into tiny pieces and mixed it together. Then I watched dispassionately as Pete ate his dinner like a dog. I heard the sound of his saliva coating the food in his mouth, sloppy with his lowness, his misery, and I felt full of the past that I had just denied, a haunted woman. I prayed for a sinkhole in the carpet to swallow me, to take me down and out of the way, and leave poor Pete to his pie and peas. I wanted to run away. I wanted to drink and smoke, smear my lipstick and ladder my tights, go out to a dirty city bar and do my worst.

When Pete had finished his dinner, he took my mashed meal off my lap and carried it through with his own empty plate into the kitchen. He came back and sat on the edge of his chair. He was looking at me with the expression of a kicked dog – it was as if he didn't trust me any more but he still couldn't help but love me.

'Do we have anything to drink?' I said before he had chance to speak.

'I think there might be some vodka in the freezer,' he said softly.

'Fancy one?'

'No thanks, but I'll get one for you if you like.'

'I'll get it,' I said, getting up.

'No it's fine, I'll get it.'

He disappeared into the kitchen, returning with a glass of vodka and orange. 'Thanks,' I said. 'Mind if I smoke?'

'It's your house too.' I heard the lump of reluctance in his throat but I sparked up anyway. I crossed my legs, clasped my hands, looked at him, my Pete, who just a week ago had slept in my arms and thought the world of me.

'Thanks for dinner,' I said in an attempt to keep the conversation on a superficial level, but it was no good.

'You remember that programme?' he said. I didn't reply but I knew which one he meant so I nodded as I sipped nervously at my drink. 'Jocelyn Bell Burnell and her pulsars.' I nodded again and took a slug of vodka. 'I think we should try and be like her.'

'You mean not give up?'

'I mean if something comes knocking in the night then you should be brave enough to let it in.'

I swallowed the lump in my throat.

'I do love you, Pete.'

'I know.'

I finished the glass of vodka-orange and got up and walked into the kitchen for another. When I came back through the hall Pete was standing on the stairs.

'I'll sleep in the spare room,' he said.

It was quite a statement and I wobbled on my feet.

'You don't have to do that.'

'I feel like I do.'

I took a sip of my drink as Pete turned his back and walked up the stairs, two at a time, as he always did, slightly more slowly than usual. I waited for the sound of his feet on the floorboards of the spare room and then I followed him upstairs and walked into our bedroom, locking the door behind me. I pulled open the bottom drawer of the chest of drawers.

I had to double check. I had to know exactly what I was dealing with. The old knickers and bras were exactly as they were. The jewellery box was untouched, undiscovered. So Pete really hadn't found anything – he didn't know about the other ring.

The next morning I woke up on the dining room table again. The tabletop creaked as I sat up. I shivered with cold. I looked out of the window, trying to work out the time of day and trying to remember what I had to do that morning. A thin blanket of cloud covered the sky, flattening the sunlight into a translucent grey sheet like the lid of a plastic box.

'Pete?' I called. 'Peter?'

An empty vodka bottle and an empty carton of orange juice lay on the floor at awkward angles, like cars after a crash. I walked into the hall just as Pete came down the stairs, his eyes rubbed raw.

'Are you alright?' I felt my dry lips cracking as I tried to smile.

'Why don't you ask the parrot?'

'What do you mean?' I said but Pete ignored me and walked into the dining room. I followed him. Pete walked over to Adrian's cage and whipped off the cover. Adrian stared out innocently.

'What are you–' I began.

'Luke,' said the parrot, in his best girly voice.

My mouth fell open.

'Pete,' I said but he had already turned his back and within a few seconds I heard his keys in the front door. 'Pete!'

'Luke,' said Adrian insistently. 'Luke, Luke, Luke.'

It was such a classic way to get caught out that I almost burst out laughing, but then I burst out crying instead.

Green tea shrimp with nano-lime

The waitress gently places a little square plate onto my place mat.

'Green tea shrimp with nano-lime.'

In the best restaurants every dish is introduced to you personally, no matter how small. On the plate is an amuse-bouche, to titillate the tastebuds. The amuse bouche is the chef's beckoning finger, their little come-hither. It's their way of defining not only their own personality and that of the restaurant but also their present mood.

I shake my head and try to snap back into professional mode. First of all: the name. *Green tea shrimp with nano-lime*. 'Nano' is surely a wry nod to the trend for 'molecular gastronomy' – that study of the scientific processes involved in cooking. I do like a chef with a sense of humour. I look down at the plate. On a square of brown toast the size of a postage stamp, a tiny pink shrimp is curled around a pea-sized blob of lime-coloured concentrate. It is playful, colourful, delighted with itself. There is a very happy chef at Bethel today. I pick up the amuse-bouche and pop it into my mouth. I chew. Open my eyes wide. Draw in some air. Chew again. Feel my eyes go wider. My jaw begins to ache, the way it does when I really enjoy something. I swallow. It is... without a doubt, *the* most exquisite thing I have ever tasted. There's something in the tea-infused toast I can't quite put my finger on. Something between the exotic tang of the green tea and the rich comfort of the wholemeal bread.

No.

Yes.

There's no denying it.

* * *

When I woke up that first Friday morning in Luke's ninth floor flat, on a pillow that smelled of spent matches, I watched him sleeping on the double futon for whole half-hour before I could move. I stared at his nicotine fingers loosely gripping the corner of the pillow, the soles of his unblessed feet poking out from the bottom of the yellowing duvet. I was rigid, awed, rapt – a riotous mix of feelings. *This is it*, I thought. *True love. How terrifying.* I thought of all the false starts I'd had up until then – the lesser feelings that had left me empty and disappointed without my knowing exactly why. The fear and excitement that I was feeling were in actual fact the same thing.

I found my knickers at the foot of the bed and tiptoed through the living area, in between pieces of paper – star maps, complex graphs, computer printouts, scribbled notes, science magazines – that were scattered across the floor like the continents of an unexplored world. I kept my feet on the gaps of floorboard around the papers, like I was a ship nosing my way through uncharted territory. A large cobalt-coloured telescope was cocked by the window, pointing over the Mersey estuary towards the sky.

When I reached the kitchen, my bare feet ticked across the cool linoleum. The CD player sat mute on the mock marble work surface next to a brittle, un-watered Peace Lily in a pot. A mug came off the drainer with gluey reluctance, sending bar flies scattering. I slowly opened a cupboard to reveal a tin of pineapple chunks and a box of green tea bags. I picked up the box of tea bags and shook it but it was empty so I looked around for the bin and spotted, in the far corner of the kitchen, a pedal bin overflowing with sandwich wrappers and mouldy paper cups. I sniffed a few times. The smell of Luke's flat was disgusting – it was as though a scientific experiment had gone wrong in there, creating a toxic cloud of cheap air freshener, dirty upholstery and cigarette ends. There was no tea, no coffee, no milk, no sunlight, no music. I had missed my job interview, I hadn't called my parents, and I didn't know how or when I was going to get home. But I didn't care. Nothing else needed to be right because nothing else mattered.

Luke woke around 10am and sat bolt upright on the futon. I was sitting reading on the windowsill wearing just my knickers.

'You,' he said. I put my bookmark into my book and smiled. His face was as creased as the bed sheets and he looked older in the morning light, but just as handsome, just as perfect. 'So you decided to stay?'

'I couldn't find my clothes.'

He reached down under the duvets, a look of mock puzzlement look on his face, and pulled out my bra with one hand, followed by my top with another. He grinned and I grinned back.

'Come and get them why don't you.'

When we were both dressed we took a walk together around the town. Luke kept taking my hands into his and blowing hot breath onto them. We passed the entrance to a nightclub, ragged with flyposters, we passed tin cans and burger cartons, odd shoes and chip papers. We walked down a side alley past an old man who was picking up pieces of rubbish and jettisoning them into a big maroon bin. He turned to face us and I saw that his false teeth were calcifying at the gums.

'Dirty, isn't it?' he said.

We nodded.

'I'm doing my penance,' said the man.

'What have you done to deserve penance?' asked Luke.

'Well,' he said, 'you know *heaven*. I can't get in the back door any more with my joints, so I'm trying for the front.'

'I'm going for the cat flap,' I said and Luke laughed and I felt pleased.

'Got a cigarette, have you?' said the man. I shook a couple out of my packet. He took one and as I sparked my lighter he cupped my hand to steady the flame. 'Soft pack,' he said, drawing back and exhaling. 'Where've you come from, London?'

We walked on, up past the Walker Art Gallery and the World Museum, past lampposts and hanging baskets, dustbins, manhole covers, and the stark Radio City broadcasting tower. We passed a group of bikers, eight of them huddled together chatting and filling the pavement, their motorbikes tethered to the railings like horses.

To the rear of Lime Street the pillars of St George's Hall were assuming their morning colours. A pigeon was standing on the head of a statue of equestrian Prince Albert, facing forwards, relishing the degradation.

We walked back down towards the water, down thinner streets where angels' faces peeped down from the architecture above. Our footsteps rang off the walls. Light descended in petrified shafts. Bar and restaurant workers swept front steps and washed windows in preparation for the day ahead. As we reached the end of the last street, the soaring white-grey of the Liver Building, pockmarked with windows and gilded with turquoise and gold, rose up out of the docklands.

We crossed the dual carriageway. Icy wind sliced in from the estuary and reeled round the red brick buildings of the Albert Dock. We were both wearing yesterday's clothes – he had put the same outfit back on too in an act of solidarity. I wore my rumpled clothes and my unclean skin like badges of honour. Luke kept looking at my face, witnessing every flash of emotion, but I tried hard to disguise my feelings, I had waited so long to feel like this. I wanted to guard them jealously for a little bit longer.

Down by the docks seagulls were calling, their voices untangling, until one, just one, was perched, hoarsely cawing, on the marooned black anchor outside the Maritime museum. I told Luke that I used to think that seagulls were angels. The way they were bigger in the flesh. The way they fought and stole.

We crossed Hartley Bridge to Railway House and round the corner of the Tate Gallery with its red and blue porthole windows, and then along the docks towards the ferry port, and finally to the bench where we sat that September morning when Luke told me he was a physicist, and I told him I was a Scorpio, and he looked at me the way you only want to be looked at when you're feeling that way too, and I didn't need any other options. I looked the same way back, and my heartbeat felt as though it was butterflying out into the universe.

'Physics has artistic potential,' he said, his eyes full of the sky's morning light, the tassels on his scarf licking his chin. It didn't occur to me at the time that he might be trying to impress me, too.

'Artistic?'

'Yes. The edges of the universe as we know it, and the smallest forces we can detect, symbolise very literally the limits of human understanding. To discover something beyond those things, to define yourself by that discovery – that's the purest form of self-expression.'

'But you didn't make the stars, you found them. So to put your name to them – well, that's just plagiarism.'

'Oh, everything is someone else's when you put it like that.' He clawed a tassel off his lip with his fingernail. 'Ideas are like energy – they can't be created or destroyed; they just change form. I think all you can hope for is to put your name to some little *story-so-far*.'

I could see that there was fire behind his eyes – small flames of emotion, ready to blaze again, given the chance.

'To plant a flag,' he continued, 'where before it seemed there was nothingness...'

I looked at his face framed by the sun and the wind and the water, and I saw how well it bore the elements – flares of hair looping around his planet-sized brain, his jaw set like a vice, the spoils of old wars in his multi-coloured eyes. My eyes followed his and I saw that the horizon was no ordinary one – it was the event horizon: the final moment before a new beginning, when we would both slip through the singularity and come out somewhere else, together.

'Why,' I said, 'that would make you–'

He cut in. 'Something like God.'

'That'd suit you,' I said.

And he said: 'I know.'

And so it began: the most affecting, most satisfying, most ruinous love affair of my life. It was love that shot through me to the very core of my being, love that made every last atom of me vibrate with purpose. It was what I had always wanted and I still wasn't ready for it.

Carrot schnapps gazpacho

The waitress comes to clear my plate. 'Did you enjoy your amuse-bouche?' she says.

I am silent for a moment before I recover myself.

'Everything is delicious.'

'Thank you,' she says, taking the plate away.

The restaurant is starting to get busier now. Diners file in – two, three and four at a time. A few give me a cursory glance as they pass but it really does feel as though this is the kind of place that encourages everyone to remain in their own little world. I see my waitress head through the kitchen's swing door – I crane my neck, strain to see behind her, but nothing. I hear a muffled phone ring. It is my mobile, vibrating at the bottom of my bag. I locate the phone and read the word flashing on the display. Ben. His ancient, unromantic name brings me back down to earth.

'Hi,' I say quietly.

'Happy belated birthday, sis!'

'Oh, well done, only two weeks late.'

'I've been busy.'

Ben's voice is ever so slightly adenoidal. It adds to my vision of him as the eternal child.

'I'm in a restaurant.'

'Oh right, sorry...'

'No, it's okay, I've got a minute. You okay?'

'Did Mum tell you that Ricky and I are thinking of buying a house?'

'Yeah.'

'What do you think?'

'I think that's the real reason you called.' There was silence at the other end of the line. 'I think it's a great idea,' I add after a few moments. 'Get on the ladder. Just watch out for snakes.'

'That's what I need to talk to you about,' says Ben. 'Do you and Pete have any friends who are estate agents?'

I dip my head and lower my voice.

'What makes you think that we might have friends who are estate agents?'

'I don't know. I thought you might have.'

'I've never been so insulted in my life.'

'What's got into you?'

'Nothing.'

'Miss Prickles.'

'I'm tired,' I say. 'Did Mum not tell you, I haven't been sleeping very well.'

'She might have mentioned something about you getting engaged. To be honest I haven't had much time to think about anything but mortgages.'

I don't bother correcting him about the fact I'm not engaged. There is absolutely no way I wanted to discuss Pete's proposal with my brother.

'So whereabouts are you looking? Still in Brighton?'

'As close to the sea as we can get. You know how much Ricky loves his surfing.'

'I know how much *you* love Ricky's surfing...'

Ricky is as buff as they come. Whenever I see him he's barely clothed and I can't say I blame him.

'Check the chimney's straight,' I say. 'Look for damp patches. Visit the area at night and weekends. Beyond that I don't really know.'

'I'll call you when you've got more time.'

'Yes, I'm going to go. My next course is about to arrive and I feel a bit, I don't know, vulgar.'

'Vulgar?'

'I dunno, like I'm showing off or something.'

'Yeah, look at you with your *mobile telephone*, you big show-off.'

'Bye, Ben.'

As though she has been waiting for me to finish my call, my waitress appears immediately with my next course on a tray.

'Carrot schnapps gazpacho,' she says, placing a shot glass – the contents of which are the same vibrant orange as her hair – onto my placemat.

'Thank you.'

I bring the shot up to my nose and sniff. The cold soup gives off a sweet, woozy odour. I angle my head and knock back the shot. It is strong, *so* strong. Flavours of soil and caramelised sugar from the roasted carrots combine with the sterile, faraway flavour of exceptionally pure schnapps. It rushes into my bloodstream and I sink back in my chair, my napkin falling from my knee.

* * *

Three days after we'd met, on Sunday afternoon, Luke and I worked our way through the remnants of his "cocktail cabinet" – a grotty kitchen cupboard containing a selection of tragic dregs: crème de menthe, pastis, peach schnapps, apple sours.

'Move in with me,' he said, chinking his shot glass into mine.

We had spent the entire weekend together, walking and talking and laughing – laughing *a lot*. It had been the most intense time I had ever spent with anyone. It was so easy between us that in a strange way I felt as though we had always known each other – I had never felt so physically comfortable with anyone. Still, it was soon to talk about moving in together.

'I don't know,' I said. 'I should probably be getting home.'

'Why?'

I couldn't think of a reason.

'Sleep on it,' Luke said. 'You'll have to leave in the morning because I'm teaching at ten but I hope you'll come back in the evening, with your bags.'

'That's ridiculous!'

'Why is it ridiculous?'

Again, I couldn't think of a reason.

The next morning I woke to find an empty space next to me and I felt momentarily vulnerable, as though I was trespassing in someone else's bed. I called out to Luke but he didn't seem to be anywhere in the flat, and I wondered whether he had left early without saying goodbye, or whether I had slept through his goodbye. I got up and pulled my phone out of my bag and checked the time. 8am. Surely it was too early for Luke to have left to teach a ten o'clock class? I walked over to the window and looked across at the river and then down to the pathway in front of the flats, where a large number of pigeons – fifty or sixty or so – were gathered around a man who was throwing down pieces of bread. The man tossed his head and stepped back, and I recognised his movements: it was Luke. I was surprised; it seemed so out of character for what I knew of him. I felt a childish delight, as though I wanted to share the moment, and so I moved my hand up to open the window and shout hello, but then I stopped. I realised that I was enjoying seeing Luke as a stranger, from the outside, when he didn't know that he was being watched. He was dressed in his jeans and a blue jumper, his blond hair bright against the concrete and grass. A plastic bag of sliced bread, the remains of our weekend breakfasts, was swinging from his hand. The other hand dived in and out of the bag, ripping the slices into chunks and then hurling it down. Pigeons swirled and scuttled in fast dark shapes around his feet, like rats before a sorcerer.

As he reached the bottom of the bag, he began to throw the bread to the birds that were furthest away, the youngest and the weakest, aiming his shots carefully so that every last bird was fed. As he leaned backwards to put more power behind his throw, I saw a look flash across his face, a mixture of determination and delight, a little boy's look, and I felt my heart melt into my stomach. When the bag was empty he shook the crumbs out over the grass and turned around. I dipped from the window and ran back to the futon.

When I heard his key in the lock I toyed with the idea of pretending to be asleep, and then decided against it.

'Morning.'

He held the empty plastic bread bag aloft.

'You caught me encouraging the local perverts.'

'Perverts?'

'Pigeons. They're all into amputee sex.'

How could I not have moved in with him? And besides, what would have been the point in waiting? I felt as though I had waited so long for something that felt right.

When I called home to tell my parents the news it was Ben who answered the phone.

'You're moving to Liverpool,' he said in a bored voice. He was in the middle of his A-level mocks.

'Yes I am. Please will you tell Mum and Dad I'll come and collect my clothes on Sunday?'

'Hup.'

'What's 'Hup' supposed to mean? Have you joined the Territorial Army?' From the receiver came the sound of slack-jawed chewing. 'Do you understand the significance of what I'm saying, Ben? I'm *moving to another city*.'

'Hup. To live with a man you've only just met. *Plus ça change*, sis. You've always been a headcase for fellas.'

'Oh-ho-ho – French tomorrow, is it?'

I was irritated but I had to accept that my brother had had a point. Since poor Roger Dunn my love life had consisted of a string of short, intensely dramatic, ultimately doomed affairs.

At university I dated a postman who lived in Belfast. Rory had dreadlocks and a "life manifesto" and the relationship worked well enough long-distance but then it turned sour when I flew over to meet his mother. Veronica had got out the best china and I could see her disappointment that I wasn't the girl who was going to turn her son back to the straight and narrow as she wearily poured my tea.

'And did you get anything to eat on the plane?' she asked. Tawny-coloured tea trickled from the teapot into the cup.

'Oh no, it was too bloody expensive – they near enough charge you for having a piss on those things, don't they. Oh god, sorry. Sorry, God. Sorry.'

The biscuit plate clattered on the table. There was a miniscule, disapproving steel figure on the end of the teaspoon. I was staying at a nearby hotel, but not that any of this mattered in the long run. I broke it off with Rory a month later when he came to Leeds for my nineteenth birthday. I was studying English literature but academia was losing its charm and I'd been predicted a low 2:2. I was also living with three thieves. One of them stole a jacket potato right out of the oven. I caught her on the stairs.

'Is that my jacket potato in your pocket?'

'No,' she said, the potato bulging in her jeans pocket, her face contorting with the heat.

I kept her talking.

The theme for my birthday party was "the Wild West" and I was wearing a thong necklace with a silver pendant in the shape of a bull's head. I drank heavily all night, I suppose I was faintly depressed, and around midnight while my friends were all dancing I stepped outside for some fresh air. I realised that I was far too drunk and wanted everyone to leave so that

I could go to sleep. What could I do? I racked my brains for possibilities: I could feign illness or start a fire.

'Come on then,' I said, sparking my left hand against the greenhouse as though my palm was the pink tip of a match.

When the devil appeared holding a bottle of tequila, I wasn't surprised to see him.

'Thanks,' I said, extracting the tequila bottle from his claws. The cap of the bottle was a little red plastic sombrero, which I filled and emptied six times before I went back inside. Over the next hour I drank so much tequila that by midnight I was vomiting into a plant pot on the next-door-neighbour's porch.

'Better out than in,' Rory said, holding back my hair.

'Get away from me, Man of God,' I bellowed, my head spinning round. 'Your mother pours tea in hell!'

My previous relationships had been just as disastrous. Before Rory there was Bernard, a socialist playwright who at thirty-one was far too old for me – a fact I enjoyed as a second-year English student. He boycotted shampoo and had once met Harold Pinter. 'Tell me something about yourself,' he said on our first date. 'Approximately half of my laughter is sincere,' I replied. He'd thought I was joking. Bernard was better than average in bed but sometimes when he kissed me his mouth felt like a beak. He also had terrible taste in music. I broke it off with him when he made me a mix tape so appalling that I didn't even bother to play it. I looked at the track listing and thought, *This shit is going nowhere.*

Before Bernard it was Joe – a bisexual graphic design student who had an attic flat and an overbite. I was having a wild time, running round Leeds in my first year at university, kissing anything that stayed still for long enough – which was a *lot*. I was craving tangibility, desperate to *feel* something, still so unconvinced that the real world could hold anyone who could truly move me. I collided with Joe in a club when I was wearing a rubber dress and no bra. He said it was the most erotic experience of his life. For me, it was mere friction. I dated him for six months and we spent a summer dropping acid at various dance festivals. I broke it off when he started calling me 'Schnuckums'.

Tomek was a Polish boy I dated from November to March when I was fifteen. He had a six-pack and an electric guitar. It was very much a seasonal romance – I told myself it was a smart move to have a boyfriend during the winter months, especially one who was used to the cold. Tomek was vastly chivalrous, leaping up to open doors or help me with my coat. He didn't utter a single word during sex and he called condoms 'sheaths' – a bad translation. I broke it off when I got my first mobile phone and discovered that he wrote entire text messages in capital letters: LIKE KIDNAPPERS' NOTES.

I hated all of Luke's past lovers with a vengeance but I wanted all the details all the same. I sensed that he played down his past intimacies, as I did. I told him about the hearts I had broken and the orgasms I had faked and he shook his fist at the sky and damned them all, half-smiling as he did so, because although neither of us said it so explicitly we knew that what we had together was so much more evolved than any of those affairs. It was pure chemistry: that rare attraction where every last one of the body's sensory detectors is satisfied, every last impulse of the brain is sparked, every last atom so powerfully pulled together that there is the fear of the obliteration of both parties – negative to positive, matter to anti-matter.

I would marvel at the solidity of his body filling up space, then displacing particles with each swing of his limbs. There was part of me that couldn't believe that he was a mere mortal, trapped in time. I would plant kisses on him from head-to-foot, lingering over his jawline, his ears, his wrists and ankles, the thick muscles either side of his throat, his thighs, the vein of his penis, the hum of his blood on my tongue.

Always in our final moments I felt myself falling and falling until I was at the hard, solid centre of the earth, where flower after flower opened in the pit of my stomach, and burned there.

* * *

Not that life with Luke was perfect – there was the excessive drinking, for a start. I'd done my fair share of student drinking but nothing could have prepared me for how much I drank when I was with him. Still, there was something so deliciously *wrong* about opening a bottle of wine at 11am on a Saturday and Sunday. I tried to keep up even though it interfered with my work, which was serving cappuccinos, pastries and toasted panini at a café to the lunching masses of Liverpool's business district every Monday to Friday.

'Alcohol was my father's master,' Luke would say, downing a glass of wine in a single, hinge-headed gulp, 'but it is my slave.'

His father had died from cirrhosis of the liver when Luke was sixteen. He didn't talk about him that often but I sometimes suspected that he was thinking about him, and I knew that he was still very angry about the whole thing. There was a hell-bent element to Luke's drinking, a self-destructiveness that took him straight to oblivion. Sometimes when he raised his glass to no one in particular and said *Cheers* I imagined what he was really saying was *I'll show you*. But they were good times, too. All weekend the two of us would sit reading, drinking and talking on the futon, taking it in turns to go to the fridge. We could get through six bottles of wine in a day and I knew that was too much, much too much, but I didn't care. I had never talked to anyone like that before, had never really appreciated the artfulness that there could be in a conversation, where pieces of speech were considered and shaped and sent out into the air, like letters. He was a compelling raconteur, a subtle comedian, but what really clinched it for me was his imagination. He made a new world for me every day in that little room.

The state of being regularly drunk soon became my norm and sometimes a whole day could pass before I realised that not a morsel of food had passed my lips. One day, after a couple of months of living with Luke, I caught sight of myself sideways in the mirror – the concave dish of my stomach, the wavering question mark of my bottom and thighs. I tightened my belt a notch, wore more make up, looser jumpers.I woke up with a hangover almost every morning.

'Who's on the throne?' I'd cry from the futon, one eye glued shut with sleep.

Through the window, as a fitting soundtrack, the apocalyptic cymbal sounds of bottle bins being emptied rang around the docklands.

'Elizabeth the Second,' would come the reply from the bathroom, or the kitchen, or the windowsill, or the end of the futon – wherever he was sitting, looking at his data.

'Okay. *O-kay.*'

Luke told me that he had been lonely before I came along. His mother had disowned him when he was twenty-one, refusing to let him return to the family home in Carlisle after he'd graduated with a first in physics from Durham. She told him that she had grieved all over again when he left to go to university and she couldn't bear to go it through that ever again, especially since he looked more and more like his father. He didn't take the news easily – he was relying on her to support him through his PhD. He smashed the mirror over the mantelpiece with the urn containing his father's ashes. His mother screamed as ash fell onto the rug and then she picked up a cold poker and tried to stab him with it. He dodged her, backing out of the room, the hall, until he was on the street, walking towards a friend's house. He applied for a PhD in particle physics at Liverpool University, where he was accepted and ended up giving a few classes a week. He hadn't spoken to his mother since. He said he had thought about sending her a postcard when he was headhunted to be a part-time researcher on the UK's nuclear fusion research programme in Oxford – but then a year had passed and he hadn't got round to it. It sounded to me like he was punishing her but I also thought he had a right to. Still, it meant that at the age of twenty-five, while his career was charging on, he didn't have anyone to love, or anyone to love him. I changed that. Within three weeks I had completely transplanted my life from Manchester to Liverpool.

Unsurprisingly, it was my grandmother who noticed the change in me first, at my uncle's fiftieth birthday party. Luke and I had only been together for two months when I asked him whether he wanted to meet my family. He said that he had too much work to do so I went to the party by myself with half a bottle of brandy for company.

They were just announcing that the buffet was open when I got to the club and people were streaming over to the long table on the far side of the room. I stayed where I was, next to the bar. My grandmother hobbled over. Even though her arthritis was chronic she was too proud to use a walking stick.

'Are you *drunk*?' she said, gripping the bar and panting.

I was drunk. Very drunk. *Wedding-drunk*.

'Only spirits I swear, Grandma.'

She laser-beam-looked me up and down and remarked: 'You've lost weight.'

'I'm streamlining,' I said. 'You should see me in the pool.'

'You're drinking too much, I can tell,' she said. 'You'll go blind. Then you won't be able to find the bleeding pool.'

'Rubbish.'

She prodded me in the chest with her fingernail. 'There was once a Russian ship where the sailors brewed their own hooch out of grain, and they made it so strong that they all burned out their optic nerves, and the ship was lost. When another ship eventually came to the rescue, the first ship had been going round in circles for weeks. Because –' she said each word like she was firing it out of a gun at my head – 'because *every sailor on board was blind.*'

'Right.' I took a swig of my drink.

'You're not even listening to me. You don't give a damn.'

'*How are you* would have been more appropriate than a stupid story when you haven't seen me for months,' I said, and walked out of the club.

My mother ran after me, trailing nieces and nephews carrying balloons with the words *You Are 50* printed on them.

'Helen!' she shouted.

'I don't have to take all this shit any more!' I shouted and I hurled my tumbler against the wall. The little ones jumped back at the shattering glass and I felt even more wretched.

I fumed all the way home and when I got back to the flat I told Luke what had happened.

'Put your coat back on,' he said.

'I'm not going back there,' I said. 'I don't want any trouble.'

'We're not going back. We're going *up*.' He jerked his thumb at the sky. 'Now put your coat on.'

We drove east of the city, deep into the Cheshire countryside, with a box of wine and a telescope bobbing about on the back seat.

'Breathe from your stomach,' Luke said and I concentrated on calming down as the lines of cat's eyes disappeared under the car.

By the time we arrived at our destination I felt better. Luke pulled into a lay-by and unclipped his seatbelt.

'Are we here?'

'We're here.'

He got out of the car and walked round to the boot. I buttoned up my coat and followed him. He wrenched open the boot and pulled out a large, heavy-duty torch. When he turned it on the yellow beam illuminated a clear circle of grey gravel surrounded by a cloudy ring. Luke handed the torch to me and I walked round to the side of the car and opened the back door. After I had pulled out the box of wine Luke reached inside the car and carefully eased out the telescope.

'All set?'

I nodded and he locked the car.

We walked to the end of the lay-by, climbed over a rickety old stile and then walked across a dark open field, my outstretched arm holding the torch to light our way, until Luke stopped about halfway across the field and looked up at the sky.

'This should do it.'

I looked up, too. The stars were crystal clear in the pitch-black. Luke set the telescope down the grass and crouched down to adjust the height of the tripod, extending the legs with three quick flicks. As I stood watching him I could feel the dew from the grass creeping up the legs of my trousers.

'You can turn the torch off now.'

I pushed the button with my thumb and the torchlight went off, leaving us in almost in complete darkness, with only the spotlight of the moon above. I could make out the small shapes of the trees at the edge of the field and in the handsome silhouette of Luke's profile was cut out like a cameo. He put his arm around my shoulders and pulled me in front of him so that I was standing between his body and the telescope. He reached around me to focus the lens and rested his head on my shoulder as he checked the view.

'Here.'

He took my hands and placed them around the viewfinder and I squinted up through the lens to see a patch of moon glowing coldly. At first I thought the expanse was featureless and I wondered why Luke had focused on it but as I looked harder I saw the shape of a wide, bluish crater scooped out of the surface.

'That's the Sea of Tranquility.' His voice was warm in my ear.

'Beautiful.'

'I like to think of it as something to aspire to.'

Jamon porridge with mustard nebulae

The maître d' shows a young couple to the table next to mine. I can tell they've been home after work to dress for dinner. He is wearing a pinstriped red shirt and she is in a low-cut sequinned top. They don't look happy. When he puts his hand on her knee she takes a sip of her drink and I see that look in her eyes of acquired deadness, something she has practised and practised until she has convinced even herself that she is enjoying life. With a jolt of recognition I realise it is something that I sometimes do, too.

'Are you ready to order?' the maître d' asks them.

'We'll both take the tasting menu,' says the man.

'Very good, sir,' says the maître d', smiling. Then he turns to me. I look down at my empty plate, embarrassed to have been caught staring at the unhappy couple and embarrassed that I am clearly so nosy.

The maître d' lights the candle on my table and I watch the wick take flame.

'Are you enjoying your meal?' he asks.

'It's astonishing,' I say, and I mean it. 'My compliments to the chef.'

'Thank you, madam,' he says, walking away from my table. 'We aim to please.' I open my mouth and close it again as my waitress arrives.

'Jamon porridge with mustard nebulae,' she says, placing a plate before me.

The plate is covered with a glass dome, a cloud of yellowish smoke swirling around inside. She replaces my empty vodka-tonic glass with a stubby glass of wine.

'Fino sherry.'

'Thank you.'

I've seen the smoke trick before. It's achieved by holding a tubular implement known as a 'smoking gun' beneath a lid or cover, pumping in smoke and then whipping the gun out quickly while closing the lid. As well as being visually effective, the food is infused with a smoky flavour. I smile as I peer through the glass, trying to make out the shape of the food inside. The maître d' walks over and removes the dome, releasing the smoke.

'Enjoy,' he says.

'Thank you.'

Acrid fumes waft up into my nostrils followed by the aroma of meat and stock, and my mouth begins to water. I pick up my spoon. Annoyingly, my phone starts to ring, so I put down the spoon. The name on my phone is Pete's. I feel annoyed that he is intruding, here, now. Slowly and carefully, feeling the alcohol in my blood, I get up from my chair. I decide that I will have a quick cigarette while I take the call.

'Do you mind if I take a moment?' I say to the maître d', rattling my packet of cigarettes as I pass.

'Of course,' he replies and his eyes flick back to the cooling food on the table.

The phone rings out. I step outside, light a cigarette and call Pete back.

'Helen?'

'Hello, Pete.' I take a long drag on the cigarette, holding the phone at arm's length so that Pete doesn't hear.

'How are you feeling?'

'Good. Drunk.'

'What's the restaurant like?'

'It's the best food I've tasted in a long time,' I say, then I correct myself. 'It's the best food I've *ever* tasted.'

He pauses. 'You're kidding.'

'No. It's incredible. It's going to get a star, no trouble.'

Then the guilt hits me. Pete has cooked for me for five years. Cooking is his passion. His pride. But in the last hour I have eaten better at someone else's table without him and now I'm rubbing his nose in it. I realise that I am being cruel so I take another drag on the cigarette and try to think of something nice to say.

'I wish you could be here to taste this,' I say, even though this is a lie.

'Are you smoking?' he asks and I hear annoyance in his voice.

'Yes.'

'I can't imagine *that's* good for your palate.'

He says it almost sneeringly and I decide to give up trying to be nice. I take a long, obvious drag on the cigarette and laboriously exhale.

'Get home safely, won't you.'

'Of course.'

'The last direct bus is at half ten. I checked.'

'I know, thanks.'

In the background I hear Adrian wittering away and I realise that my safe little home, just a few miles away, feels a lot more distant than my life with Luke. I don't want to go home. I want time to slow down. I want this meal to last and last.

'I think you should get a cab,' says Pete. 'Or I could come and get you if you like?'

'No, no thanks, and don't worry,' I assure him, because I want the conversation to be over so that I can get back to my food. 'I'll make the last bus.'

I turn off my phone so that there's no chance of me being disturbed again. I want to enjoy every last scrap of this evening.

Back at the table my porridge is still steaming. Miraculous. The oaten grey mixture is riddled with chunks of ham and specked with tiny yellow dots. I plunge a spoon deep into the porridge, scoop up a mouth-sized portion, close my lips around it and pull out the spoon. The porridge sets off a chain reaction in my mouth. As the yellow dots crackle and explode on my tongue I realise that they are mustard-flavoured popping candy. Ingenious. It's an incredible sensation – as though a thousand hot little stars are being born on my tongue.

* * *

As I got closer to Luke, the rest of the world retreated. When I glanced beyond the bounds of the flat it was as though I was looking down the wrong end of a telescope. At the café where I worked, I doled out hot drinks and sandwiches while avoiding eye contact with the customers. I allowed only their blurred outlines to enter the periphery of my vision. I saw them all as pretty and simple and well behaved, like faraway galaxies. By contrast, my personal life was vast and affecting. I sat beside Luke on the futon and I felt the space between us, full of power and possibility, and I imagined that all around the universe was gathering, swirling and redefining itself. As to how it would eventually settle, I didn't know.

Every Tuesday Luke drove to the research centre and stayed until Thursday. I put a brave face on as I waved him off, resigning myself to tea and toast and the depressing drone of morning television until my shift started. The time apart killed me – not only did I miss him terribly but I was envious of his exciting mission: to recreate the stars on earth.

Luke was part of a team attempting to replicate solar fusion to provide an alternative source of energy. Fusion, Luke explained to me, was the process by which the sun converts hydrogen atoms into helium, a heavier particle. The mass change resulted in a blast of heat and light, which could be used to drive steam turbines and generate electricity. Fusion was cheap, efficient and much better for the planet than fossil fuels. The team were still developing the technology but Luke didn't seem to think they were too far off building a plant capable of providing electricity to the grid.

'Give me five years,' he'd say, as though it would be his own personal achievement.

He was developing "solenoids" – long cylinders of magnetic coils stopped up at each end with magnetic mirrors to confine the hydrogen while it was squeezed and heated. The machine that the solenoids formed part of was called a *tokamak*. It sounded dangerous and exciting – like a monster from a storybook – and I was desperate to see it.

But it was six months before I accompanied Luke to Oxford and even then I wondered whether I had almost forced him into inviting me. He had turned down an invitation to my father's birthday meal – the tenth invitation he had turned down in the short history of our relationship. I texted my mother: *Just me, as usual, thanks* and then I had a flash of paranoia. Had his feelings changed? Had things moved too quickly in the beginning after all?

'Why don't you ever want to meet my people or introduce me to any of your people?' I said.

Luke looked up from the paper he was reading and eyed me darkly. 'I don't have *people*.'

'You have friends at work.'

'Don't be petulant, Helen. It doesn't suit you.'

'I think it does, actually.'

He laughed. 'Oh come to Oxford with me then. Next week maybe? Then you'll see how dull it is and realise you have nothing to be jealous of.'

'I'm not–'

'Oh yes you are, cupcake.'

The following Tuesday I sat beside him on the three-hour drive, bones shaking, cheeks gibbering, as the balding tyres of his decrepit hatchback struck every bump in the road. I felt the thrill of rough fabric on my shoulder blades as they poked through the back of my vest. I heard the grind of the worn cogs in the gearbox. I revelled in the thought of the two of us combined there in the car's captive air.

But things weren't as I expected and I was surprised when Luke took the turning for the centre of town at the motorway roundabout.

'I thought the fusion centre was south?'

'It is but we'll be staying at a college of the university with the other part-timers. I go into work from there – you knew that, didn't you?'

'I don't think I did.'

'Sorry, sweetheart.'

I couldn't hide my disappointment.

'So I won't get to see the tokamak?'

Luke glanced at me as he changed gear. 'Did you really expect...? Oh honey, I'm sorry, it's like Fort Knox at the facility. Sometimes I'm not sure whether they're going to let *me* in. I thought you just wanted to meet my colleagues, we usually decamp to the pub on a Tuesday evening...'

'So what am I going to do for the rest of the day, and tomorrow?'

'You've brought some books, haven't you? And Oxford is a great town to explore. There's lots to do.'

'Okay.'

I felt stupid, as though I had changed my own shifts around and made a lot of effort for nothing. When I had fantasised about our trip I had imagined Luke giving me the guided tour of his fusion kingdom and telling me how everything worked, while his colleagues looked on and saw that there was a person at home with whom he shared absolutely everything. Now it seemed that I was still going to be kept in the dark about one of the most important areas of his life.

Things got progressively worse. At the college we were assigned the most hideous room imaginable, with two glum twin beds pushed together, a lopsided sink and nasty floral wallpaper that was smeared with grease around the light switch. I remembered the halls I lived in at university in Leeds – those bleak little cells stacked up on top of one another like a game abandoned by a bored giant. Luke dumped his bag on the bed, clipped his security pass to his jacket lapel and kissed me goodbye.

'It's the pub over the road, The Shakespeare –we're usually finished around seven. Shall I just see you in there?'

'Sure.'

After Luke had left I took a walk around the town, bought a coffee in a paper cup and sat thinking by the river. My disappointment was intense and so I began to over-analyse. Were the cracks beginning to show? Would this relationship go the way of all the others? I couldn't bear the thought but I couldn't shake it, either.

Around teatime I made my way to The Shakespeare and sat at a little round table in the back corner of the pub. By the time Luke arrived I'd had three vodka-tonics and a shot of sambuca. I was reading *Rebecca*, which I used to read every year, and I was so engrossed in the book that I didn't notice him walk into the pub until he was practically standing above me.

'Here she is!'

I looked up to see Luke beaming down at me, flanked by two other men with security badges clipped to their coats. I put down my book and stood up.

'Hello.'

I stuck out my hand.

'Helen, this is Alastair and Tony. Alastair and Tony, Helen.'

Alastair had his hair scraped into a ponytail. Snags of hair sprayed out through the centre of the ponytail, making him look like some kind of monkey-eating eagle. Luke introduced Tony, a stocky man in his late forties with a subtle suntan, as one of the world's most renowned physicists. When Luke asked what everybody would like to drink, Alastair and Tony ordered a Guinness and I asked for the same. The two men hovered awkwardly on the other side of the table while Luke went to the bar.

'Do you want to sit down?' I asked Alastair, who seemed the more approachable of the two.

'No,' he said, his bun jiggling as he shook his head. He gave Tony a sidelong glance.

'Are you sure?' I said.

'Well,' Tony picked at his shirt collar, 'it's just that our usual seats are over *there*.' He nodded towards the front of the pub.

'Oh, shall we all move then?'

Alastair exhaled and Tony dropped his shoulders as they both visibly relaxed.

'Would you mind?' said Alastair. 'I didn't want to cause a fuss, it's just that...'

'I understand completely.'

I collected my things and followed Alastair and Tony to the other side of the pub. They were an eccentric bunch, Luke's colleagues. They all seemed to be out on the edge of the world on their own little orbits – and I had only scratched the surface. As Luke handed me my pint I felt a little tap on the side of my boot. I jumped and looked down. It was an apple.

'Is that an apple?' I said.

'I think so,' said Luke, bending down to pick it up. The door of the pub was open a crack – an apple's width, in fact – and as we stared, the door opened fully and a girl appeared.

'If that had been a grenade, you'd be dead by now,' she said triumphantly.

'Helen, this is Kat,' said Luke. 'She's a complete lunatic.'

Kat walked over. She looked younger than me, nineteen or twenty, and I guessed she must be an early graduate. She had tattoos all over her forearms – Latin phrases and Egyptian hieroglyphs – and her ears were pierced through four times on each lobe. She took the apple from Luke's hand and dropped it into a carrier bag. From the same bag she extracted a packet of cigarettes, which she handed to Luke. 'Surely,' she said, 'it would be more accurate to describe me as a *sol*atic.'

The door of the pub burst open again as though it had been kicked, to reveal a tall woman semi-silhouetted in the doorway. As the shape of her appeared, everybody stopped talking. The woman stepped inside and pointed at Kat. She was almost six feet tall, with long red hair and pale skin.

'*You* were supposed to wait for me.'

'Sorry!' said Kat. 'I had to do a last-minute fag run.'

The woman moved closer. 'Duly noted.'

I put my hand on Luke's arm.

'Lily,' said Luke, 'this is Helen. Helen, Professor Lily Collier. Lily's the centre director.'

The woman flashed me a serpentine grin. 'Also known as the one who gets all the credit.'

Her handshake was firm, smooth and cool. She looked to be in her late forties, maybe fifty, with a thick Scottish accent and a high forehead that gave her a Renaissance air. Her hair was a deep auburn – sun and earth mixed together. She had metallic blue eyes and wore layers of black clothing beneath her science whites, like charred silk flower petals beneath bandages. She had a fierce, damaged look about her and I recognised her instantly as a force to be reckoned with.

Lily went to the bar and came back holding a steaming white mug that had a label on a string dangling over the side. As she pulled up a stool I got the impression she didn't often join her staff for an after-work drink: she didn't have a regular seat for a start.

'To what do we owe this pleasure anyway?' said Kat, slurping her pint and wiping away the froth from her top lip with her thumbnail. 'Are you firing us or something?'

'No.' Lily turned from Kat to look at me. She held her left wrist with the first two fingers of her right hand as though she was taking her own pulse. 'I've come to see the girl who's managed to tame our Luke.'

I thought: *She's slept with him.*

Luke snorted and I felt my cheeks redden but I was determined not to be undermined. Lily reminded me of someone although at the time I couldn't think who. An electricity hung in the air like heavy rainclouds, ready to crackle and burst. I felt an intake of breath around me, the rainclouds swollen, heaving with foreboding.

'We tame each other,' I said.

Lily turned to look at Luke. 'How romantic.'

I thought: *She's definitely slept with him.*

She held the label of her tea and swirled the bag around the mug. Luke stood up and noisily collected together the empty glasses from the table. 'Can I get anyone a drink?' he said.

I nodded. Kat shook her head.

'Yes please,' said Tony.

'Alastair?'

'Yeah,' said Alastair. He tapped his empty pint pot thoughtfully. 'I think I'll move on to red wine. I should get in practice for France, I suppose.'

'Are you emigrating?' I said, glad of the chance to change the subject.

'No,' Alastair coughed and looked guiltily at Luke. 'We're all moving there,' he said slowly.

I saw Lily smirk into her drink as she took a sip. Luke turned to me.

'The research programme is transferring to the south of France sometime in the next few years. I haven't decided whether I'm going.'

I felt my stomach fall three feet, to the floor.

'We're desperately trying to persuade him,' said Lily, squeezing the teabag against the side of the mug with her fingernail. 'But we've never been able to make him leave Liverpool so we're not holding out too much hope.'

'I teach in Liverpool,' said Luke, the glasses rattling between his fingers.

'You could just as easily teach down here.'

'I like the North.'

I didn't like the speed with which Lily and Luke were arguing, as though there was nobody else in the room. It was a very strange feeling, that of being around Luke and not being included in a conversation with him.

I quietly downed drink after drink for the next two hours, smiling politely whenever one of Luke's colleagues made a joke. I was reeling from what had been said. I ignored Lily whenever she made a cutting comment, and I even ignored Luke when he laid his hand next to mine on the table and rested his little finger on top of my little finger.

When we got back to the halls I couldn't help but bring up the subject of France.

'When were you going to tell me?'

Luke slammed the door of the room.

I stepped back.

'Why are you behaving as though you've been *shown up*?'

He looked at me, his eyeballs quivering, and I saw that he was almost as drunk as I was. There we were: two drunk and angry people, taking the evening's tension out on each other.

He ripped off his shirt and trousers and got into bed with his boxer shorts on. Once he was in bed he turned away from me, towards the wall, and pulled the duvet over himself to form a blank, immovable lump of pure rage. I undressed and got in bed next to him but when I put my hand on his shoulder he shrugged it off.

'Leave it, Helen.'

'You don't want to talk about it?'

He snorted. 'Just let me sleep. I'm up early.'

I tucked myself in on the other side of the bed and closed my eyes, but it was no good. I lay awake all night, turning the events of the evening over and over in my mind. In the darkness, alone, my anger mellowed. Luke was right. What business was it of mine where he might be next year? We'd been together a matter of months. Everything had happened so quickly, my feelings had grown huge and uncontrollable, and now it was as though I wanted all of him – his heart, his soul, his future. Lily's words rang in my ears: *The girl who's tamed our Luke*. I knew then who she reminded me of. It was another woman with a knife for a tongue. My grandmother.

* * *

I made myself a ham sandwich yesterday afternoon because my stomach was gurgling so loudly that I knew I had to eat something. I opened the breadbin and took out two pieces of bread. From the fridge I took out ham, butter and wholegrain mustard. I picked a tomato out of the bowl next to the egg caddy. Pete and I had recently had a conversation about how putting tomatoes in the fridge impaired their flavour and had designated a bowl especially for tomatoes, which we kept on the work surface. As I looked at the bowl I felt guilty and sad.

I roughly sliced the tomato into six pieces and spread butter onto one side of the bread and then mustard onto the other. Then I laid two slices of ham and three slices of tomato on one piece of bread, and pressed the other slice of bread on top. I cut the sandwich in half. Adrian squawked.

'Troublecauser,' I said, tossing him a slice of leftover tomato.

I heard Pete's key crunch into the lock.

'Hello?' I called.

Pete came through to the kitchen carrying a square cage filled with navy blue felt cloth.

'What's that?' I said.

'This little fellow,' Pete said, 'needs a home for the night.'

A quivering pink snout emerged from between the cloth in the cage, followed by a fuzzy black and white head. 'Oh god,' I said. It was a baby badger.

'Mike found him on the road by the power station,' said Pete. 'His mother had been run over by a lorry. The refuge centre can't take him for a few days so I said that we could take care of him in the meantime.'

'We don't know what to do with a *badger*!'

Pete patted a piece of paper on the top of the cage. 'Mike's given me full instructions.'

Adrian hopped to the nearest chair and squealed. The badger disappeared back inside the cloth. Pete took hold of my hand.

'Helen, I'm really worried about you. I'm really worried about *us*.'

The badger emerged again, its immature nocturnal eyes struggling to endure the harsh halogen spotlights.

'Well, Pete, this is a subtle move,' I said.

Pete put the cage down on the floor. Adrian jumped down to inspect it.

'*Adrian! No,*' I said.

Pete let go of my hand to pick up Adrian and put him in his cage. Adrian squealed louder.

'What's that?' said Pete, nodding to the sandwich on the work surface.

'I haven't eaten all day. I thought I probably should.'

'Are you hungry? I could–'

'Not really.'

'How can you not be? You haven't eaten properly for days.'

'I don't know.'

Pete filled the kettle with water from the cold tap. He placed the kettle back in its cradle and flicked the power on. 'So what do you think about the badger?' he said as the kettle began its preliminary rumble. I looked down at the cage.

'We can't nurse that creature – at least, I can't,' I said. 'For a start, I've promised Keith I'll review a restaurant tomorrow night. You know, Bethel. The new one that's supposed to be *all that.*'

Pete looked at the untouched sandwich on the work surface. 'How are you going to review a restaurant when you can't even eat a sandwich?'

I didn't answer. He pulled his lips inside his mouth and took my hand again.

'Do you want me to come with you tomorrow?'

The kettle shook in its cradle, a rush of steam clouding the dark tiles on the wall. I knew that Pete's question was loaded with other questions, such as *Do you still love me?* and *Does it still matter to you whether I love you?*

'Do you?' he said, looking at my face.

The question hung in the air between us. He let go of my hand.

'Helen, are you having an affair?'

I laughed.

'Don't laugh,' he said. 'Are you?'

'No.'

'Swear. Swear on your mother's life.'

'I swear on my mother's life. I'm not having an affair.'

'So who the hell is Luke? Adrian hasn't plucked that name out of thin air...'

Hearing Pete say Luke's name made me shudder. Just the sound of it made me feel as though a veil had dropped between two worlds: my past and my present. Luke's name was out there, flying round the room.

'Someone from a long time ago.'

'How long ago?'

'Aeons. Light years.'

I knew that I was trying to convince myself as much as anyone. I was trying to put distance between myself and Luke for everyone's sake.

'From the black hole?'

'Yes.'

After he had called Mike to get him to come and collect the badger cub, Pete was very quiet the rest of the night. We ate an Indian takeaway in silence and he wouldn't let his leg touch mine in bed, even when he was asleep.

Deconstructed Lancashire Hotpot

A man in a baseball cap walks past my table on his way to the toilet.

'Can you get *over* this place?' he says. He is American. 'Five years I've lived here and like nothing. Then, out of nowhere, this!'

'It's unreal,' I say, smiling.

Meanwhile the waitress has taken away my cleanly scraped porridge plate. So far there has been no sign of the miracle worker in the kitchen – not even the top of a head visible in the porthole window. I wonder if the chef is a man or a woman. There must be at least two or three of them in there. Every detail of every dish is executed perfectly. I play with the fork for my next dish and wonder where the food will transport me next. The American man comes out of the toilet and heads back to his table.

'Enjoy,' he says as he passes.

'Thanks. You too.'

The couple at the table next to mine are still sitting in silence. I watch the kitchen door and my waitress emerges seamlessly, carrying a plate of food. Mine, I hope. She walks towards me, past other waiting tables, increasing the likelihood of the food being mine. Good, good. When she arrives by my side I smile up at her gratefully.

'Deconstructed Lancashire Hotpot with Beaujolais,' she says, placing the glass and the plate precisely in front of me. Sometimes in restaurants plates are delivered to the table so carelessly that they hang off the edge of the tablecloth, threatening to fall into your lap, but here immense care is taken when it comes to things like plating up and placing plates at the correct angle.

'Thank you so much,' I say, picking up my knife and fork.

'Deconstructed' is right. The thin slices of beef look raw, like carpaccio. The potato is deep-fried, sprained in tight curls. I dip my little finger into the sauce and taste it. Garlic caramel. Delicious. Difficult to get right. The dish is accompanied by a single oyster on the half-shell and a tiny bottle of Tabasco. The wine is a light red colour against the candle wax.

* * *

One day after sixth-form college I found myself suddenly standing outside my grandmother's house. I hadn't consciously thought about travelling there but somehow I had managed to catch the bus to Burnley and walk across to her housing estate without realising what I was doing. By the time I came to my senses and looked at my watch it was five o'clock. I unlatched the gate and immediately Grandma's dog, Shandy the Second, bolted out from behind the house and dashed to the gate, barking and spinning like a multi-headed Cerberus at the gates of Hades.

'Grandma!' I shouted, lingering behind the gate because I wasn't convinced that Shandy the Second wasn't going to attack me.

She opened the door. 'Come on in,' she said, unsurprised to see me. Her apparent ease made me instantly uncomfortable. Was she expecting me? A more disturbing possibility entered my thoughts. Had she somehow *summoned* me? I walked over to the door, the little dog trotting at my heels.

In the living room, which was as hot as a blast furnace, she ushered me into a high-backed armchair and disappeared into the kitchen. Shandy the Second lay across my feet so that I couldn't move while she was gone. When my grandmother returned she pushed a thin china mug of volcanic tea into my hands.

'I'm glad you're here,' she began. 'There are some things I want to tell you.'

She bent low to turn down the gas fire. The orange flames turned violet and then pale blue, until only five rows of red heat remained. I looked around the room. My grandfather had been dead two years that winter, and the house they shared, where my father had grown up, had become my grandmother's castle. Remnants of my grandfather – the fire irons, a ship's brass porthole, a doll in Portuguese national dress – were polished and positioned and angled like trophies in the crevices of the room. On the metal base of a lamp was a fridge magnet decorated with a religious poem: *God grant me the serenity to accept the things I cannot change, the courage to change the things I can, and the wisdom to know the difference.*

'What kind of things?'

My grandmother sat herself down on the other side of the fire in an almost identical chair. I thought we must have looked like a pair of big pot dogs: Gog and Magog.

'You're sixteen, Helen,' she said. 'It's time for some home truths.'

Great, I thought, *a lecture. Just what I need in the middle of my A-levels.* I took a sip of hot tea and felt it sear my soft palate so I held it there in my mouth and nodded.

A gentle smile appeared on my grandmother's lips, as though she might be remembering a stolen summer's day from long ago, and then she said, 'Your grandfather was a bastard.'

I spluttered the tea down my blouse. As I attempted to put the cup down safely onto the carpet I spilled a hot slug on Shandy the Second, who howled and scarpered into the hall.

'Gran!'

'Well he was.' She calmly took a sip of her own tea. 'I know you and your brother have it in your heads that he was an angel, but let me tell you something: he was far from it.'

'Why? What did he do?'

'He had an affair.'

A bar on the gas fire blew out and relit itself.

'An *affair*?'

It was indeed a bombshell. Affairs were things that happened on TV and in other people's families – more exciting families than mine.

'Yes,' said my grandmother. 'I got onto it when he started being dominant in bed, like an old dog with a new trick. I confronted him and he crumbled. He could never hide anything from me for too long. No one can.'

'When did it happen?

'Oh, early on. Before your father was born.'

I imagined my grandfather standing there in the shameful ruins of his marriage. My gallant grandfather, who we all adored, who sang at the beginning and end of every day, like a bird. The story in the family was that he saved her a seat on the bus to the mill every morning, since he got on two stops before. He had taught me how to whistle and how to take a photograph, his eyes slightly phosphorescent like the opals from the spread of gemstones in the Encyclopaedia Britannica. I wondered whether my grandmother was lying. I hoped she was.

'She was another winder at the mill,' my grandmother went on. 'Lottie Aspin, that was her name. She was a friend of mine, but not a close friend – one of those that never quite breaks through.' I nodded although I couldn't imagine my grandmother having any close friends at all. 'Your Granddad and I had been married seven months. Your father was two months in my belly.' She paused and looked at my face and then, satisfied with my expression, she continued. 'Anyway,

144

a year or so later, when your father was a baby – and *what* a baby, he looked like Princess Margaret! – well, it all came out. He told me how he'd been in the pub after work and she'd arrived, and they'd got talking, and she was *ever* so impressed with the fact that he was a warp dresser, and before he knew it he was back at her sister's house unclipping his braces.'

I hated the fact that I had started to believe her.

'I punished him for a long, long time. Then I realised I couldn't hate him for it because it wasn't his fault – he was just weak, as all men are. And in some ways it made life easier because his other faults paled into insignificance. All his shitty little habits like leaving the top off the toothpaste and asking where the back door key was. All the things that, over decades, send married people over the edge. I rose above them all from that point on because of how thoroughly he'd disgraced himself.'

I didn't know what to say. I retrieved my half-empty cup of tea from the floor, checked the temperature and took a contemplative swig.

'Anyway,' said my grandmother. 'Here I am, still. So I won, didn't I.'

I didn't answer. I drained my cup.

My grandmother stood up and walked over to the window. She looked like a statue of a conquering noble man, sated with victory. I saw that she was still furious with my grandfather and I wondered whether she was simply trying to ruin my good opinion of him now with this poisonous outpouring. But how could she have invented so many tiny little details if it wasn't true?

'Why are you telling me all this, Grandma?'

'You think love is easy.'

'I don't.'

'Yes you do.'

'No I don't.'

'I'm not arguing with you,' my grandmother scoffed. 'I'm just telling you that it isn't. It's the hardest test of your life.'

'Maybe you'd think differently if you'd sat a Latin exam.'

She pretended to ignore this comment and continued to stare out of the window into the middle-distance.

'Given my time again, I wouldn't have a husband. I'd have a butler. Someone to iron my clothes and chauffeur me round, and no bloody aggro.'

'But then none of us would exist. My Dad, Ben, me...' My voice trailed away.

She smirked into her teacup.

'Oh.' I looked down at my shoes, dejected. I realised that my grandmother wished us all away just as I had often wished my family away.

'Shall we have our tea?' she said brightly, her mission accomplished. 'I've hotpot in the slow cooker.'

I looked towards the kitchen, where two white dinner plates were warming on the top of the radiator, propped up against the wall like blank plaques.

'Thanks, Grandma, but I'm not really very hungry.'

'Don't start that. I see that starting in you.'

'What?'

'Martyrdom.'

'I'll never be a martyr,' I said. I looked at her and thought, *You don't really know me at all.*

She forced a dish of hotpot in front of me but I could barely eat it. I couldn't get my head round it: her apparent delight in being evil.

When my father picked me up there was a questioning look in his eye, an unspoken enquiry as to why I had gone to see Grandma. He was terrified of her, too, and it wasn't exactly as though she and I were close. Seeing my father nervous made me nervous so I said: 'The thing about Grandma is she thinks she's got everyone sussed.' He seemed to relax a little.

Bands of light like beams from a lighthouse flashed through the windows as buildings passed between the moving car and the setting sun, turning my father's hair red – gold – red – gold – red. I looked at his patchy sideburn and the half-hearted jut of his Adam's apple. As I studied the imperfections of my father's face I wondered what secrets he kept in his head, what wars had raged between him and my mother on their own private battleground, what they had never told me about each other, what they considered sacred. I wondered whether being in love with the same person for ever and ever always involved living a lie of some kind or other.

Roast pheasant with spiced prune mincemeat

As I chew the last piece of beef I think about what the memory of my grandmother might be telling me. I slowly wash the meat down with the last mouthful of red wine. Individually, the flavours are untamed – together they are sublime. I know that for the first time on a job I am savouring where each taste takes me, appreciating how my senses are being coaxed.

I look over to the next table. The unhappy couple are inspecting their amuse-bouche. Strangely, they don't seem to have the green tea and shrimp concoction – they have instead a little flat doughy disc, a blini, topped with a freckled whitish pate and a strand of fresh chive. He is the first to pincer the blini between his oar-like fingers and bring it up to his lips. His reaction isn't one of someone overly impressed. He puts his head on one side and makes an appreciative noise as he chews. Then she tries it. As she bites her face changes dramatically – she looks to one side, at me, to hide her face in shame because she is enjoying the blini so much. I look away. I give it a few seconds before I peek back and her head is back on her shoulders, her eyes closed, her face displaying the most holy sweetness. She is lit from inside. Her partner is looking at her as though he doesn't know her. '*Sarah,*' he says, and the hand goes to her knee again. She fixes herself and looks at him as though she knows him too well, as though she has finally come to her senses.

My waitress picks up my empty plate and wine glass. I snap my head back round. 'Excuse me, I wonder if you could tell me–' I say but she is gone. I notice that it is getting busier still. Perhaps they just ran out of shrimp.

Another glass of red appears on the wine-spotted coaster. This one is darker in colour. Brooding almost. The colour of blackberries and sparrow's eyes.

'Roast pheasant parfait with spiced prune mincemeat,' I hear my waitress say. 'Shiraz.'

'Thanks.'

I try the wine first. It is rich but not too tannic – spicy and gamey. The doll-sized portion of food looks surprisingly hearty. I carve off a piece of roast drumstick and smear it with a dollop of sticky warm fruit. The combination cloys in my mouth. It is sweet, rich, exciting, poignant – simultaneously full of promise and tinged with tragedy. It tastes like Christmas.

*   *   *

Luke hated Christmas.

'It's a con,' he said, when I asked him how he wanted to celebrate our first festive season together.

'I've had some good Christmases,' I said. As I said this, I realised that I hadn't thought about my devil for a long time.

'Let's keep it lo-fi,' said Luke.

So when 25th December rolled around I didn't go home to my family. I slicked on some red lipstick and roasted a turkey crown, which we ate on the futon with two bottles of ready-mulled wine heated up in a saucepan.

I imagined my family sitting there in their paper hats, thirty miles away. My mother would be avoiding the gravy and cream, dressed up in dangly earrings and incongruously also wearing her many-times-through-the-wash slippers; my father would be meticulously cutting his potatoes into squares and suggesting which films they might want to watch on the

TV; Ben would be gobbling up anything and everything in sight and irritating everybody by inventing worse alternatives to the punch-lines in the crackers; Grandma would be having her usual livid staring contest with the Queen during her speech. I imagined them all trying not to look at the empty seat at the table, the extra sprouts, the unopened presents under the tree. It would be as if I had died, or gone to prison.

I tried to brush those thoughts away and remember that the fun of Christmas was false. I had always hated sitting around a table with my family. It was agony.

I bought Luke an antique brass orrery that year. It was a beautiful thing, a scale model of a planetary system, each planet on its own brass rod connecting it to a central ball, the Sun, and through this to the other orbiting bodies. Turn one and you turned them all. Its movement was perfectly smooth – *symphonic*, Luke called it. At three feet wide it dominated the living area. He bought me an illustrated copy of Edgar Allan Poe's collected works, filled with spidery drawings, plus two designer nail polishes, one a shade of deep plum and the other a sort of rotten fig. He painted my nails that evening with the dark figgy colour. I held out my hands as steadily as I could after so much hot wine, enjoying the accurate way he covered each of my crescent moons with an unnatural shade of purple-brown. Then he held my hands and blew gently on my fingertips until the polish was dry, and I knew in that moment that I would have sacrificed all the family Christmases to the end of time for that sense of communion – that two-way trance.

New Year's Day felt similarly hallowed. We took a blanket to Formby beach and waited for the sun to set, lying there freezing in our anoraks and jeans. We took off our shoes and socks and rolled up our skinny jean-legs. I was admiring his toned calves, his rough heels. I was the drunkest I'd ever been – beyond wake-drunk, even.

I said: 'I think I've known you before, in another life.'

I was expecting the usual cool, measured response but instead he replied: 'They'll keep meeting, our souls, you know.'

But then he turned down the invite to have dinner with my family on New Year's Day.

'We could just go for a few hours,' I said. 'I'll do the talking.'

'I haven't got much time off work. I wouldn't mind relaxing.'

'You've had two weeks almost.'

Luke tossed his head.

'Look, I've not got the greatest memories of New Year, okay?'

I remembered that his father had died in early January.

'I'm sorry,' I said. 'I didn't think.'

'It's okay.'

Valentine's Day and Easter came and went, and I didn't visit my family or invite any of them to the flat in Liverpool. A studio flat wasn't really the sort of place you could play hostess anyway. We had roughly ten metres square to live in and, as the months passed, the dirt and mess seemed to be getting worse. The paintwork was chipped, the windowsills were dusty, the floor covered in discoloured cracks, which spewed out silverfish when it rained. On any given day the following flotsam might be strewn about: a fax machine, a printer, a dead cactus, a single brown German-made sandal, empty wine boxes and bottles, empty cigarette packets, empty lighters, books, magazines, papers and DVD box sets. On the windowsill there was a red and gold pincushion, a tub of cocoa butter moisturising cream, a fluorescent orange felt tipped pen and the TV remote control. The usual data sheets and highlighted printouts were scattered across the less-worn end of the rug, along with three or four astronomy magazines. The kitchen was only relatively tidy because we barely used it. Bacterial flora – if not quite fauna – was rife. Even then, glasses and cups were hard to come by. We had a cooker, a

CD player, a kettle, a mismatched pair of plates, and a vertical stack of watercolours that Luke had turned to face the wall.

With the flat in such a state, a visit from my parents would be unthinkable. I could see them huddling together like vulnerable animals at a stagnant watering hole in the Serengeti, suspecting that just out of view, lions were gathering to circle them. I could almost see that anxious-tempted look in my mother's eyes as I offered her the first biscuit from a fresh packet, my father standing by regarding the futon. 'So this is where you sit *and* sleep...' I'm not sure they'd have approved of Luke anyway. My family's idea of a good man was someone who kept his head down and took care of his car. Luke was as far away from that kind of man as you could get.

I told myself that Luke and I didn't need other people. When we were together every hour was loud and round – every cubic centimetre full of wonder. Every day arrived like a surprise parcel in the post, full of shiny things. Who needed Christmas?

Langoustine mint roll

'Langoustine mint roll,' says my waitress, placing the little creation in front of me, 'and a glass of Sancerre.'

'Excuse me,' I say and as she looks at me I notice she has an unusual little glint in her eye like a slice of mirror – the result of laser surgery, perhaps. 'I'm sorry to bother you...'

'Of course, madam, if you can just give me a few minutes. As you can see we're rushed off our feet at the moment...'

'Sorry, of course.'

I look around at the busy restaurant but I also resent being made to feel inconsiderate. The waitress disappears in the direction of the kitchen. It could just be coincidence, I think, taking a sip of wine. It could just be a string of coincidences. I can rationally evaluate this whole experience if I try; I'm just not sure I want to.

The white wine's acidity cuts through the remnants of game on my tongue, clearing the way for the delicate shellfish before me. I press the sponge roll with the back of my fork. It has a good resistance. I turn it around on my plate, looking at it from all angles. It is a simple dish. A dish that doesn't flatter or deceive. It looks like a savoury Swiss roll – a piece of pale yellow sponge rolled around chunks of light flesh and a mint-dashed cream. I cut it in half. Bring it up to my lips. Close my eyes. Forget all about my questions.

*   *   *

I was standing in a production line making prawn and egg sandwiches when I realised I was too drunk to be at work.

It was the afternoon of a derby match between Liverpool's two major football teams: Liverpool and Everton. The café where I worked was owned by a woman called Lucy. She was in her early thirties, blonde and willowy, and she liked me a lot. I had blown her mind when I told her that her body contained a small amount of every single element on the periodic table – something Luke had recently told me.

'Even gold?' she said, rinsing the drip trays from the post mix with sloppy-handed disbelief.

'Even gold,' I replied. 'A very small amount in the pit of your stomach.'

'Well would you believe it? Here's me, walking round like a branch of H Samuel all these years and not even knowing it...'

Lucy's mother was a Liverpool fan and her father was an Everton fan. This caused ructions within the family – especially on derby days, when Lucy attempted to keep the peace by hosting her extended family at the café. She bought a limited amount of alcohol and assembled a stodgy buffet, uniting the lot of them with sandwiches and cakes presented on an exactly equal number of blue and red paper plates.

I had been out with an old friend prior to my shift – a real one-off. The days, weeks and months had flown by and I had lost touch with almost all of my friends. Initially I had ignored Ruth – who was then training to be a barrister in London – when she texted me to say that she would be passing through Liverpool for a conference and asked whether she could stay, but then I changed my mind. I thought that it might be an interesting experiment. I hadn't seen her since the night I'd met Luke but I was interested to see what an outsider from my past might make of Luke, especially as he hadn't met my family.

I wore a red top and a grey skirt when I went to meet her – with red shoes and a lot of eyeliner. I felt energetic and Ruth's eyes widened when she saw me.

'You look very – alive,' she said, sitting down again and taking a fast, sucky sip from a frosted orb of Chardonnay. We were in a nice place.

'Thanks,' I said. 'I feel it.'

'I'm a plant,' Ruth said. 'That's the conclusion I've come to. I have no emotions.' What she really meant was, *no sex life.*

'Actually they've proven that plants respond to stimuli,' I said, because I had nothing to lose. 'Their chlorophyll rate goes through the roof when a previous molester walks into the room.'

'Shit,' she said, taking a proper swig of wine. 'Does your boyfriend have any single friends?'

'Sorry,' I said, because he didn't have any friends apart from his work colleagues.

I stayed drinking with Ruth until quarter to two, when I looked at my watch and realised I should have been at work an hour earlier. I gave her directions to the flat and told her that Luke was expecting her, and then I made my way to the café.

Lucy was furious when I arrived and set me to work chopping egg and red onion. I tied on a cotton bandana to keep the hair and sweat off my face, and it was soon soaked. Laura, the other girl who worked there, had covered for me in my absence and was taking her frustration out by slamming dollops of mayonnaise onto oven bottom muffins. Meanwhile Lucy laid the tables and attached red and blue bunting to the café walls with drawing pins. We worked in silence while we got up to speed. Somehow I didn't cut myself with the knife, although I did start mindlessly eating the ingredients.

'I'm not sure the red onion goes with the prawns,' I said to Laura. 'I think spring onion would go better.'

Laura looked at me like I'd just grown a tail.

'Helen, I don't really think you should be dipping your fingers into the sandwich filling.'

Lucy came into the kitchen as we made up the last sandwich.

'All done in here?' she said. 'Good. They're about to arrive. Helen, hot drinks duty, please.'

The coffee machine at Lucy's Café was a complex creature, with pipes and taps coming out at all angles, like obscene tentacles. I wasn't entirely convinced that it wasn't alive as I watched it steadily breathing out steam and shuddering. It gargled out shots of espresso readily enough but whenever I wanted to steam or froth milk it hissed at me so forcefully that it almost blasted off my bandana. *Give me a break*, I begged, twisting the knob for hot air. There was soon a backlog of orders and then more kept coming. I was so overwhelmed that I accidentally left a teaspoon in the bean grinder and the contraption almost blew a gasket.

'Helen,' Lucy said, turning off the grinder just as the metallic crunching reached an ear-splitting crescendo, 'can I have a word?'

The toxic smell of burning plastic pervaded the café. Helen's rowdy extended family had fallen silent and were staring at me, triangles of egg and prawn sandwich in hand. I made a fist and dabbed at my brow. Then I followed Lucy into the kitchen.

I took off my bandana and blew my wet fringe out of my face.

'What's going on?' said Lucy. 'What makes you think this is okay?'

I knew that the job didn't mean that much to me, and that knowledge made me reckless.

'I'm sorry, Lucy.'

'Helen, *look* at yourself.'

Laura stuck her head round the kitchen door. 'Lucy, we've run out of white wine,' she said.

'Already?' said Lucy. 'Decant apple juice into some of the empty bottles. See if they notice. Or maybe we could just wring out Helen – she seems as though she's soaked up a few gallons of the stuff today.'

Laura disappeared and Lucy turned back to face me.

'I'm just being honest, Helen. I can usually smell the booze on you. It's been that way for a while.'

'Only on Mondays though, right?'

Lucy smiled. 'Tell you what, why don't you take the rest of the day to have a think about whether you really want this job.'

I heard a deeply amused drunken voice come out of my mouth: 'I don't really want this job.'

As I walked out of the door I felt totally out of sorts – exhilarated but also worried about what I was going to do. I bought a bottle of brandy to steady my nerves from an off licence on the way home. As I walked along the docks, the side of the brown bottle pressed against the thin white plastic of the bag, stretching it into translucence, like a vein under skin.

When I got up to the flat I heard raucous laughter through the front door. As I opened the door I saw Luke and Ruth move slightly away from each other on the sofa as they caught sight of me, although neither of them stopped laughing.

I stood in the hallway for a moment. 'Where's the party?'

'You're home early!' said Ruth, her eyes wide and shiny.

Luke stood up scratching his chin, and Ruth started chewing her fingernails. She looked nervous and excited. There was a strange atmosphere in the room, false and staged, and I felt as though I had just walked onto the set of an amateur theatre production. I sensed that something wasn't right but I didn't know whether I was just unsettled from the events of the afternoon.

'Who's for brandy coffee then?' I said, shaking the bag in my hand.

'Yes please!' Luke clapped his hands.

Ruth nodded uncertainly. 'Just coffee for me please. I probably shouldn't drink any more.'

I followed her gaze over to the kitchen countertop and saw that they had worked their way through half a bottle of gin while I had been at work.

Luke went to use the bathroom, giving me a peck on the cheek as he passed. While he was out of the room Ruth said, 'He's special, isn't he?'

Not lovely or nice but *special*.

I felt a sick feeling hit my stomach as all the possibilities rushed through my mind: had he charmed her with stories about his youth, or with details of his work – but still that didn't explain the suspicious mood of the room, which led me to the worst possibility of all: had he tried to kiss her?

I took the bottle of brandy out of the bag and set the kettle boiling, glancing at Ruth now and then to try and work out what exactly was going on as she silently reapplied her lip-gloss. When Luke emerged from the bathroom he sat back down beside her and said: 'Ruth's been whinging about how she can't get a boyfriend.'

'Oi!' Ruth punched him lightly on the arm and Luke assumed a defensive karate pose.

Were they flirting with each other, in front of me? I couldn't believe it.

'Right,' I said, staring at Ruth. She looked a total idiot, giggling like a schoolgirl in her expensive suit. I was glad then that I had been fired from the café – who knew what might have happened if I had left Luke and Ruth alone together any longer.

'I've told her that she's a formidable woman, and the right man is just around the corner.'

I nodded in agreement.

'Oh I'm not that formidable,' Ruth said, flapping her hand in Luke's face, 'it's only family law.' But I could tell she was thrilled.

'Nonsense,' said Luke. 'You should be very proud of yourself. Shouldn't she, Helen?'

'Absolutely.'

I took three mugs over to the sink and rinsed them under the hot tap. Maybe it was the mood I was in but I couldn't help but feel as though Luke's comment was loaded. As I unscrewed the cap on the brandy I saw Ruth getting up off the futon. I looked up to see her picking up her briefcase and holdall.

'Well, I suppose I should go and check into a hotel.'

I put down the brandy. 'Are you not staying here?'

Ruth looked embarrassed. 'I'll be fine in a hotel.'

'But why?'

She slung her scarf around her neck. 'I didn't realise it was all one room,' she said quietly.

'We've got an airbed. I can set it up in the far corner.'

'It's absolutely no problem for me to get a hotel.' She smiled. 'It's been so lovely to see you, Helen, and to meet you, Luke.'

Luke stood up and gestured towards the kitchen. 'One for the road?'

Ruth shook her head. 'No, I really shouldn't. Big day tomorrow.' She walked towards me.

'Okay then,' I said and I was secretly relieved. She kissed me on both cheeks.

'I'll call you when I'm next in town,' she said. 'Or if you ever find yourself in London...'

I nodded even though I couldn't see myself ever being in London – I felt entirely without prospects at that point.

Luke saw Ruth to the door as I stirred brandy into two mugs of coffee.

When Luke returned he was grinning wildly. 'Well, *she* was awful,' he said.

I took a step back. 'You looked to be getting on a house on fire.'

'She was bearable for a few hours,' he said, taking a slug of his brandy coffee. 'But I can see why she hasn't got a boyfriend. Desperate vibes.'

I narrowed my eyes. 'You don't have to lie to me, I know you enjoyed her company.'

'Would you rather have come in to see us having a fist fight?'

I had a choice at that point, as you do in those moments when you feel the heat rising and you're spoiling for a fight: you can either blaze up or go Zen. My eyes bristled with the perverse urge for damnation.

'I'd rather not have come in see to you pawing each other like dogs on heat.'

Luke put down his mug. 'Jesus, Helen. What's wrong with you?'

I squared up to him; angry, desperate. 'Why did you have to get drunk and flatter her like that?'

'I was only trying to make her feel welcome.'

'You made me feel uncomfortable.'

He snatched up his mug, coffee spilling onto the counter. I could tell he was going to bark and spit back. 'Do you know how hard that shit is for me? Of course I got drunk. So what if I flattered her? I felt like I was killing time when the truth is I'm BUSY. And I gave up MY AFTERNOON for YOUR FRIEND.'

The air boiled in the room around us.

'Why couldn't you just have a normal conversation with her like a normal person?'

'Was my little act not good enough for you?' He slammed down his mug, spilling more coffee. 'My work is very important, and I don't think we have the room for guests, but maybe if you'd *asked* me instead of just *telling* me it was happening, once you'd decided to do your little domestic bliss test on us, on me … as it turns out I think I performed rather well.'

I didn't know what to say to this because he had hit the nail on the head so spectacularly, so I started to cry hot, pointless tears – and then I was furious with myself for crying, which made me cry harder and hotter still.

'How *dare you* invite whoever you want here and then criticise my behaviour!'

'I'm sorry,' I bleated amidst the tears.

He was right, of course: it wasn't my flat, it was his. I had to remember that it didn't matter what we looked like as couple from the outside.

'I lost my job,' I said, not so much as in explanation for my outburst but out of resignation to the fact that he had won.

'Ah, sod it,' Luke said, coming towards me and putting his hand on my neck. He picked up my coffee mug and pushed it into my hand. 'We'll get you another.'

Are you not even going to ask me why? I thought the words but I didn't speak them. And then it struck me. It was all in those words that Luke had just said: *We'll get you another*. My work was as trivial and pointless to him as it was to me.

We had make-up sex but I was distracted. What I couldn't bear to admit was that I was becoming frustrated and threatened by one of the very things that attracted me to Luke: his lonely, devout ambition.

After my first visit to Oxford had gone so badly I vowed never to go back, but when my twenty-second birthday fell on a Wednesday and Luke was due to be away, I changed my mind and suggested myself that I should accompany him on his next trip.

'Are you sure?' Luke said. 'We can always celebrate on the Thursday night when I get home.'

'I'm sure,' I said. 'I like your work colleagues. It'll get easier as time goes on.'

I had already decided that if Luke decided to move to France I would offer to go with him. What did I have to lose? It wasn't though I had any real ties in England. This was dependent of course on whether he wanted me to go with him, but I couldn't see why he wouldn't. He told me that he loved me and I knew that I had to try and fight my insecurities and just believe him. The little problems we had would iron themselves out. If we lived in France then seeing my family wouldn't be an issue. I could take some time to work out what I really wanted to do and make a fresh start, maybe even go back to college for a bit. Best of all, Luke and I could build a new home together, a home that we were both comfortable in, where we could both feel safe. If France was the future I might as well get to know his work colleagues better in the meantime.

But when Lily turned up at the pub again I realised it wasn't going to be that easy.

'Happy birthday,' she said as she handed me a blue alcopop. 'Eighteen, is it?'

'Twenty-two.' I put the alcopop on the table, next to my empty wine glass.

She was clutching her usual mug and the white paper label dangled on its thin string over her thumb.

'What *is* that?' said Kat, who was sitting in her usual place at the other side of the table, next to Alastair. 'It stinks.'

'Smells like mint tea,' said Tony.

'It's green tea with mint,' said Lily. 'I bring my own bags.'

Kat raised her pint. 'I prefer the cooking lager.'

Lily raised an eyebrow and took a sip of her tea. 'My regards to your liver.'

Luke started to stand up from his stool. 'Do you want to sit down, Lily?' he said. 'Helen and I aren't stopping long, we're going for a meal.'

'Very nice,' said Lily. 'KFC?'

'Excuse me a minute,' I said, standing up and pushing past Luke and Lily. 'I'm going to the loo.'

But Lily followed me into the Ladies'. As I sat on the toilet I heard the door open again and I thought *That's her*, and when I came out of the cubicle I saw that it was – she was standing by the sink, holding her hair in place on top of her head with one hand, like a world-weary nightclub singer. She had brought her drink into the toilet, just like my mother had told me never to.

'What did you study at university?' she said, releasing her hair and letting it fall down over the straps of her vest onto her bony shoulders. 'It wasn't science, was it?'

I scrubbed my hands together under the hot tap.

'Oh, lots of things. How to wear a tight t-shirt. How to down a pint. How to identify a dickhead.'

'You know, you remind me a lot of myself, when I was younger,' she said.

That old chestnut, I thought. I knew what Lily was up to – she was trying to put me in a box, to pigeonhole me, to file me away like the results of some experiment, so I said: 'I have brown hair,' by way of disagreement.

'Are you familiar with Schröedinger's Cat?' Lily asked, perching on the porcelain sinktop. I saw that she was gearing up for a speech of some kind, something that she was prepared for, and I wasn't. I instantly felt at a disadvantage. I felt as though I had said everything that I wanted to say to her and now I just wanted to get out of the bathroom as quickly as possible. I shook my hands and held them under the automatic drier.

'No,' I said, raising my voice over the sound of the hot air from the drier. 'Is it a fusion-related in-joke?'

'Pretty much,' said Lily, taking a swig of tea and showing no sign of going anywhere. 'Schröedinger's Cat was a thought experiment designed by the Austrian scientist Erwin Schröedinger to illustrate the problem with the Copenhagen interpretation of quantum mechanics being applied to everyday objects.'

'Right,' I said, nodding my head when in fact I was at a loss to grasp what she was saying. I pulled my hands from beneath the drier and the stream of hot air quickly stopped.

'In the experiment, a cat is contained in a sealed lead box with an unstable radioactive source governing the release of a poison that will kill the cat. The source is random once the box is sealed so you no longer know whether the cat is alive or dead – until you open the box, that is. The Copenhagen interpretation of quantum mechanics implies that after a while the cat is *simultaneously* alive and dead, because it relies on the idea of quantum superpositions – the combination of all possible states of a system – an idea which only collapses at the exact point of measurement, i.e. when we open the box, we see that the cat is *either* alive or dead.'

It was complicated stuff but I thought I knew what Lily was talking about: once you pin something down there's no point any more. But I didn't understand how this related to me, in that moment – unless, I thought, unless all of my suspicions *are* true and Lily has slept with Luke, and she is trying to make me feel even more excluded from their world.

'Luke and I went to an interesting conference together on the subject last February,' said Lily, as if to confirm what I was thinking. 'In London.' She paused to drink her tea. 'You should ask him about it.'

So Lily *was* trying to compete with me where Luke was concerned, that much was obvious now, and something *had* happened between them in the past, while they were in London, I thought, probably in some horrible little hotel. It must have been around the time I'd met Luke, angrily reading on that train, he must have been travelling back from spending time with Lily. My imagination whirred and a sequence of pictures rolled through my mind like an old silent movie. Luke had been with Lily the day that I'd first met him. They had been at the conference together, then they had gone out for dinner, had too many cocktails back at the hotel, had sex, and then an argument. He had gone to Euston to catch the late train back to Liverpool, but there hadn't been a direct one at that late hour, so he had got on the next best thing: a train to Manchester. And he had sat on that train, on the whisky, on the rebound.

'Ignorance is bliss,' I murmured.

Lily smiled. 'You really are a funny kid,' she said. 'But you should open the box before you get hurt.'

'The thing about me, Lily,' I said, emboldened by the wine and still determined to save face, 'is that I believe in true love. I don't need other possibilities. The cat will always be alive.'

'If you want to believe that, then believe it,' said Lily but I could see her eyes had darkened in livid defeat. 'Just know this: however important you think it is, what you think you've got, here's the killer: the universe is indifferent.'

As I turned my back on Lily I felt her eyes, red hot with hatred, boring into the back of my skull, willing me to drop dead. She stayed in the Ladies' while Luke and I gathered our things and left the pub, but she remained on my mind throughout my birthday meal.

In our room at the university halls that night, Luke fell asleep quickly, his snores loud and round. I locked the door and pulled the desk chair across the room and positioned it by the bed. I sat myself down. I didn't want to sleep so I dug my fingernails into my palms and pinched my arms every time I felt myself dropping off. Even though the door was locked I still felt the need to keep some sort of vigil, to stand guard over Luke and our love. I felt it coming out in me: possessiveness – the kind that only rears its head when you sense a threat. After Lily's attempt at an attack I felt as though Luke and I were the last remaining two of an endangered species.

Wild Scottish salmon with vanilla foam

As the couple at the next table start their second course I see that once again it looks different to my shot of carrot vodka soup. It is instead a shot of green liquid topped with foam. The woman knocks it back, and when her head bows back down she has a look of steely resentment on her face. She slams the empty glass on the table, slaps the man across the face and storms out of the restaurant. The man begins to weep. The maître d' hurries over and gently escorts him out. 'Of course, sir, no charge, sir...' he is saying. I'm not sure what to make of this, but before I have time to really consider it, my next course arrives.

'Wild Scottish salmon with vanilla foam,' says my waitress. 'The wine is a Pinot Noir.' I'm still staring at the door. 'Sometimes,' my waitress says, 'the food is so good that people are overwhelmed.'

'Right,' I say. I sit there, zombie-like, as if I am stoned. This really is the strangest place. Then I look down at the plate of food and I forget about the rest of the room.

I tease apart the fillet of salmon and soft coral flakes slide across the thick, primrose-coloured sauce that has been swiped across the plate to hold the fish in place. The foam on top of the fillet is light but still has substance and a faint shine. In the mouth it has a hint of vanilla, of summer, and sun cream and short nights.

* * *

There hadn't been an eclipse visible from Britain for ten years when Luke and I went to Skye. We decided to camp in order to see more of the night sky, so the day before our trip we visited a camping shop to buy the necessary equipment. It was a new thing, shopping together, but it wasn't an entirely pleasurable experience. There was an old sign in the camping shop window that said: *NOW IS THE WINTER OF OUR DISCOUNT TENTS.*

'Ha,' said Luke, pushing open the door.

We found an assistant over by the Thermos flasks. He looked malnourished, with a beauty spot on his left cheek and a name badge that said *Ian*. He looked at us with a forced sort of expectation, the way people do in shops.

'We're looking for a tent and a double sleeping bag,' said Luke.

'This way, please,' Ian said with a little jerk of his head and we followed him across the shop. 'What sort of weather are you expecting?' he asked.

'Scottish,' said Luke. 'Four seasons in an hour.'

We stopped by a line of sagging sleeping bags, like empty carcasses hung up on hooks. Luke snatched down a grass-coloured bag with a darker green lining.

'We'll take this one, please,' he said without smiling, 'and we're in a rush.'

I took my purse out of my bag. 'I want to get this.'

'No, no,' said Luke.

'Yes.'

'No.'

Ian looked uncomfortable and so I stopped arguing and allowed Luke to pay.

We left at dawn the next morning. The car was cold so I took regular slugs from a bottle of Jamesons between my knees, to warm me up. I know that I was a bad passenger. I winced when Luke overtook lorries and gripped the dashboard when he accelerated round corners on country lanes.

'You are a control freak,' said Luke, giving me one of his wild, dark stares.

'Takes one to know one.'

When we reached the ferry terminal at Mallaig, we parked the car and got out to buy tickets. Luke put on his woolly hat and I thought he looked younger, innocent almost, and I thought of the young man he'd once been – living all alone after his mother had kicked him out, trying to find his own way at university, forced to support himself, discovering the stars one by one. I stood outside the ticket office and bent one knee and put my foot on the wall, my fringe dropping down over one eye as I smoked. I pretended not to notice him until he was right beside me, waving two tickets in his hand.

On the ferry we bought hot chocolate and I poured whisky into the paper cups. Then we stood on the stern and watched the mainland recede in the swollen grey sea. We lit cigarettes with waxy little matches and blew the smoke out over the gutsy wake and it was so cold we couldn't tell where our smoke ended and our breath began.

'We might pass out if we're not careful,' I said.

'Don't you love the idea of a sea burial, though?' Luke said. 'The way they say: *Until the day that the sea will give back her dead*. It seems less final somehow.'

We stood there, arm in arm, on what felt like the brink of infinity. My hand shook in the cold wind as I drank my whisky-chocolate. Across the deck I noticed a couple of other people who looked like they might be astronomers, too.

'They'll kill you, you know!' shouted one of the men, nodding at our cigarettes.

'Oh I certainly hope so,' said Luke. 'I'll be asking for my money back otherwise.'

The crossing took us to the southernmost point of Skye, to the Sleat Peninsula. It was a short drive from the ferry port to the campsite. We followed the coast road, along the crashing cliffs and pebbled bays, from where the nearby Isle of Eigg's northern lighthouse was just visible, swathed in sea mists. The car tyres sprayed up arcs of gravel on the driveway, and then we stopped. The campsite was near-deserted apart from a couple of campervans. It felt like we were in the first scene of a disaster movie.

We parked up outside the office and stepped inside. 'Welcome,' said the man behind the desk. 'Just one tent is it?'

'Yes please,' said Luke. 'Two nights.'

'Twenty pounds please. If you could fill in this form...'

I held out a ten-pound note, which Luke refused with a vertical palm. 'I've got this.'

'But I want to go halves.'

'Buy me a drink.'

'We've brought all our booze.'

'So work it off.'

The man behind the desk rustled his paperwork and pretended to ignore us as we riffed away.

'There's a word for that.'

'Socialism?'

We parked the car by some trees and I unpacked our luggage from the boot while Luke pitched the tent. We had travelled light – just a rucksack, a cool box and a bag of telescope equipment, a pair of jeans each and a few tops and jumpers, tracksuit bottoms, long johns, walking boots, deodorant, toothpaste, toothbrushes. Luke had the tent up in no time, and we changed into our walking boots and braved the toilets together. The bathroom was lined with horizontal planks of wood, like a sauna, and the toilet worked by means of a macerator, which let out a throaty roar when the chain was flushed. As I sat on the loo I noticed that the wooden planks were covered with dark, beady knots.

Before it got dark we lit a fire in the charred pit outside, using newspaper pages scrunched into sweet-shapes as kindling. I hung a torch from the centre of the pole inside the tent.

'Don't turn it on yet,' said Luke. 'Insects.'

We sat in the doorway of the tent, finishing off the bottle of Irish whisky and listening to the night sounds of the surrounding woodland. I was convinced that I could hear the sea.

When I woke up I was alone outside the tent, and one side of my face felt squashed and sore. The fire was still smouldering – cracks of hot pink slicing through the white embers. I loosened the door flap and shuffled backwards inside the tent, where Luke was sleeping. The torch was still on.

'Luke!' I whispered, nudging him gently.

'I didn't want to move you,' he said. 'And the fire was warm.'

He was lying with his arms folded above his head, like a baby. I crawled inside the sleeping bag next to him. When I awoke for the second time it was to the sound of buzzing. I looked at Luke and his eyes were open, his face unreadable still, less than a foot from mine.

'What's that?' I hissed.

'A fly?'

'Optimist.'

The buzzing stopped.

'I don't like it when they go quiet,' Luke said. 'It means they're planning something.'

The buzzing started again.

'There!' yelled Luke, escaping from the sleeping bag in a hop, skip and jump movement and tearing open the door flap.

'Aaaaagh!' I shrieked, following him just as ungracefully out into the sunlight.

We stood awkwardly in front of the tent, where the fire had by now fizzled out. Luke was wearing his tracksuit bottoms and a hoodie. I was wearing the same clothes as yesterday. I sheepishly tugged down my dirty t-shirt. The wasp crawled round the edge of the door flap and flew away towards the trees.

'You're my hero,' I said, wiping the sleep out of the corners of my eyes with my cuff.

As the time of the eclipse drew closer we gathered the equipment together and headed for the highest point of the island.

'You know, this will be the last eclipse I'll really bother with,' Luke said. 'I feel as though I've pretty much ticked that box.'

I wanted to ask him how that felt, to have something worked through and sealed up, but the idea of starting a conversation about the end of something made my stomach shrink. All of the huge things surrounding us now that we were far away from the flat – the sea, the sky – were starting to scare me, and I could understand why in ancient times, an eclipse was seen as a sign of the onset of the apocalypse. There was a very odd feeling in the air, an anticipation of something impossibly dramatic.

When we reached the plateau we found a patch of grass and smoothed out the hairy tartan picnic blanket. Fields surrounded the plateau on three sides and to the fourth lay the sea. I unpacked the box of wine, two plastic glasses and a paper bag of smoked salmon we had bought from the shop at the campsite.

'Keep your eye on the ball,' said Luke, nodding at the sun while he fumbled about in his rucksack.

I twisted the little tap out of the box of wine and pressed the button until a weak stream of wine trickled out.

'I suppose now's the time to tell you that technically this isn't an eclipse,' said Luke. 'It's an occultation.'

'Then you brought me here under false pretences and I demand to be taken home immediately.'

'Strictly speaking, the term is a misnomer,' Luke went on. 'An eclipse occurs when one object passes into the shadow cast by another. Like when the moon disappears at full moon by passing into the Earth's shadow – that's a lunar eclipse. So, technically, what we commonly call a solar eclipse actually amounts to an eclipse of the Earth.'

I handed him a glass of wine and we tapped our beakers in a mute cheers.

'It's just what I call a little over-dramatisation,' I said, 'and that's fine by me.'

Luke smiled. 'When I was younger I always found the sight of the horizon very comforting. It's what they prescribe for seasickness, you know, because it helps your brain process the movement – informing you that beyond the motion there is a still point; there is calm and stability.'

'Are you talking about when your dad died?'

It was the most direct I had ever been about the subject and I wasn't sure how Luke would take it, but it had been on my mind so much that some part of me was goading me to throw it all up there, everything between us, the scariest deepest stuff, and see how it all came back down.

'Yes,' he said and I could tell he was thinking as he spoke. 'I suppose I am.'

It felt as though he was letting his guard down and I wondered whether this meant we were growing closer or drifting apart. We sat in silence and watched the sun move across the sky, but I felt as though I'd had a glimpse of someone else behind the image of himself Luke polished and presented – and he was shit-scared, just like me.

'An eclipse can only ever happen during a new moon,' said Luke, snapping back into lecture mode. And he chickened out, just like me, just like that.

He told me all about eclipses then, that the dark grey region below the moon was the umbra, where the sun was completely obscured by the moon. The small area where the umbra touched the Earth's surface was where the eclipse would be seen – on this occasion, the umbra would take in Scotland, Iceland, some of Greenland and a lot of the North Sea. The larger, light gray area was the penumbra where a partial eclipse could be seen – but this was nothing in comparison to what we'd see: blackout in the middle of the day. In any given year there were at least two solar eclipses and as many as five. I didn't know how many eclipses I had lived through – total or partial – and I didn't know how many I had missed.

As I sat with Luke drinking plasticky wine and eating smoky fish, I learned that the sun's distance from the Earth was about four-hundred times the moon's distance, and the sun's diameter was about four-hundred times the moon's diameter, and that because these ratios were approximately the same, the sizes of the sun and moon as seen from Earth appeared approximately the same. I learned that total eclipse occurred when the moon was closest to earth on its elliptical orbit – or at its perigee. I learned that total eclipses would recur at any given place, on average, only once every three hundred and seventy years. The total eclipse only lasts for a few minutes at any given location, as the moon's umbra moves eastwards at over a thousand miles per hour. Due to tidal acceleration, the orbit of the moon around the Earth becomes approximately three-point-eight centimetres more distant each year. It is estimated that in six hundred million years, the distance from the Earth to the moon will have increased by twenty-three thousand, three hundred kilometres, meaning that it will no longer be able to completely cover the Sun's disk. The fact that the sun will increase in size over this timescale makes it even more unlikely that the moon will be able to cause a total eclipse. Therefore the last total solar eclipse on Earth will occur in slightly less than six hundred million years.

I filled glass after glass and handed them to Luke as he spoke. Shortly after 2pm, the moon began to slowly inch across the sun. By this point we really were *wake-drunk*, ballooning in our seats on the ground, grabbing one another to speak.

'Look!' I said, clutching his collar. 'It's starting!'

'Here,' said Luke, reaching into his kit bag. 'All the cool kids are wearing them.'

He passed me a pair of what looked like sunglasses, except they were much thicker.

'Certified solar filters,' he said. 'I find they're more involving than a pinhole camera.'

I put them on and made a peace sign. We sat side by side, my right thigh along his left, our walking boots lined up like odd feet.

'I think we made a pinhole camera once at school,' I said. 'A camera obscura.' I enjoyed saying the words.

'I bet you were an astonishing little girl.'

I blushed. 'I was hit and miss.'

'You went to a good school, though?'

'Oh, the best.'

'Did you enjoy it?'

'I once wrote a poem about it called 'The Pleated Hell of Doing Well',' I said. Luke laughed. 'Whatever you do, don't say the word.'

'What word's that?'

'*Ungrateful.*'

'I won't. I'll just say astonishing and leave it at that. The rest is your own opinion of yourself, and you don't deserve it.'

But despite the compliment or maybe even because of it, I felt my deepest insecurities rising, all the old feelings of alienation and inadequacy. I stopped myself and looked around, outside myself. The daylight was getting dimmer as if the sky was overcast, and yet I noticed that objects cast sharp shadows. I had my solar filters at the ready.

'You say when,' I said.

'I will,' said Luke. 'You'd be surprised how many people get caught out. They know not to stare at the sun under normal conditions because it's so bright, but with so much of the sun covered during an eclipse–'

'Don't you mean an occultation?'

'It's easier and more tempting to stare.'

'Even thought it's rude?'

'The only completely safe time is during totality. But either side of totality is the most perilous time, because your eye is tricked.'

'Tricked?'

'When the sun is full you usually only glance at it, and even then the pupil will close down and reduce the brightness of the scene, allowing less harmful light into the eye. But if the eclipse is near total, the low average amount of light causes the pupil to open. Unfortunately the remaining parts of the sun are still just as bright, so they are now brighter on the retina than when looking at a full sun. As the eye has a small fovea–'

'A *what*?' I was giddy, reeling, taking the mickey. I was so very drunk.

'A small fovea, at the very back of the eye. The name comes from the Latin for 'pit'. It's the best part of the retina and you use it for your most detailed vision. The tendency is for your eye to track images onto this which, during an eclipse – if you let the brightest sunlight in – can cause a lot of damage.' The sky grew darker still. 'Now, the first thing of interest will be Baily's Beads,' said Luke. 'When the shrinking visible part of the photosphere – the disk of light also known as the sun–'

'I know what the photosphere is,' I said, my tongue stuttering over the word.

'Oh do you? That's good. Well, when that becomes very small you'll see little blobs of bright light, caused by the sunlight still being able to reach Earth through lunar valleys, but no longer where mountains are present.'

Luke put on his own solar filters and turned to face the sun. There was a mere quarter of it left, the moon obscuring the rest. We watched the mottled sphere of the moon creep further still. The moon covered all but a clipped yellow fingernail of sun and then the fingernail was gone. Birds from nearby trees started twittering and calling, confused. A few spattered out from the trees in jagged flocks. My own animal instincts prickled. The hairs on my neck stood on end, my shoulders hunched, my feet tingled – all of me ready for flight. It was the most unnatural thing I had ever seen. The sun shorn of its beams. Disastrous twilight.

On the left hand side of the almost-obscured sun there was a last bright flash of light, and then there was a moment of complete and utter silence, as though the world was taking a breath. I held my own breath too.

At that instant I felt a tapping on my arm and so I turned and peered down under the filters. There was a small red box on my knee. I removed the solar filters. Just then, the sun disappeared in the sky. I looked up. Our nearest star, our source of light and life, had been replaced by the cold silhouette of the moon. The sky darkened in a matter of minutes. Around the edge of the moon's silhouette there was a small ring of light, the corona – the only reminder that the sun was actually still there, hiding from the world, out of sight. I looked back down at my knee, took the box into my hand and opened it. A diamond solitaire was inside, sitting in a slot of cream silk.

'The world is round, but you turn me on,' Luke said. He was looking at me as though nothing else mattered – the sun coming back, the end of time, nothing.

'I like this star better than the old one.'

I slipped the ring onto the third finger of my left hand and kissed him.

'Look,' said Luke, pointing towards the moon. 'A solar flare. Normally you can't see the chromosphere because the photosphere is much brighter. Because of where the sun is in its cycle the corona is small and symmetric today, but sometimes it can be large and fuzzy. It's difficult to predict.'

'You're more difficult to predict,' I said, still admiring the ring.

He turned to look at me and smiled a lupine smile. 'Then you'll never be bored.'

There was a whoop from the field behind. We turned round to look. The shape of a man was dancing with the shape of a woman. The woman was twirling her scarf around her head. In the distance, the shape of a horse looked on.

'Pagans,' said Luke.

'Seriously?'

'Yep.'

'Are they going to burn us to make the sun come back?'

'Well, this *is* an island...'

I poured us both some more wine. 'Better make sure we're nice and flammable, then.'

The shapes in the field behind stopped dancing and sat down. The world around me looked like a primitive puppet theatre, with shapes on sticks whirling in front of oil lamps and candles. I saw it was an old, old place, of grinning faces and false beliefs. I looked down at my ring and saw how it caught the tiniest rays of light, trapping them, reflecting them forwards and backwards through its intricate prism. We sat on the hill for a few minutes more, staring into the hissing black hole where the sea must be, the wind pulling our hair out of our hats, buffeting our arms and hands, wine spilling down our fronts. Then Luke instructed me to put my filters back on. Sure enough, seconds later, a flash of light appeared on the right hand side of the moon. The sun was coming back. Beads of light started to appear, and then, finally, a yellow-orange curved slice of sun.

'The shadow bands!' said Luke, leaping up.

'What?' I said, feeling the unfamiliar weight of the ring on my finger as I moved.

'They look like dark waves, like the ripples you get on the bottom of a swimming pool. They occur just prior to and just after totality. Shit shit *shit*.'

'Sorry.'

'No, I didn't mean–,' Luke sat down and put his arm around me. 'Look, it doesn't matter.' He took my face in his hands – my ordinary face, pale as a planet, that emitted nothing and reflected everything. 'Those are just the special effects,' he said, jerking his head at the reborn sun. 'I look at you and I know myself.'

No one had ever said anything like that to me before and no one ever would again. I was thrilled from top of my unremarkable head to the tips of my unremarkable toes. I knew that there were galaxies that could unfold beneath a single fingernail, within a single strand of hair.

We watched the sun continue on its path across the sky until eventually it came to rest on the horizon and sat there, steady and unblinking, like a bubble in a spirit level. Lily was so wrong, I thought. The universe wasn't indifferent. It could see us, and it was on our side.

Ballotine of hogget with quince

My hands are clenched into clammy fists. I open them and press them onto the tablecloth either side of my empty plate, where they leave irregular spots of sweat on the red cloth.

'Ballotine of hogget with quince jelly,' says my waitress, out of nowhere. 'The wine is Rioja.'

Hogget is a peculiar meat, like black pudding – another old-fashioned delight that has recently enjoyed a renaissance. It's best not to analyse a black pudding unless you're in biology class but hogget stands up to some scrutiny. Somewhere between mutton and lamb, it was once a staple of the British diet but, like mutton, lost out to lamb years ago – something lamented by many critics since as an older meat it has more flavour.

In the dish before me the hogget is served as a ballotine – a poached, boneless cylinder, secured with string. The meat has been flattened, stuffed with herbs and then rolled into a tight little bundle. I've always found ballotines romantic, the way they're parcelled up like presents. I slice it in two. The meat has texture and heft, the fibres coarse but well-woven.

The quince has been made into a reddish jelly, cut into a square-inch block. I know that it will be sweet but not too sweet, there will be a hint of preservation, of maturity. The Rioja Gran Reserva has spent two years aging in an oak barrel. Two years – almost as long as I spent with Luke. It's a long time, long enough to fall in and out of love, to travel to hell and back.

* * *

The last time I saw my grandmother she was making a cup of tea in my parents' kitchen. I was twenty-three years old and weighed just eight-and-a-half stone.

I had planned to go home to show off my engagement ring but as I had stood in the lounge brandishing my left hand my mother and father had looked at my face with what seemed like concern, and my brother, who was home from university for reading week, had just been plain insolent.

'Bit small, isn't it?' he said, scrutinising the diamond, his hand on his hip. 'I thought he was the *grand fromage* of particle physics, this *Luke*?'

'It's bigger than your brain,' I said. 'What can you possibly be *reading* for a degree in Sport Therapy anyway?'

So my big news turned out to be a bit of an anticlimax, but I reminded myself that my family weren't really enthusiastic types anyway – even when it came to things they enjoyed, such as television. So I decided that I would get through lunch with them as quickly as possible and then I would run as fast as I could for the train back to Liverpool.

I went into the kitchen to fetch a glass for the half-bottle of brandy that I'd bought from the off-licence at the bottom of the road.

'Alright?' said my grandmother, without looking up from the teapot she was stirring.

I stood by her at the stove and poured myself a three-finger shot. She put the lid back on the teapot. Then she said: 'I've clocked it though, don't think I haven't.'

I put down the glass of brandy. 'Clocked what?' I said.

'*Clocked what*, would you listen to her. Clocked that bloody big diamond ring, that's what.' She transferred the teapot to a plastic tray.

'I'm engaged to be married,' I said.

'Well, I'm glad to know you haven't just been on the rob.'

'His name's Luke.'

'This is the one you've been living with, is it?'

'For six months.'

'Oh aye. The man no one's met. The stranger at the gate.'

This was a judgment but it was also the truth and I hated her for it. And I hated Luke too in that moment, for being the man that refused to meet my family.

'I should have known,' I said. 'Why can't you just say *congratulations*? Why do you have to have a dig?' I was babbling, running away with myself now, avoiding the fact that she had touched a raw nerve. 'But that's too much like admitting someone else might know more about the world than you, isn't it? You don't need to meet Luke to know that he's wrong for me because you know everything about everyone, don't you, Grandma?'

She looked shocked. I had never spoken to her like that before. I felt vaguely ashamed but at the same time I couldn't help but feel furious. What right did she have to criticise my relationship? She had already admitted that her marriage to my grandfather had boiled down to nothing more than pettiness. Was she jealous again, or just enjoying being spiteful?

'At least I didn't just marry the first boy who was nice to me on the bus,' I said, screwing the lid back onto the bottle of brandy and pulling on my coat.

'Sod off then!' she shouted after me as I ran. 'Sail away for a year and a day, and see what happens!'

Approaching Liverpool from the west, there's a section of track between Edge Hill and Lime Street that passes between stone walls some twenty metres high. The walls are thunder-grey, dark with moisture. Patches of rust and moss drip down in tombstone-sized slabs; ferns and lichen froth out of the cracks. Lily of the valley flowers nod over the top of the walls, like a reminder of heaven. There are drainage portholes at eye-level, sharply dipping down to black. Lighter-coloured gouges, deep and diagonal suggest that something huge and mechanical has once scraped through the gap. The train feels tiny by comparison – a toy entering the battlements of a giant's castle. After three tunnels, each longer than the last, the bone-grey arch of Lime Street looms, like the skeleton of a dinosaur.

When I got to the flat I told Luke what my grandmother had said.

'She's senile,' he remarked without looking up from his sheet of data.

'She's not senile,' I said. I felt I had to defend her somehow.

'You can get away with murder when you're senile. It's the only thing we've really got to look forward to.'

I wanted to say, *She's always been like that*, but I was also sick of thinking about my grandmother so I said: 'And what about you, my darling?' I said. 'What grand plans do you have for the thin end of this mortal coil?'

'Why, I'll shed this man suit and make for the great beyond!' And he got up off the futon and ran around the room on all fours, nipping my bottom with his fingers as he passed.

I kept my frustrating lack of conclusions to myself. My grandmother was out of touch with my life and she couldn't handle it; that was all I needed to know.

In the end, I had taken the job at the bookshop. It was a bijou place owned by a woodlanderish man in his mid-fifties. During the interview he had rolled his Rs theatrically and described himself as the *prrroprrrrrietor*. William was his name. He had grey mutton-chop sideburns like a butcher and on his way to and from work he wore a straw boater with a navy ribbon around it. I liked his style.

'Why did you leave your last job?' he asked.

'They asked too many questions.'

'What, like when can you start?'

'Just like that, yes.'

The bookshop was called The Ginnel, an old Yorkshire word for alley, although it was situated on a major road. The shop was gloomy and oppressive at first with a dark, narrow entrance hall, but beyond that it opened up into a welcoming, snug little lamp-lit space that felt like a place in which to shelter from the storms of life. It was easily twice the size of the café and it was divided between two rooms: Fiction and Non-Fiction. I had never in my life seen so many books. The rooms were packed floor-to-ceiling – with shelves stacked on top of shelves, and books piled on top of books, and tinier books stacked on top of those – all making great elongated pyramids of leather and board spines, punctuated with the odd modern dust-jacket. Hints of dark-stained wooden boards were visible in the corners of each room, but otherwise the floors were covered with two huge Persian rugs, worn away in patches to bone-coloured string. Random chairs – a Van Gogh, a dining chair, an overstuffed easy chair – were scattered around to encourage browsers, and a deep green Swiss Cheese plant enlivened the central archway between the rooms.

William was more of an obsessive, compulsive reader than I had ever been. In between assisting customers, he read a book a day. He read stood next to the till, bobbing from foot to foot, occasionally he would slap the table with his hand when he found a bit he liked. He had an interesting system – reading two or three books on a similar theme one after the other. The day I started working for him he told me that his current theme was Victorian Archaeology and I saw that he was reading a book called *The Victorians and the Ancient World: Archaeology and Classicism in Nineteenth-Century Culture*. A title and a half. I was suitably impressed and said so, which I could tell was partly the point. William was, among other things, a drama queen and a show-off.

William liked his mornings to himself so he opened the shop from lunchtime until 7pm – which was a much more realistic shift for me. I started at 1pm and was never late, although usually the remains of a hangover clung to me. I would sniffle and stammer my way through the first few hours until, after several glasses of water and a couple of coffees, I came into my own around mid-afternoon.

There was a bunch of regular customers who used the shop like a private library. They would ask for new books each week and sit for hours in the easy chairs and on the rugs. In addition, the occasional lost or adventurous shopper – the shop featured in a few of the more indie tourist guides – would wander in. And, last but not least, there were the students who seemed to feel edified by the atmosphere of the place. To start with, they would look tired and hopeless, as if they were disillusioned with the world and everything in it, and then, once they had rested their bags on the backs of chairs and started exploring the shelves, I'd watch them gradually relax. Soon enough, they would be working their way through a haphazard stack of books, occasionally breaking their reverie with a beatific smile when they discovered a collected works of Dante or Dickens. They rarely bought anything – the odd £1 or £2 paperback – but their gratitude meant the world to William, because essentially the Ginnel was a refuge more than a shop.

It felt as though it was all going so well but then one afternoon William caught me off-guard with the question: 'Your fella's into cosmology, isn't he?'

'How do you know?' I said, pausing on a stepstool, a copy of Shakespeare's sonnets in my hand. It was 2pm and I'd only had one coffee since waking up. My head was still throbbing. I wasn't ready for conversation.

'You keep buying books that I don't see you reading,' William continued. He was right. I'd been using my staff discount to treat Luke to a book I thought he might like.

'He's a physicist,' I said, turning back to the shelf and putting my fingers between two books to make a space. I slotted the book on sonnets into the gap and stepped back down.

'Why don't you take this one for him? On the house.' William proffered a gold-embossed red leather book towards me. As I moved closer he opened it to the flysheet: *A Mind as Brilliant as the Stars: The Life of Galileo.*

'Thanks, William, but I really couldn't.'

'Why not?'

'It looks... valuable.'

'Well, it is. But he'll look after it, won't he?'

'He doesn't always look after books.'

It sounded silly out loud, there in the mature, grown-up environs of the bookshop. I'd been so impressed by Luke's rock and roll behaviour at the beginning of our relationship but now in the cold light of day it seemed a little bit silly.

I saw that William was looking at me curiously. 'He looks after *you* though, doesn't he?' I studied his face, wondering whether this was a come-on, but I realised that it wasn't – William just liked me and cared about me, even though he barely knew me. It was purely platonic. 'I've known a few destructive types in my life,' he said and for once I wasn't dreading a lecture. 'A few years ago,' he went on, 'before I opened this place, I worked my way up to the position of publisher of a magazine. But then the management started making cuts, something about the advertising migrating, how they hadn't predicted it – we never got the full story. The media group had decided to focus on what it called its 'core products', and the magazine I worked for wasn't one of them. Their plan was to lose people and transfer the rest to lower-paid jobs elsewhere but first they asked for voluntary redundancies. I thought long and hard about it, and then I decided to take the package. Around about the same time, a painter friend of mine came round for dinner. I told him what was happening and he sneered at me and my choices – he disapproved of my ever being there, you see. He left after dessert and we never spoke again. A month later I packed up my desk and left the magazine. I spent the next two years trying to work out which was worse: a corporate arsehole or an artistic arsehole.'

'And what did you decide?'

'That the corporate has it, but only by a whisker.'

'Is that why you opened a bookshop?'

'Partly.' William handed the book to me. 'And I still want your boyfriend to have this.'

'Actually, he's my fiancé.'

'In that case, I *really* hope he looks after you.'

I spent the rest of the afternoon trying to work out why I hadn't minded William's input. I decided it was because he didn't laud his knowledge over me like my grandmother or the teachers at school. He didn't have anything to prove and I realised that I admired this about William. It was a rare quality. The only other person he reminded me of was, weirdly, my father.

My phone rang as I walked home and I expected it to be Luke, asking me to pick up some wine from the off licence as I passed, but when I looked at the screen I saw that it was my mother. We hadn't spoken since I'd stormed off before Sunday lunch the other week.

'Helen!' she said, sounding surprised when I answered, and then: 'You've upset your grandmother.'

'She's upset me.'

'Oh, *Helen*.'

'I was thinking, you should all probably meet Luke and see what you think. There's a nice pub by the dock...'

'Ben won't come,' my mother said. 'He's torn a ligament. And your Grandma's in hospital.'

'How come?'

'She had a thrombosis and they've kept her in because they think she might have another.'

'Oh.'

'Your father's been spending a lot of time at the hospital. We'll both be going again tomorrow at three if you want to come.'

'Maybe,' I said.

I think I really did intend to go. But that night I got so drunk that I overslept and didn't wake up until two in the afternoon the next day. I called my mother to let her know and she just said: 'Not to worry. Come next week.' But I didn't go the next week, or the week after.

Later that month I noticed William watching me as I rang up a bill on the cash register. I raised my eyebrow and he went back to unpacking the boxes of new stock that had just arrived.

'Mind if I take a cig break?' I said to him after the customer had left.

'You can take a lunch break,' he said.

'I had my lunch before I came in.'

'What did you have?'

'Black coffee.'

'I've got some manchego cheese sandwiches in the fridge. You can have them.'

'Thanks, but a cig will do me just fine.'

'A biscuit, then?'

'William! I'm not your pet dog!'

But the next day I caught him staring at me again, this time from behind a pillar as I put another sale though at the desk.

I looked at him and he hid, like a child. I shoved a book into one of the small paper bags and as I did so my engagement ring slid off my finger and rolled off the cash register onto the floor. The customer, a young woman, stooped down to pick it up and handed it back to me.

'Thanks,' I said, slipping the ring back onto my finger and giving William, who had poked his head out from behind the pillar, a hard stare.

When the customer had left William cornered me in the Non-Fiction room.

'You don't eat, do you?' he said.

I felt disappointed and self-conscious. I looked to one side.

'I once knew a man who moved to L.A,' William said, in his usual tangential way. 'He started out on a macrobiotic diet. The diet starts by eating just one bowl of brown rice per day. Then it moves onto other things like tofu, vegetables and fish. But this friend of a friend in L.A. just stuck with the rice, a single bowl every day. He thought it was giving him clarity – and to look at him, well, I have to admit, he did look *in-the-know*. But he was slowly starving to death. You know, they say starving is one of the most pleasant ways to die. Very gentle. You lose your pain sensors before it gets too bad. But you die nonetheless.'

'I have no intention of dying, William,' I said.

'Try eating more than you drink then.'

'Excuse me?'

'I can smell the drink on you sometimes, Helen. It's not pleasant. It's really not good for you to be living this way. I've been watching you deterior–'

But I didn't let him finish. 'Why don't we take a moment to look around us, William, and see how many of these great works have been inspired by over-eating, compared to those inspired by intoxication of some kind or other... Then we'll reassess your argument. Now. Let me see...'

'Don't you try and pull that one.'

'Pull what one?' I could feel myself getting angry and hot.

'So what great artistic creation are you currently working on, to justify this quest for clarity? Come on – what can the world expect?'

I opened my mouth to speak and closed it again. Then I held my hands up.

'I'm sorry to put you on the spot,' William said. 'I just feel as though I'm watching somebody becoming very ill.'

'You don't have to be so dramatic, William.'

'I beg to differ. I think it is rather dramatic to see someone lose a stone in a matter of weeks.'

'I haven't lost a stone.'

'You look gaunt and tired and run-down. When I gave you that book for your boyfriend–'

'Fiancé.'

'*Fiancé*. I was hoping it would let you know that someone cares about you, that someone was there if you ever needed to talk. But if you're not even going to admit that you've got a problem...'

'I don't have a problem.'

'Well there you go. I'm telling you that you do. If you disagree then there's really nowhere for us to go here.'

I took a deep breath and raised my hands. 'I understand, but I don't really think you've given me much of a chance,' I said. When he didn't reply I picked up my jacket and walked out of the shop.

I half expected William to come after me but he didn't. I cried a little on the walk home. I was upset about losing my job this time, much more upset than I had been about losing the job in the café. I'd liked working for William, I felt as though we had started to get to know one other. And he was right: what was I working on that was of any worth? What *was* my excuse for bumming around, living the way I was living, other than love – and was that enough?

I woke abruptly in the early hours of the next morning, at 3am, when a storm was raging over the estuary and a particularly violent gust of wind had shaken the windowpane. I realised I was alone. Luke hadn't yet come home, so I got up off the futon and went over to the window. As I was looking out over the water, the sound of the front door opening made me jump. 'Luke?' I called.

'Hello, yes it's just me,' he said, shaking off his umbrella and walking towards the window. 'What are you doing still up?'

I thought about telling him about the storm waking me, about the fact I'd lost my job again, but nothing else was as pressing as the fact that he had been out all night. 'Where have you been?' I said sharply, in a voice that was almost my mother's.

'We hit ten megawatts today,' he said. 'There was a bit of a celebration. I brought you some trifle.' He held up a plastic tub filled with pink goo.

'There was trifle?'

'There was *champagne*.'

'Oh.'

'Lily's been asking when you're going to come to Oxford again,' said Luke. 'I think she wants to be our friend.' The word 'our' stuck out like a dirty white flag.

I said: 'I think she wants to be your friend more than she wants to be my friend.'

When he didn't answer I felt a tiny, new feeling – one I couldn't put my finger on at the time but now identify as vertigo. I wondered whether Luke and Lily had been sitting together at the party, whether they had danced, whether they had clinked glasses, whether they had embraced as they said goodbye.

My mother called me again the next day – two phone calls in two days was more than we'd had in a month, so I knew she was worried about me.

'How is everything, Helen?' she asked. I translated 'everything' as meaning 'your relationship' – after all, there wasn't much else going on in my life.

'Fine,' I said, which presumably she translated as 'just okay', because then she said:

'Helen, are you sure you're happy?'

'See, that's it just there, Mum,' I said. 'That's why I can't talk to you about things. You've made up your mind about him before you've heard what I've got to say.'

'Sorry, love,' she said and she sounded genuinely confused. 'I didn't mean it like that.'

'It's okay,' I said, and there was silence for a moment. I wondered whether I was being paranoid after all and then I realised we had never made it past this point before – usually I would have hung up by now – but we were still there, connected to each other, on the silent phone line. 'How's Grandma?' I asked.

'Worse,' said my mother. 'If you do get a chance to get over to the hospital, I know she would really appreciate it. Your father would appreciate it, too.'

'Mum, did Dad ever have any female friends?'

'Female friends?' she said. 'Your father? No!'

'Do you think that's a generational thing?' I said. 'There's a woman who works with Luke, she's called Lily, and she's always giving me a hard time.'

'So this Lily,' said my mother after another moment of silence, 'does she have a boyfriend?'

'No, I don't think so,' I said. 'But I'm sure it's not as simple as that.' I wasn't even convincing myself.

My mother made a harrumphing noise, as though my comment didn't compute. 'Watch her,' she said. 'When it comes to men and women, it's usually *that* simple.'

Rhubarb iced tea

'Are you ready for your palate cleanser?'

I look up and see that my waitress is standing close to me, looking at my face, studying me almost. She looks to the maître d', who is also close by and looking at me, and she nods. I realise I am gripping the tablecloth and I relax back into my seat. Satisfied, the maître d' moves away.

'Rhubarb iced tea,' says my waitress, setting down an espresso cup filled with pink liquid.

I take a sip. The iced tea washes my mouth clean, and I feel refreshed and ready to go on.

* * *

When she called to tell me that my grandmother had died my mother sounded like a lost little girl who had dialled my number by accident. As I hung up the phone I felt a flood of guilt followed by a great and deep longing to be with my parents. Even in my grief I couldn't understand why I wanted to be with them so much when I had spent most of my life trying to avoid them.

'I want you to come with me to my grandmother's funeral on Wednesday,' I said to Luke. I heard the fear in my voice and I suspected Luke did too, and it made me angry to hear myself sound so weak, like I was begging for something – especially when I knew that he would probably refuse anyway.

'Wednesday I'm in Oxford,' he said, without looking up.

'So tell them you need to take compassionate leave.'

I felt that I was ready to blow. Surely he couldn't refuse to meet my family now! A thousand feelings were stirring within me and I knew if Luke continued to be so disagreeable I wouldn't be able to keep a lid on them.

'One of us taking a day off work is enough,' said Luke. 'We've just had a monster gas bill.'

I had been too proud to tell Luke yet that I had lost my job at the bookshop. I had been leaving the house every day as normal and then going straight to the library instead.

'It's important to me that you come,' I said, trying to stay calm, but feeling the writhing mass of emotions rising within me: hatred, panic, fear, irritation – all those hungry old demons.

'It doesn't seem like the right time to meet your family,' he said calmly. 'Now can we talk about something else, please?'

'So when would be a good time? I said. 'Because I've been letting you off the hook a while now.'

'*Letting me off the hook?*'

I suddenly had his full attention. He looked at me and I didn't blink.

'Luke, we're engaged. You have to meet my family. It's as simple as that.'

It felt like the bravest thing I'd ever said but I knew that I was also angry at myself for not having seen my grandmother before she died. I was looking for someone to kick out at, to maul. I was angry, really angry. I tried to hold it together but I knew any moment I might burst. What would come out of me? What would spill over the tiles? Blood? Bile? Or fire, pure fire? And despite all of this I still couldn't quite believe that I felt such anger for the sake of a woman of who had so often sought to make me miserable in one way or another.

'You know I don't do families,' said Luke.

'I know you don't do families. You don't have to regularly do families with me. *I* don't want to regularly do families.' I couldn't control the words coming out of my mouth. It was as though I was speaking in tongues. 'But now and then. Or even just this once.'

'Next time,' he said. 'Now let that be an end to it.'

'What, next time my grandmother dies?'

'No, next time you need a scapegoat.'

Well, I thought, *I'm on the edge now, I might as well jump off*. 'You don't give a fuck about anybody else when it comes down to it, do you?' I said. 'And you've always got your trump card: your dead Dad.'

There was a terrible silence while he answered. 'I think,' he said, 'that you need to take a good, long look at yourself, Helen Burns.' He had never used my full name like that before. 'I support you, *us*, in this flat. I pay the bills, I work all hours, and still you're giving me a hard time.'

I saw that his eyes were almost black with rage. I saw my own face in the half-mirror of the window, ugly with fright.

'What do you want to do with your life?' he said, as though he had nothing to do with me. 'You can't live in my shadow forever. What is it you really want? Come on!'

I had no answer. He shook his head angrily and flew out of the front door. I heard him clattering down the stairs. The fury I felt followed him out of the room, like a fire following its source of oxygen. I went and sat on the futon and cried cold tears of defeat. I was right, he was right, oh, but it was all so wrong.

Hours later, Luke finally returned. I had washed my face and steeled myself with a glass of hot port – but I wasn't going to apologise. Luckily, Luke apologised first.

'I'm sorry,' he said. 'I didn't mean to say all that. I wish I could make it to the funeral, but I can't.'

'It's all right. I'm sorry too.'

I really was. I knew that we had struck each other deep that day, and it had been agony, but there was a beautiful clean feeling of absolution in the aftermath.

Later, as I lay awake next to Luke, I decided that the following week I would start looking for a new job, maybe even start a college course in the evenings, study something vocational.

I didn't drink at all on Thursday night and set my alarm clock for nine o'clock the following morning. When Friday arrived I awoke fresh and ready – and alone, since Luke had gone to Oxford after all. I brushed my teeth and my hair and I put on a black dress, smoothing out the creases against my body. I bought a bottle of straight cola for the train journey.

When I arrived at the church I didn't join my family in the pew but instead watched the ceremony from the back of the hall, beside a statue of St Christopher. I could see the backs of my family's heads and I tried to pick out other people I knew by their hairdos and hats. The man who'd given out the hymnbooks sidled up to me.

'You know, St Christopher was the patron saint of–'

'Of travellers, I know.' I smiled at the man so that he wouldn't think I was being rude.

'Yes he is,' he continued, undeterred. 'That's why you find little statuettes of him on dashboards. But did you know that his sainthood was revoked due to lack of evidence as to his existence?'

I didn't reply. I was too distracted by the back of my father's head, which had drooped lower with the prayers, like an old bloom. Ben and my mother were standing either side of him, holding his elbows. *I should be down there with them*, I thought. *But here I am, watching from afar.* I walked over to a statue of St Dominic and sat on the plinth. Without thinking, I lit a cigarette.

'I'm sorry,' said the man with the hymnbooks, back at my side, 'you're going to have to go outside to smoke that.'

'You mean that's not an ashtray?' I said, nodding to the font.

'That's a font.'

I looked at his face – it was an open, honest face. I wondered whether I could really love a face like that if I really tried.

'Sorry,' I said. 'Churches make me nervous.'

I walked outside and smoked the rest of the cigarette.

At the interment I went up to my family and kissed them in turn. 'Helen,' said my father, in surprise. I held his hand as they lowered the coffin. I looked at Ben's ill-fitting suit, my mother's silver sandals, my father's trim fingernails – and I felt a sudden impulse of love for them all. But nevertheless we were a family, together, quiet at the graveside, thinking the unthinkable: the size of her, the life of her, shut up in that box, descending.

The wake was at my grandmother's house, which felt doubly empty without a dog of some description since Shandy the Third had been taken in by a kindly neighbour. I avoided alcohol as well as food and instead drank cups of tea. When people shook my hand I smiled, although I knew I couldn't be as selfless as my parents were being. They were chatting and mingling with the guests, saying things like *Yes, she was, wasn't she, so full of life*. I instinctively knew they would have much preferred to be somewhere quiet, at home, not speaking, just processing their loss.

When everyone had gone my mother approached me with a sausage roll on a napkin.

'What are you doing with that?' I said to her.

'You're going to eat it.'

'I don't–'

'Just eat a little bit. Then I'll show you something.'

It was pure bribery but I forced a few mouthfuls down. Then my mother and father led my brother and me out through the back door of Grandma's house, down the tangled garden path, and stopped at the padlocked door of the old creosoted shed. Ben and I exchanged a look that said: *Are they crazed with grief?* My mother took a bunch of keys out of her pocket and tried a few in the padlock. On the third try the lock sprang open.

The four of us could barely fit beyond the doorway. Inside the darkened shed, hundreds of red candles were sticking out of the ground at various angles. As my eyes adjusted to the light I saw that there were floppy green leaves at the top of each stick, and then I saw that they weren't candles at all but sticks of rhubarb.

'Rhubarb,' I said.

'That's right,' said my mother. 'Your grandmother was giving it away to all the neighbours.'

'Who'd have thought it.'

The four of us stared at the bright red sticks illuminated by tiny shafts of light through the rotting wood planks of the shed walls. I realised my grandmother had liked to feel important. When she put the knife in it wasn't just to cause destruction so much as it was a way of asserting herself. Being a bitch provided the things she craved: power, fun and freedom. As I stood there I became aware of the roles that my family and I had allowed each other to slip into down the decades, and how as a result we barely knew each other. The unconditional love within families meant they were often the last people to work each other out. It was a little bit like blind faith.

When I got back to Liverpool, Luke was waiting for me at the flat. He had bought a bottle of wine and some chocolates, and he immediately got up to run me a bubble bath.

'You're back early,' I said. I was pleased to see him even though I felt as though I had a slightly different appreciation of our relationship since being at home.

'Yes,' he said. I saw guilt in his eyes and I knew that he was sorry. 'How was the funeral?'

'As good as they get,' I said, smiling. I didn't want him to feel bad any longer. It felt like a good thing that I had gone alone, that I had spent that time with my family, just the four of us.

'That bath should be full.'

'Why don't we both get in?'

He sat between my legs and as I bathed his head I felt a single bubble travel the length of my spine, up towards my neck, where it was lost to the air. I unhooked the bottle of body wash from the shower attachment and squeezed a blob of blue liquid soap into my palm. I was still feeling numb from the day, from the past few days.

'Where's your engagement ring?' Luke asked. I heard a tendril of panic curling out at the end of his sentence.

'In my bag,' I said. 'It keeps falling off.'

'Right.'

After the bath, swaddled in towel turbans and soft jersey pyjamas, we read poetry to each other on the futon and listened to the deep, electrical whirr of the weather outside. Luke told me he loved me over and over, and I felt hopeful that something in him seemed to have shifted between the row and now, and that similarly something had shifted in me since the funeral. I should have told him everything about how I was feeling but something was still making me hold back. I should have told him that when our little world was split, for any reason, even for an instant, it felt as though a chain reaction was spreading out through the cosmos, to the furthest reaches of the universe, to the dust from the dawn of time, and everything in between was spinning off. But instead I turned it all inside. I knew that I wanted to stay with him, even though it was difficult, I really wanted to work things out. I just didn't know whether I was actually happy any more.

99 Revelations

'Your dessert,' says my waitress, presenting me with a cone of ice cream in a neat little vase-like holder. 'We call it Ninety-Nine Revelations.'

The scoop of ice cream is the size of a golf ball. There is a thin chocolate flake poking out at a jaunty angle and the ice cream is covered in a bright pink sauce. I look around the restaurant. No one else has such a dessert. In fact, no one is eating anything I have eaten. Stranger still, no one is eating anything that anyone at another table is eating. How can a chef make an individual selection of dishes for every group of diners? It's preposterous. I stand up. I want some answers. The maître d' looks over, concerned.

I look down and notice that a drip of ice cream has fallen from my cornet and has landed on the red cloth, staying there, pert and perfect, wasted. I sit back down and pick up the dainty silver teaspoon.

The ice cream is made with clotted cream. It turns to liquid in the heat of my mouth, dissolving on my tongue. I snap off a piece of the wafer cone. It is saltier than I expected. The sauce is cherry. Rarer than raspberry, and deeper. It tastes of childhood. Of promises broken.

* * *

'I lost my job at the book shop,' I said to Luke a few weeks after my grandmother's funeral. I was sitting on the futon, kicking the big brass orrery with my foot to make it move – so that I might at least rule that small, perfect world. I had decided that my next job had to be something I chose to do, and found myself, rather than just fell into, and I felt proud of myself for making this decision.

'How come?' asked Luke softly, walking over and stilling the orrery with his hand.

I told him what William had said. When I had finished recounting the story I kicked the orrery again, causing it to spin wildly.

'Hey,' said Luke softly. 'The man leads an insular little life. You gave him something to think about, that's all.'

'But don't *I* lead an insular little life, too?'

'Well, why don't you see this as a positive thing?' said Luke. 'The chance to start doing what you really want to do.'

'I've made an appointment at the job centre next Wednesday,' I said, without admitting the fundamental flaw in my plan: I still had no idea *what* it was I wanted to do. Still, I felt as though I was doing something pro-active for once.

'Good for you,' said Luke.

I walked over to him and pressed my face into his shoulder and he leaned down and kissed my neck. I looked over to our reflection in the darkening window and I saw myself being kissed by the man who *got me*, really got me, and I grinned.

I spent the next couple of months making plans and enquiries as I weighed up all my options. I had good language skills but I didn't want to do anything too interactive. I thought something in the city centre would suit me, something involving research, or cataloguing information. Maybe working in a library, or for the council? *Sooner or later the right thing will come up*, I told myself. It didn't have to be a fully formed vocation, it just had to be a start: a step in the right direction while I worked out what it was I wanted to do.

Early evening. I remember the smell of spring slipping through the open window – the world outside suddenly fecund. Luke and I had been for a walk along the docks, the tassels on his houndstooth scarf tickling my shoulder. We had stopped for a drink at a waterside bar, smoked a packet of ten between us. He had smoothed my hair off my forehead and kissed my closed eyelids once, and then twice. It felt as though we were closer that we had ever been. Luke had been asking questions about how my family were doing and he had been supportive when I ordered a couple of college prospectuses that day. We had got back from our walk and cooked pasta, followed by a punnet of cherries – a simple, fast, happy dinner for two people in love with much to do and so much to talk about. He had fed the pigeons our leftovers and then had set about the washing up, and he was singing at the sink. When a fax started to come out of the machine, I said 'I'll get it' because I was closer as I sat reading on the futon.

The cover sheet emerged: FROM LILY. 'It's from Lily,' I shouted and he stopped singing. Turned off the tap. Dried his hands. Quickly, too quickly.

The next page began to chug out from the machine. It was a mottled image, swimming with blacks and whites and greys, making barely distinguishable shapes.

'I think it's a telescope image or something,' I said, as he made his way over to the machine.

Then I read the writing printed across the top: the previous day's date, and the word COLLIER, Lily's surname.

When the image was fully revealed, it looked like a negative photograph, except it was too fuzzy for that. There was a large, light patch in the centre that looked like a little frozen prawn, curled round on itself, alone in a black sea.

'No,' said Luke, his face blank, his voice emotionless.

'Is that an *ultrasound* image?' I said.

'No,' said Luke again but it wasn't in answer to my question.

'It *is*,' I said. 'It's a scan of a foetus. Why would Lily be sending you a scan of a foetus?'

Luke ripped the page from the fax machine and screwed it into a ball. He clenched the ball of paper in his fist.

I looked at him, waiting, waiting, for whatever would come next. For a split-second, infinite possibilities hung in the air between us. I read the look on Luke's face, his trembling hands, his mouth trying desperately to find the words as the possibilities reduced and reduced and reduced and suddenly became one horrible certainty. I covered my hand with my mouth as my entire body threatened to flip inside out. The cosmos shuddered and then collapsed: the baby alive inside Lily was Luke's.

I ran into the bathroom and threw up everything I'd just eaten. Lumps of semi-digested cherry spattered across the toilet bowl. When I came back into the living area, Luke was sitting on the futon, his head in his hands. He raised his head and I saw he was crying. It was the first time I had seen him cry but I felt nothing. My body was freezing cold. It was as though I had chilled myself to ten degrees below zero, because the truth, the reality, was so horrific that if I erupted I was frightened that my anger wouldn't stop.

'I didn't want you to find out like this,' he croaked and threw his eyes around the room.

I wiped my mouth. It all began to make such horrible, perfect sense. The guilt in Luke's eyes when I had returned from the funeral. The way he had been more loving towards me since that day. I felt numb, as though my life wasn't my own, as though I was simply a casual observer. I raised my head and assumed the blankest of looks.

'Save it,' I said, in a voice that wasn't mine.

Luke looked at me. I had seen this expression before, except not on his face – on the faces of other people; more specifically on the faces of actors playing plaintiffs in the docks of courts on TV. It was the look of a condemned man.

I went over to the kitchen area and lit a cigarette on the gas ring of the hob. I inhaled and Luke moved himself round on the futon so that the cupboards of the kitchen were between us. I knew that I should be feeling pain but I just couldn't seem to, instead all I felt was a vague, detached enjoyment in the fact that I had the upper hand in the situation, and Luke was hanging on my every word, my every blink. I blew smoke out hard through my nostrils and the plumes rose either side of my face, like tusks.

'Three months ago, I slept with Lily,' said Luke, from the other side of the cupboards. 'I know I was a complete idiot.'

I still didn't feel anything.

'Was that the only time?'

'No,' he said. 'I slept with her years ago, when I first started at the centre. And then another time when we were in London at a conference.'

Still, nothing.

'The same night you met me?'

'No,' he said, smiling, bewildered as he realised that this was something I had believed for some time. 'I was in London for something else that day.'

So I had been half-right. 'Oh.'

'I don't love her.'

'Well you'd better start.'

My voice remained calm. Really I felt quite calm. I almost wanted to laugh at how little his words were hurting me, and how much they were obviously hurting him – he could barely speak.

'She told me she was pregnant last week,' he said. 'I didn't want it to be true, but I wanted to tell you in my own time.'

The cigarette burned in my hand. It seemed strange that everything could go on. How oxygen could keep fuelling a fire, how the air could go on moving in and out of my lungs, how Luke could keep talking and talking.

'The research facility is transferring in late summer,' he went on. 'Lily's moving to France with the others.'

'You should go too,' I said in the same voice I didn't recognise.

I didn't feel as though I wanted to salvage anything at all. I didn't want to be his friend or a stepmother – none of these things.

'Is that what you think?' he said. 'That I should go?'

I heard absolute despair in his voice, and I looked at him and nodded.

In the lift on the way to the street, descending nine floors, I stood there with my small, hastily packed bag and looked at my expression in the mirror of the lift's interior. I thought about what Luke had told me, about not wanting it to be true, and about the possibility of living that lie. I wondered whether I was glad of those last few happy months together. Whether honesty could actually be a selfish thing, when it was motivated by guilt. Was confessing to infidelity, if that infidelity had already come to an end, something that people did for their own peace of mind, rather than some notion of the general good?

The lift stopped at the ground floor, and I walked out of the block of flats for the last time. I didn't know where I was going. I felt as though I had been exiled from my own life. Stepping outside the building I felt a new sense of reality – as though everything I had experienced before had fallen away behind me in fragments and I knew I simply had to keep walking forward because behind me was nothing but an abyss leading straight to hell.

As I approached the zebra crossing over the dock road I noticed a man who was walking ahead of me. His feet moved in a strange way, inwards slightly and over each other, like a wind-up toy's. I was repulsed and enamoured at the same time, and then I felt an intense embarrassment and I didn't know why. I followed the man over the road and up the main street into town. The man stopped at the foot of a ladder. I stopped a little way behind. A window cleaner was standing at the bottom of the ladder, swinging a wet cloth back and forth, back and forth – higher each time. He was looking at a bucket hooked at the top of the ladder, leaning against the window of a building, and it soon became apparent he was aiming to get the cloth in the bucket. A woman with a pushchair stopped beside me and the window cleaner lost his stroke momentarily to smile at her, and then he started swinging the cloth again, back and forth, back and forth. I looked at the woman and her baby turned and peered out of the pram, like a concerned cherub. The window cleaner finally released the cloth and it flew up and up to the top of the ladder, landing neatly in the bucket, and then we all stared at the bucket, as though it had just burst into flames.

* * *

I was eleven-and-a-half years old when I learned that a betrayal was a special kind of lie.

I was sitting at the dining table, doing my homework. Ben kept asking me to help him with his sums and I pretended to mind but really I was enjoying showing off to him.

'So three sixes are eighteen,' he said, looking at me incredulously.

'Uh-huh.'

He scratched the answer onto square paper. I noticed that he'd started chewing his fingernails down past the midway point, making his fingertips look rubbery and unreal. I turned my attention back to my comprehension exercise. Just then our mother emerged from the kitchen with an uncharacteristically vivacious look on her face.

'Cherry cocktails, kids!'

She was holding two dishwasher-scarred tumblers filled with a puce-coloured liquid. The tumblers were decorated with sparklers, foil cocktail umbrellas, and little green and blue plastic mermaids.

'Wowee!' said Ben.

He closed his exercise book and my mother ceremoniously placed a pink drink in front of him. I looked at her suspiciously. She put a drink down in front of me. From the rim of the tumbler a green plastic mermaid hung stiffly, like the masthead of a ship. Behind the mermaid, the drink slowly swirled. A thin scum of sediment had risen to the surface.

'*Cherry*?' I said.

The sparkler in the tumbler fizzled out into a thin pillar of grey ash and fell onto the table.

'Drink up!' said my mother. I watched Ben drink first and, when he didn't retch, I took a sip.

'Yummy!' said Ben.

But the drink wasn't sweet, it was watery and slightly bitter.

'It's not cherry,' I said. Ben stopped drinking and looked at me, a sheer pink moustache across his top lip.

'It's cherry *flavour*,' said my mother.

'It tastes like medicine,' I said.

Ben looked at my mother, unsure.

'Oh, alright then – it's *worming solution*,' said my mother.

'*Mum*!' said Ben, and he pushed his drink away.

'It's vile,' I said.

'Helen, you have to drink it and that's the end of it. There's threadworms going round school.'

'Oh I'll drink it alright,' I said. 'Now I know what it is I'm dealing with.'

I pulled the tumbler towards me and removed the mermaid and the cocktail umbrella. Then I downed the drink in one long, breathless intake.

Over the course of the next week I exacted my revenge, which was to adjust the bathroom scales by small, almost undetectable increments every day. I came home from school as normal and went to use the bathroom, locked the door and got on my hands and knees to nudge the dial along half a pound. Then I flushed the chain and went down to do my homework at the table with Ben. I waited until five o'clock, which was the time my mother weighed herself, and smiled to myself as I heard her horrified gasp travel through the gap in the bathroom door and down the stairs. On the seventh day, she stormed down the stairs and flung open the dining room door. Ben dropped his pencil in alarm.

'WHO has been fiddling with the scales?' she shrieked, looking at me.

'Not me, Mummy,' Ben said. He looked as though he was about to cry.

I widened my eyes and said nothing. My mother flexed her fingers and stared at my throat.

'You,' she said, 'are a *very difficult girl.*'

Coffee & petits fours

Neither a scrap of cone nor a drop of ice cream remains on my plate when the waitress comes to take it away. I sit back in my chair. I can't feel sorry for myself, I have no right to. It isn't as though I am an innocent victim in the story of my life. I know that I am not innocent, that I have never been.

I start remembering all of the very worst things I have done. I think about my grandmother lying in a hospital bed with no one to hold her hand. I think of Pete sitting opposite me in that Italian restaurant all those years ago, trembling as I toyed with his heart, like it was a soft little dessert on my plate. I realise that I am thoroughly ashamed of myself. I feel tears prick the backs of my eyes and threaten to roll down my face. But what good would that do now for anyone?

'Coffee with petits fours,' says the waitress, placing a miniature cafetiere on the table, along with a plate of four tiny cakes: a ginger biscuit, a peach tartlet, a macaroon, and a madeleine.

I blink to stop the tears. And then I realise that I have seen cakes like these before.

*   *   *

After I left Luke I couldn't bear to leave Liverpool immediately, so I checked into a B&B on the other side of town. It was a dirty, forgotten little place but it was only £16 a night without breakfast, which I didn't want anyway. I went to bed at 8pm and woke at 5am, and when I ran out of white wine I went to the corner shop for more. I felt ragged and lost, a moth without a flame. I tried to avoid eye contact with the B&B owner, who eventually threw me out after the second night even though I was booked in for three.

'Sorry, love, it's just– well, we can't have drugs on the premises,' she said. She was nice enough.

'I don't take drugs,' I said, wringing my thin hands and rubbing my arms. I was itching for a drink. I realised I couldn't look any more like an addict if I'd tried.

'Well whatever it is,' she said, 'we can't have it here.'

I checked into a cheap hotel. I thought I might be less conspicuous there. I was aware of the woman in the next room having sex three times in the space of two hours before it dawned on me that she was a prostitute. The thought of sex sickened me. It was an empty gesture, like drinking, just another way for people to fill a hole. I heard the speed of the woman's transactions, the door open and close, the chest of drawers rattle, the bed thump, the door open and close again. I imagined the scenarios as each man came and went. I couldn't see how sex of that kind, of any kind, could be exciting. I felt the worthlessness, the tragedy, in how quickly the customers threw their clothes back on and exited into the hallway – I imagined them still yanking up their flies as they stepped out onto the street.

I stayed in the hotel for two nights, smoking and drinking and thinking, mulling over everything that had happened, trying to make sense of it all. But I felt as though Luke was everywhere I turned. He was still all around me, a very real presence. I heard his voice in every song on the radio, to the point where I had to turn it off to check that he wasn't standing just outside the door of the room, softly talking. Similarly, as I approached every door, I imagined him standing behind it, sometimes until I was so thoroughly convinced that when I pulled the door open Luke would be on the other side that I would jump, startled, by the empty space. I smoked cigarettes and the smoke from the cigarettes floated around and touched everything in the room except me. It would be a long time before I could touch myself again.

On the third day at the hotel I returned from the off licence to find the manager waiting for me at reception. 'Ms, er, Bovary,' he said.

'Yes?' I said, clutching my bag to my chest.

'I'm afraid the cleaner has reported the smell of cigarette smoke in your room.'

'There's a perfectly good reason for that,' I said, and he looked momentarily relieved, really he was just a man doing his job. 'I've been smoking in it.'

He grimaced. 'This is a no-smoking hotel. We're going to have to ask you to leave and charge you a cleaning bill for the room.'

'Do you mind if I slit my wrists first?' I said. 'It's not really the kind of thing a person wants to do at home...'

I was over-reacting, behaving like a stroppy teenager in front of people I hardly knew. But I felt as though I was so completely alone. I was so unlike every other person in the world and I was convinced that everyone was hell-bent on attacking me. I packed up and left the hotel immediately, and in. the end they didn't charge me for the cleaning. I think they realised it could have been a lot worse if I had chosen to kill myself there and then. But the truth was I couldn't even imagine doing anything as energetic as killing myself, I was so exhausted. I wandered Liverpool for another day, half-drunk and half-hungover.

When you're all cried out, two things will break you: a kind word or the sound of your mother's voice. My pride told me that I shouldn't really answer the phone when it rang.

'Helen?'

'Mum?'

'What's wrong, love?'

I lost it for about ten seconds. Of course, my mother assumed the worst.

'Helen? Have you been *run over*?'

The absurdity of the suggestion brought me to my senses. I wiped my eyes and my nose. I cleared my throat. 'I'd hardly answer the phone if I'd been run over, Mum.'

'Where are you?'

'Liverpool.'

'Are you hurt?'

'Just upset.'

'Is it your fiancé?' I couldn't answer this and she didn't push it. 'Come home, love. Just come home.'

When I arrived at the house in Manchester it was Ben who answered the door. He was up from Loughborough for the weekend. He stood in the doorway holding a packet of coconut macaroons, and he slowly looked me up and down.

'Shit,' he said, 'Gandhi had better legs than you.'

'You know, Ben,' I said, 'it is customary to *host* a thought in your head for a split-second before allowing it to exit your mouth.' He smirked and offered me a biscuit. I shook my head. 'Got a boyfriend yet?' I said.

'Got a few.'

'Come in, love,' said my mother, pushing Ben out of the way and taking my bag. 'Sit down. I've put the kettle on.' I saw her anxious eyes flicking over what was left of me as she emptied out my washing onto the living room floor, sorting it quickly into coded piles: whites, darks, brights, delicates. She was wearing a peach-coloured vest top I hadn't seen before and the nude colour against her skin made her seem naked and vulnerable. I couldn't put my finger on what I was feeling, I had felt so distant from her up until that point. But now it was as if I could see her from the outside, as a person operating in the world, rather than just my bossy, diet-obsessed mother. Suddenly, I saw the shape she cut, and it was a good shape, and after all the years of fighting her like a cat at a mirror, I finally saw my mother right the way round. I saw how when the shit hit the fan, she could make worlds turn. It wasn't just crisis management. It was grace.

She left the room and returned, minutes later, handing me a cup of tea and two coconut macaroons on a saucer. She sat down and looked into her own cup of tea as she drank it, pursing her lips in that simian way she had about her when she ate and drank. Somehow the passing of the last two years, and all the shattering events that had taken place – my moving away, my behaviour at family gatherings, my engagement, the death of my grandmother – had ultimately changed nothing. My mother forgave everything in an instant and with so little fuss. I was taken aback.

'What happened?' she said after a minute or so.

'I asked for it,' I said. 'I stuck my head above the parapet.'

'How do you mean, love?'

'Sorry,' I said. 'I'm tired, that's all.'

She showed me to my old bedroom, which had been refurnished beyond all recognition and now had a medieval French theme complete with fleur-de-lys wall stencils. My head had hardly hit the bolster cushion before my mother started talking again.

'Do you need a different pillow, Helen?'

'Your tea's not milky enough, I can tell.'

'That mashed potato isn't from a packet, you know. I mashed it with my own fair hands.'

'Take off your tights and I'll wash those too.'

'Did I tell you that Cathy down the road got divorced? You *do*. Blonde hair. Two sons, Tom and Jake. Goes to the same keep-fit class as me. You know, *Cathy*.'

But even though it was annoying, I was so weary and drained that I passively lay in bed and let myself be talked to and looked after. I stayed for a couple of days and then I borrowed the cash to rent a bedsit in a cheap part of the city, a student area where everyone and everything was so lively that it was easy to play dead. I was shown round the flat by an avuncular Pakistani man who told me lengthy tales of the worst tenants he'd had: a girl who removed all the light bulbs and hung black drapes at the windows so that she could breed spiders, a man who had all-night parties and played drum-and-bass music so loud that teacups came off hooks in neighbouring flats, a family of three that turned out to be a family of thirteen.

'I'll be very well-behaved,' I assured him. 'You'll have to come round and see how nice I make the place.' He never did, but I did work on making the place nice. I bought a new doormat and a wooden toilet seat. I lit vanilla-scented candles. I unpacked my things into the wobbly chest of drawers. I considered buying a clothes rail.

In the initial period after a break-up there is much to do. The logistics of moving, sourcing an income, recovering a social life – all of these are very good ways of occupying your attention, of taking you away from the truth. Then, when everything settles, when it all goes quiet, that's when the real heartbreak begins. When the decorating was done, it hit me. I couldn't bear to unpack the remaining bin bags. It all suddenly seemed very futile.

Still, I knew I had to start earning some money to make the rent, so I signed up with a temping agency. They assigned me to various businesses for weeks at a time. It was basic administrative work – typing, filing, stuffing envelopes – and I kept my head down and my hands busy. I moved from company to company, a nameless, faceless drone. When I heard the permanent employees bitching, I didn't get involved.

'That's got to be the best thing about being a temp,' a young clerk said to me as I filled my plastic cup at the watercooler, 'you get to avoid the office politics.'

I smiled but didn't say anything. The truth was, I couldn't bear the daily chitchat, the emotional shipping news, the *How are you*? It wasn't the office politics that killed me so much as the small talk.

'The thing I've noticed about you,' said the boss of one company, a woman in her late thirties with a photo of a baby in a ballpool on her desk, 'is that you don't have an agenda. Most of them out there,' she motioned beyond her open office door, 'have their own agenda.'

My mother called every lunchtime to check on me. I always lied and told her that I was fine. 'I'm fine,' I said in my most fine voice. When really I was bone-sad. Bone-sad, lost, and fucked six ways from Sunday. But *fine*. I was coping, working, functioning, but then whenever I felt pain of any kind – a hangover, say, or someone being rude to me in a shop – I was reminded of the fact that I was operating on a very sheer level of pain. I was reminded of the feeling of extreme isolation I had felt as a child. A kind of grief is the best way I can describe it, as though I was frozen with effort.

At weekends I barely left the bedsit as I drank so much I couldn't walk. Strong white wine was the fastest way to oblivion for me. I sat all night on the scratchy sofa and called to the empty darkness, thinking about Luke and Lily. I thought about her belly swelling under the continental skies. I thought of her appealing to the heavens, and the heavens answering back, while I sat in a broken chariot with all my devastated fairytales coming back to haunt me. I was mute, immobile. It was the thought of the life inside Lily that killed me, not only because it was a symbol of love and love had betrayed me, but because my insides felt uninhabitable, even to myself.

I travelled around on buses and every window I looked through, every house I saw – I imagined a different life for myself, a parallel life where things had worked out differently. *I could live there*, I thought, staring into a compact little council house with net curtains or a listed suburban semi with an antique doorknocker, *I could live there, or there, or there – anywhere but here*. I was up and down, up and down, moving from philosophical to furious in a single morning.

I was polite at work but I wasn't interested in making friends. And who would have wanted a friend like me? A girl with a brand on her palm, afflicted with that fatal flaw: the homesickness of the heartbroken. Even the simple dance of avoidance with strangers on the street had me in torment – when they stepped the same way as me again and again, instead of avoiding me, I felt surplus, in the way, unnecessary. As though the world would work more efficiently without me.

Six months or so after Luke and I had split, and a few temping jobs down the line, I started working as a secretary to the editor at a local newspaper, which had offices in Manchester city centre. I enjoyed travelling in and out of the city every day, and the editor was always saying how pleased he was with my work. I was impressed by how hardworking and committed the journalists were. They worked long hours with few breaks but it didn't seem like drudgery. There was something driving them all on – a nose for a story, that bloodlust. I was intrigued.

When Keith offered me the job of restaurant critic I quickly found a new sense of purpose in research. It was the best method of distraction I had found yet and it was strangely energising. I had good study skills from school and spent hours reading cookery books and the recipe pages of the Sunday supplements. I watched TV cookery show after TV cookery show. I bought every weird-looking vegetable I could get my hands on, every herb, every spice. I became gradually able to detect fine details: cooking methods, cuts of meat, seasoning combinations. I soon built up a portfolio, and I pitched myself around as a freelancer. I fired out article after article from my soggy little bedsit, writing anything and everything for whoever would hire me, often working for free. Food reviewing became my own little kingdom, and it was mine alone. It was nothing to do with Luke, nothing to do with my family. It was something I could do and do well. I felt as though I had a secret again.

I developed a regular circuit around the local park. I enjoyed those walks – the mysterious light of the woods, the roguish squirrels, the chubby-cheeked ducks, the blackbirds shuttle-running over grass, the bees pollinating flowers. It was reassuring that the natural world worked so efficiently while I was safe, writing, in my own little corner of it. I would start by the car park and head down past the golf course, veer round the café and then the meadows with the horses and the horse chestnuts, circumnavigating the boating lake and back round to the cycle racetrack. I walked every Friday night before I went home to drink and I came to appreciate subtle changes in the landscape as the world turned on its axis. The way the light altered with the seasons as the planet made its orbit around the sun. How the birds and insects adapted to the shift of the gloaming – that magical time between day and night when it sounded like chaos in the trees but, if I listened carefully, I could hear each and every bird sing its own song.

Months passed and then, one Friday evening as I was walking my usual route, I saw a girl sitting on the grass verge by the lake, a man at her side. There was something that just didn't look right about the scene. I held back, keeping my head down, but as I got closer, I saw that she was trying to get up. They both looked in my direction and then the man waved. I was in two minds, but then – *What the hell*. I waved back. They beckoned. She was resting on one arm, pointing at her leg and calling. He started jogging over to me and I walked to meet him.

'Ho there!' he said.

'Hello.'

'She fell,' he said, gesturing behind him, and we ran back to where the girl was sitting.

'I think I've broken myself,' said the girl when we reached her. She was clutching her leg at the knee and there were patches of damp from the grass on her jeans but she was smiling. Her expression was steady and peaceful, her smile steadily glowing in the wan evening.

'Oh dear,' I said.

'Do you have a mobile phone we could borrow?' the man said.

'Not with me, I'm afraid.' I patted my pockets. 'But do you think you can walk? Can I help you to your car?'

'We came on the bus,' she said, 'and I weigh eleven stone. So a whippet like you has no chance. But thanks.'

'No problem.' And then, before I'd really thought about it, I said: 'I could wait with you, if you like, while you –' I looked at the man, 'go to get help?'

They looked at each other. She smiled. Looked back at me. 'Thanks. That would be great. If you're sure you don't mind?' She gritted her teeth at a sudden pain in her leg, then recovered herself. 'I didn't mean to disturb you.'

'I'm pretty disturbed already.' I grinned and she grinned back.

Kate. My first proper friend, and proper she was – *is*. When I sat down next to her I didn't imagine I could ever really love anyone again, but as we got talking, I realised I could. Kate told me that she worked as an editor at small academic publishing house in Manchester, and we talked about the books we'd read. Now and then she gripped her leg and grimaced and I'd ask her if she was okay and she'd say *Yep, yep, it's passing, there it goes*. I could see that she was tough. She was also nice at the same time, not to mention curious – I sensed she was open to suggestions, to other opinions, to the world at large. 'So what do you do with yourself?' she said.

'I review restaurants.'

'Cool.'

'Yeah,' I said and I realised then that it was quite cool, and I felt proud of myself.

'Where do you live?'

'Fallowfield.'

'On your own?'

'Yes.' I instinctively decided not to reveal anything about the past few years. It seemed far better to blot Luke out from the Book of My Life now, to cover his name with indigo ink, a sea of forgetting.

Kate carefully considered everything I told her. I felt a generosity of spirit emanate from her, something I had never really appreciated before. I knew this was the starting point from which I could return to my life. Slowly, slowly, my soul began to sip the medicine from the spoon.

It was a few weeks later, Kate was still on crutches, and we went to the cinema. That's how I met Pete – and, once more, I fell. Except this time I fell into an ordinary life with an ordinary man and an ordinary job, and sure enough, as the months went by, I thought about Luke less and less. Gradually, I could be introduced to someone with the same first name as him without feeling a pain in my chest. I could read about the new probe to Mars without skipping supper. I could see a waddling toddler grab for furniture without willing it to miss and lose its balance. I could even stop at three drinks and, gradually, I felt as though a curse was lifting.

I had taken to having lunch with my parents every Sunday. It felt like a normal thing to do, reassuring and regular.

'Dad,' I said one Sunday afternoon, 'I'm sorry I didn't go and see Grandma in hospital.'

'Take some flowers to the grave,' said my father. 'That'll do me.'

As the weeks passed I started speaking to Ben regularly on the phone to find out how his degree was going. I grew a herb garden on the windowsill of my bedsit. I grew out my fringe. I also grew to understand that Luke's decision to go to France had been the right one. I accepted that if he had stayed, or if I had gone with him, I would have punished him every day. Without ever using Lily's name directly, I would have fought with his affair behind my words, behind my eyes. I realised that I would not have been able to forgive him, and so our relationship had to end, and that was alright. Only just alright. But just alright was enough. It was all I could manage.

I started to eat more fruit, pulses and yoghurts. Breakfast cereal containing bran. I developed a three-step skincare regime. I took multivitamins with cod liver oil. I saw people standing outside pubs at lunchtime – people who had been there since opening time and would be there until last orders, or until they dropped – and I pitied them.

When the purple pâtisserie box rolled into the newspaper office on the postal room trolley, it was eagle-eyed Keith who spotted it first.

'Cakes from France,' he said. '*Someone*'s letting their new position go to their head...'

'I didn't order them,' I said. 'Here, take them. You'll appreciate them more than me.'

Keith shared the cakes among the features department. I had already removed the letter. I could only presume that Luke had seen one of my reviews online and found the newspaper's postal address via the website. I couldn't understand why he had sent me the box of cakes – there was something so ridiculous about it.

I took the letter into the ladies' toilets and locked myself into a cubicle. My stomach twisted with anger as I ripped open the envelope. The letter was handwritten – Luke's spidery scrawl defaced the bleached parchment. I read it quickly.

He wrote that he wasn't living with Lily but they were on "good terms" and he was trying to be a father to his newborn daughter, Astrid. He said that he wanted to get back in touch. He said that he missed me. He sent all his best. Not his love but his *best*. I was unmoved and I felt pleased with myself that I was unmoved. I screwed the letter into a ball and flushed it down the toilet. I pictured it drifting down the sewers and slowly disintegrating in the sea.

When Pete asked me to move in with him a few months later, I told myself that it made good financial sense. My parents came to see the house that we had bought together and their relief was tangible. We showed them the loft conversion plans, the butler's sink, the sash windows, the Egyptian cotton bedding, the TV attached to the wall.

'Like a painting,' said my father, beaming.

'Funny you should say that,' said Pete, 'because it does have artwork settings.'

'Get away.'

Pete pressed the remote control so that an image of a blossom tree appeared on the television. He pressed it again and the screen became a blazing fire complete with crackling twigs.

'It's nice to see you settling down, Helen,' my mother said.

Even though I didn't really know it, that's precisely what I was doing. *Settling*.

Hard cheese

I feel the need to speak to Kate. I turn on my phone and scroll through my contacts for her number. When I locate it I stand up, shakily at first, my head a punch bowl of many different types of booze. I motion with my phone at the maître d' as I pass – *making a phone call* – and he raises a saintly palm.

I step outside the restaurant and press the green dial key. After a few seconds I hear the flat, regular appeal of the ringtone, and then Kate's familiar voice.

'Helen?'

'Hi.'

'How are you?'

'Fine.'

'*Are* you?'

I bite my thumbnail hard and then pull it out of my mouth. The tip of my thumb is yellow-white. 'No,' I say, 'not really.'

'Where are you?'

'I'm reviewing that new restaurant, Bethel.'

'Is Pete with you?'

'No, I'm here on my own.'

'That's very brave.'

I straighten my back and take a deep breath. Now, I think, is the time to start opening up. I feel as though I want to tell Kate everything.

'Kate,' I say, 'there's something I've never told you.'

'Try me,' says Kate. 'Because there's something I've never told you.'

'Well,' I say, 'there was a time when, I … Well, when I … when –' I swallow. My mouth is dry with the heat of what I am about to say. 'I was … well, that is to say, I imagined myself –'

'I was a lapdancer,' Kate interrupts. 'For two months. In Dublin. I'm not proud of myself but I was only seventeen and I didn't take my knickers off and touch my toes.'

I'm stunned. 'I was … Well,' I said, then I stop and swallow. 'I've not been right lately,' I said.

'I know,' said Kate.

'I think things started to go wrong when Pete proposed on my birthday. It made me start asking myself whether I was really where I wanted to be. I'm nearly thirty now. I should know, shouldn't I?'

Now it's Kate's turn to take a breath.

'Want to know something, Helen? I've never been one hundred per cent convinced by you and Pete. There was always something nagging away at the back of my mind whenever I thought about you two being together forever.'

'Really?' I exclaim, and I wonder whether I am being juvenile after all. The sound of my voice echoes around the canal basin, startling a couple of pigeons on the buildings opposite. 'Well, that's the shocker of the lot.'

My head is suddenly ravaged with the thought of it. Adrian, the house, our friends, our families – everything I have known for five years – cleaved in two.

'You were heartbroken when we met, Helen, weren't you?'

I swallow. 'How do you know that?'

'You had that sick-hungry look about you.'

'I was engaged to someone but he got another woman pregnant. I've never wanted to talk about it.'

'I didn't pry because I got that.'

'I love Pete,' I say, 'I do. But it was different with the man before. I can't explain it.'

225

I start to cry and stop myself.

'So this other bloke,' says Kate. 'Where is he now?'

'Last I heard, he was in France.'

'Are you going to get back in touch with him?'

Now that I can allow myself to, I think about the possibility of Luke. I know that I haven't felt real since he touched me, that my physical presence was defined by his touch, as though my atoms have been scrambling to recombine ever since. But despite all this we weren't ever truly honest with each other, and what good is that? It was selfish of Luke to send me the pâtisserie box, to tell me that he missed me. It demanded something, it was an imposition. And what did he get from me? It seems stupid now, but at the time it had seemed like exactly what he deserved: a piece of hard cheese. I dried a large hunk of Cheddar on my kitchen windowsill for two days, Googled the address of the research centre, then posted the cheese off in a jiffy bag.

I hear James call Kate's name in the background.

'Well, there's a three-seater sofa here with your name on it,' Kate says.

'Thanks, you're a mate.'

'Call me tomorrow.'

'I will,' I say. 'Oh, and Kate.'

'What?'

'Slut.'

I hang up the phone and see that a text message from my mother has arrived. I open it and see that it was sent an hour ago. *Are you home yet? Pete v upset.*

I call my parents' house.

'Mum?'

'Helen?'

'Yes, it's me.'

'Are you at home?'

'No, I'm still out.'

'Have you spoken to Pete?'

'Yes, a little while ago.'

'He's very upset.'

'I know.'

I hear the line crackle as my mother loops the phone cord around her finger. 'We've been worried about you, Helen.'

'Who's we?'

'Me and your dad.'

'Oh.'

'We were worried you were becoming ... sad, you know, like before.'

I swallow hard. 'I'm not sad, Mum,' I say.

'Good.' She is relieved.

'Anyway,' I say, 'I'd better go. I'll call Pete when I'm on my way back to the house. I won't be long now.'

'Bye then, love.'

I press the red button to end the call.

The maître d' holds the door open for me. I thank him and turn my phone off again. When I look up I see that customers are paying their bills and leaving. The restaurant is quiet again. The bartender and waitress are moving at a slower pace. I don't know exactly how long I've been in here but it feels like a lifetime. When I get back to my table, the place setting has been cleared. There is only one thing on the clean tablecloth: a fist-sized lump of flaky cheese.

I blink. There it is still. A piece of cheese. I blink again.

Suddenly, I feel my birthmark spark into life with that old, old feeling. I clench and unclench my fist and the warmth spreads through my limbs, flooding my veins, lighting up my brain. I look at the table. There's just no way – I blink again. No one else could have –

I look over at the porthole in the kitchen door. I have to know.

I leap up and bolt in the direction of the kitchen. As I start to run, I see the maître d' swivel at his lectern and start to run after me. The waitress turns on the other side of the restaurant and begins to run after me, too, but I am too fast for them. I feel as though I am shedding layers as I run. I feel as though I am my true self as I barge through the kitchen door.

When the door swings open I stop dead and clap a hand over my mouth.

The kitchen is empty. There is not a soul in sight. The surfaces shine. The gas rings are flameless. The cooker hoods and dishwashers are silent. The ovens are dark. The pull-down sink sprays are dripless. Stacks of clean crockery gleam in the semi-dark. The racks of pans and rows of knives are all perfectly in place.

On the far side of the kitchen I see the outer door swing shut and, just before it closes, a plume of smoke curls round and then whips out into the night.

The searing heat on my palm reduces to a boil, then a simmer, then a steam, and then my hand feels normal again.

The maître d' and waitress are hot on my heels.

'Madam, you can't come in here,' says the maître d'. His voice is breathy and high-pitched.

'Where's the chef?'

'Chef has gone out for a cigarette.'

'Please take your seat,' says the waitress.

'Yes, please take your seat, madam,' echoes the maître d'. 'We would like to offer you a digestif on the house.'

I nod slowly. I need to calm down, to think carefully and rationally about what has happened. It is the end of the night, that's why the kitchen is scrubbed down. The chef is having a cigarette. The cheese might have been simply misplaced on its way to the garbage. All of this is perfectly plausible. I allow the two of them to lead me, one either side, back through the empty restaurant.

Back at my table, the piece of cheese has been replaced by a bulbous glass of golden liquid. As I take my seat, the heady aroma of the liquid wafts up into my nostrils.

Whisky. I haven't had whisky in a long, long time. I bring the glass up to my face. It's not just any whisky. It's single malt. Old. I inhale and as the particles fill up my head and all my senses.

I see Luke holding his little girl in his arms and rocking her to sleep. I see the smallness of him, his humanity, his sacrifice. I see now that he is no longer the negative centre of his own space, sucking in everything around him.

I see my grandmother sitting at a table in a social club. She is about my age. Her hair is pinned up on top of her head and she is wearing a blouse with shoulder pads in it, the fashion of the day. She is laughing. One of her arms is forward on the table, around a pint of stout, her favourite tipple. Her other arm is around the shoulders of the person next to her. She has the entire club under her spell.

I see my parents on the day they met. My father sloping along the wall by the bus stop, my mother in her cowl neck jumper and her tube socks. Sparks fly between their eyes.

I see Keith out drinking with a woman who isn't his wife. He moves forward to fill her glass, entering the outer circle of the perfume she casts, his hand vibrating with pleasure.

I see Ben on a beach watching a figure ride the crest of a wave, dipping and rising in the foam. I see him blow a kiss towards his love, giving it all, everything he has.

I see Kate in a blunt blonde wig, whirling round a pole, about to escape through the hidden trapdoor in the centre of the stage.

My birthmark tingles as I tip the whisky glass towards my lips. As I do so I hear a voice, calling my name, over and over. *Helen*, it is saying. *Helen, Helen*. It is getting louder.

'*Helen!*'

I move the glass away from my mouth and turn in the direction of the voice.

'Helen!'

It is Pete, over by the door. The maître d' is restraining him. I shake my head and come to my senses.

'She is not Helen, sir,' I hear the maître d' say firmly to Pete. 'And we are closed.'

'Helen!' Pete is looking at the whisky. His eyes are empty as water. 'Don't drink that!'

'Sir, I must ask you to leave,' says the maître d'.

'That's my wife!' The maître d' releases him.

'I'm not his wife,' I say. I put down the glass of whisky. The maître d' takes hold of Pete again.

'Don't drink it, Helen, please!'

'Sir, it is just a whisky...'

'She's missed the last bus. I've come to take her home.'

I look at the glass. I know that it contains more than whisky. It contains a choice. I can see in Pete's face that he knows it too: whether I choose to drink this whisky or not is cosmically significant.

I pick up the whisky and tip the glass from side to side. I don't want to cause Pete any more pain. He is a generous, caring man. He would never hurt me, and I would never need to wonder about him. He is an open box. It would be so easy, right now, to put down this glass and get into the car and go home with him. I could drink a pint of water to help with my hangover and put on my pyjamas and climb into bed and sleep for eight long hours. I could do that for another five years, another fifty. It wouldn't be perfect, because nothing ever was, but Pete's love was something I would always be able to rely on. How could I risk being with someone like Luke again, someone who hurt me so much, who forced me to forget myself?

I feel as though the universe is waiting for my decision. I look from Pete to the whisky, from the whisky to Pete.

Glenmorangie, 25 years old

Peat. Charcoal. An intense smokiness. Stone fruits and dry spices. Resin, fungus, roots, decay. The forest floor. Burnt sticks.

The whisky reveals everything as it fills up my mouth and slips down my throat. I feel its heat enter my bloodstream and travel up to the crown of my head, down to the soles of my feet, along to the palms of my hands.

The Gaelic 'usquebaugh', meaning 'Water of Life', phonetically became 'usky' and then eventually 'whisky', one of the most sensuous words in our language. I take another sip.

Oak decaying to sweet maltiness. Almost chewy. French toast and black tea.

The whisky distillation process is lengthy. The liquid that comes off first is no good. You have to be patient if you're a distiller of whisky. You have to catch it when it is in its prime, before it runs off into nothingness again. I think about how nothing lasts forever, how you have to catch what you can, while you still have time.

I drink the whisky until it is gone, until Pete is gone.

* * *

The last time I saw the devil I was in the bar of Lime Street Station, Liverpool.

It was just after my mother had told me to come home. At that point going home felt like the only thing to do, so I dragged myself and my hastily packed holdall to the station. I squinted up at the black departures board covered with lit-up yellow letters and saw that the next train to Manchester was in three quarters of an hour. Antsy with indecision, I looked around the station. *What to do, what to do.* Did I want a cigarette? I didn't know. A sandwich? Definitely not. Tannoy announcements echoed around the cavernous foyer and the shifting firmament of the departures boards flickered with updates. After standing there and fidgeting for five minutes I eventually decided to have a couple of shots in the bar instead of buying a bottle to drink on the train. That way I would have time to sober up in time for my arrival at my parents' house.

The station bar, The Crossroads, was carpeted and brightly lit. Foggy plastic stands excitedly advertising drinks offers stood in the middle of the little round tables. *Happy Hour, 5-7pm! Buy two glasses of wine and get the whole bottle free!* The chairs were upholstered with the same frayed, dated carpet as the floor. The whole place smelled like a damp dog. There was a single barmaid behind the bar, brushing her teeth at the sink. She stopped brushing when I reached the counter.

'Yesh?' she said with her mouth still full of water and toothpaste. There was a streak of whitish dribble on her chin.

'Which whiskies do you have, please?'

She waved the toothbrush round in the direction of the optics like a game show assistant showing off a range of electrical goods, then she spat in the sink. I strained to make out the labels on the bottles. Bells. The Famous Grouse. Glenfiddich. Then I saw my favourite.

'A large Highland Park, please,' I said. 'No ice.'

She wiped her mouth with the back of her hand and took a brandy glass from the tray fresh out of the dishwasher. She poured whisky into the double metal measuring cup and then tipped it into the glass. Then she placed the glass in front of me. 'Four-sixty.'

I took the glass in my hands. It was still warm from the dishwasher. I handed her a five pound note. 'That's right.' She didn't say thank you. When I had sat down I glanced back over at the bar and saw that she was applying make up, using the back of a CD as a mirror.

I sat staring into my glass, swirling the amber liquid round and round. Every sip warmed me from the inside out. I remembered how much I loved whisky. It was the closest you could get to smoking without actually lighting up, the closest thing to bodily contact without actually being touched.

I finished the whisky and went to the bar to order another. This time I didn't tip. As well as warmth and comfort, the whisky was filling me with something else. It was a growing sense of indignance. The indignant feeling soon developed into one of outrage, and I realised that I was angry, really angry. The rage I had so far managed to suppress was brimming up to the surface. But I wasn't angry at Luke – no, I was angry at someone else: the person who had first led me to believe that there was a better place for me, my own universe, and yet here I was, more alone than I'd ever been. It had all been a trick. A great big cruel trick.

'You!' I said furiously, swirling the whisky and staring deep into the glass. 'This is all *your* fault!'

My birthmark obeyed with a stab of heat, which grew and grew. In the bottom of the glass, beyond the whisky, the face of the devil began to appear, swimming in the oily glass. I slammed the whisky down on the table.

A red finger emerged from the glass followed by a knobby wrist, a slender arm, a scrawny bicep. The rest of his body proved difficult through such a small portal. His torso and head were stretched so forcefully that they became nothing more than a long, thin strip of spaghetti-fied flesh. The last body part to come out was his left leg. When he had fully materialised, he stood towering above me on the table. He was wearing Luke's favourite pair of trousers. I stood up and he stepped down from the table, so that we were facing each other in the bar. My hands flinched as I thought about the unfairness of how I had been left behind while Luke and Lily had gone on to do important things together. Where was the justice in that?

'My soul's my own now.'

I tossed my head and glared at him. I felt as though my anger was seething out of me from several places – my mouth, my eyes, my palm. He bowed his head in acknowledgment. I was glad that he looked dejected. I felt better. There was nothing more to say so, ignoring him, I reached for the whisky on the table and downed the remainder, baring my teeth after I knocked it back. Then I grabbed my holdall and ran in the direction of the platform, leaving him standing there. As I crossed the threshold of the bar I didn't look back but I did hear the sound of a hundred glasses shattering, followed by a girl's voice: 'Fucking dishwasher!'

Rosemary truffles

In the quiet of the deserted restaurant I run my finger around the lip of my empty whisky glass until it emits a high vocal hum. The maître d' appears at my side.

'Will there be anything else, madam?'

'Just the bill, thank you.'

'Right away.'

The waiting staff have gone home. The candles are all snuffed out. The other tables have been reset for tomorrow's lunch service. Over by the door, the till bleats out my bill. I take my purse out of my bag. The maître d' brings over my bill and places it on the table. A piece of white paper is folded in half, held down by three odd-shaped brown cubes.

'Are those truffles?'

'Yes, madam.'

I look up into his prism-filled eyes, the light inside them ricocheting into infinity. 'I don't need to tell you how good this has been.'

'Thank you,' he says.

'I don't normally do this, but I'm actually reviewing,' I say, sliding the bill out from beneath the truffles, 'and I can tell you now that it will be a glowing write-up.'

The maître d' smiles. 'The chef has some time now, if you wanted a word.'

I look towards the kitchen door. The porthole window is blind with darkness. I look back to the maître d'.

'No thank you. I think I have everything I need.'

When I am out in the shadowy street I find myself walking towards the canal. It is a cloudless night and as I walk along the towpath I see the stars trapped in the still water. I pop a truffle into my mouth. The soft cocoa opens and dissolves into warm rosemary – a refined balance of warmth, coolness and resinous herb. I smile slowly as I feel the intense, satisfying naughtiness that the taste of chocolate always brings.

A week later

I sit at the breakfast bar smoothing Adrian's feathers while Pete ladles watercress soup into two bowls.

'You shouldn't have gone to any trouble.'

I haven't seen Pete since the night we broke up. I've been staying on Kate's sofa. I wanted to come round and get my things while he was at work, I thought that would be easier, but he insisted on seeing me, so I said I'd come on his day off.

'It's no trouble,' he said. 'It's just soup.'

Pete hates me, even though this goes against his better nature, and who could blame him? I know that it will take him a long time to forgive me for what I've done and this fact hurts, even though I know that I've done the right thing. Maybe in the future we'll be able to do that polite thing that exes do where we meet for coffee on neutral territory and wish each other all the best. Maybe eventually we can even *mean* it – maybe one day, but not yet.

Pete drizzles truffle oil over the soup.

'Thanks,' I say as he hands me a bowl.

I dip my soup spoon into the grassy green liquid and bring a mouthful up to my lips.

'It's really good,' I say. 'There's some rosemary in there?'

'Yes, a bit.'

'Delicious,' I say, and Pete looks pleased. It's good that we are communicating like this, although I know that despite all my knowledge, food is still a language that I am not fluent in; that I have never really practised.

'So you're all packed up?' Pete says.

'Yes, I think so.'

The boxes in the hire van in the driveway are going into storage – I don't know yet how long for. My immediate necessities are stuffed into an eighty-litre rucksack in the hall.

'Do you know where you're going?'

'Not really.'

I know that this is the last lie I will ever tell Pete. The truth is that I am going straight from the storage unit to the airport because I have a ticket for the three o'clock Air France flight to Vinon-sur-Verdon via Paris. There is nothing positive to be gained from giving Pete this piece of information because it is over between us. I would only be easing my own conscience and that wouldn't be fair.

Pete puts down his spoon. 'I'm not an idiot, you know.'

'I know you're not. I'm sorry, Pete.'

After we have eaten, I say goodbye to Adrian and kiss Pete on the cheek. I hold back the tears because I know that it wouldn't be fair to cry in front of Pete now.

'I'll be in touch,' I say as I climb into the van. 'Let me know when you've spoken to your solicitor.' He nods. I pull my seatbelt across my chest.

I look in the wing mirror as I drive away and see that he is waving but his eyes are shining.

As I wait in the departures lounge at Manchester airport I sip a black coffee and watch the list of destinations creep slowly up the screens. Each name of a place suggests possibility and freedom, but now there is only one destination for me. When the Paris flight is called I make my way to the gate and perch on a chair, shaky with adrenaline, anxious for the waiting to come to an end. I spring up when the gate is open and am one of the first through into the tunnel. Walking down the tunnel I resist the urge to break into a jog. There is not long to go now, but I wish I had rocket boots to get me there faster.

I order a vodka-tonic on the flight, just the one, to calm my nerves. The man next to me orders a gin and we smile at each other as though we are sharing a moment, two strangers having a drink together on a plane. He is in his mid-thirties, thirty-five or thirty-six, the same age as Luke will be now. He is wearing a corduroy suit and has a stack of newspapers on his tray table. One of them is the paper I write for and I wonder whether my review has been printed today, and whether Keith published it verbatim, laden with hyperbole. The man holds up his gin and I hold up my vodka and we gently tap our plastic glasses together and say *Cheers*.

'Business or pleasure?' he says, removing the black stirrer from his glass of clear fizz and placing it on the stack of newspapers.

'Hopefully pleasure, but I'm not sure yet.'

'Isn't that always the way? You can't plan pleasure. It's all about the moment.'

I smile and sip my drink and turn to the window. The man shakes out a newspaper. I watch the clouds skim past the wingtips of the plane and feel as though I am close to some kind of peace, whichever way it goes in France. I know that if it doesn't work out there, if the Luke I find isn't the Luke I want, then I am strong enough to be on my own again.

At Charles de Gaulle I follow the signs for *Connecting Flights*, along the capillaries of escalators and wood-lined walkways, until I reach a small, bright gate at the far end of a terminal. This time the flight is too small to require a boarding tunnel so when the gate is open I walk down a few flights of stairs and across the tarmac to a propeller plane bound for the south.

The flight is short and the seats around me are empty. The other passengers appear to be holidaymakers, they have stowed their straw hats in the overhead compartments and they chatter excitedly about the beaches and restaurants they will be visiting in Provence. I don't order a drink; instead I take sips from the bottle of water in my bag and try to read an article in French in the in-flight magazine.

When we arrive in Vinon I collect my bag from the carousel and step outside the airport to smoke a cigarette. I unfold the map on the back page of my guidebook and scour the place names so that I can plan a route for the last leg of my journey. A man asks me for a light and as I grind the wheel of the lighter with my thumb to make a spark, I ask him how to get to the town where the research centre is based. He asks me whether I am a scientist and I shake my head, *a friend of a scientist*, and he sucks on his cigarette and beckons to the map.

'Stylo?' he says and I shake my head and pat my pockets.

The only pen I can find in my bag is a thick black felt tip. He takes the felt tip, pops off the lid and draws a black circle around the words *St Paul-lez-Durance*.

'Voila, *Cadarache*,' he says, batting his cigarette ash off the map and smudging the line of black pen into a grey halo.

I sit on the bus with my rucksack on the seat next to me. The pretty southern countryside passes in a flurry of cottages, blossom trees and butterflies until we reach the mouth of the Rhône and the dark forests that sprout around the river's source.

The bus driver looks surprised to drop me off here, a young woman with a rucksack. He asks me whether I am a student as he swings the bus into the stop. I shake my head and thank him as I hop off the bus. It is hot, so hot on the roadside and I reach into my bag for some sun cream as the bus pulls away.

I can see the bright yellow buildings of the fusion centre a short distance away. It is set back from the road and surrounded by a high metal fence. I walk along the fence towards the buildings, enjoying the feeling of the sun on my skin. When I reach the entrance gate the two men in the security cabin look at me suspiciously and so I flash them my most charming smile.

'I have an appointment with Mr Smithy,' I say in my best school French and then I realise that he will be a doctor now and so I correct myself. 'Sorry, *Doctor* Smithy.' The men look at each other, nod and disarm the turnstile to let me in.

'You'll need to sign in at reception.'

'Of course. Thank you.'

The tall blocks of the research centre loom larger and larger and I think how incredible it is that these simple-looking buildings can contain such fundamental things: a machine that can replicate the action of the sun, and the only man I have ever truly loved.

The reception is at the end of a thin gravel path next to a car park. The woman on the desk looks up at me and smiles.

I try to sound calm and collected. 'Doctor Smithy?'

'He doesn't work here any more,' says the woman. She speaks slowly.

My heart sinks. Then, without really knowing why, I say: 'Lilith Collier?'

The woman nods and picks up a phone. I hear her say Lily's name and the words *fille* and *Anglaise*. I imagine Lily at the other end of the line, making the necessary deductions, flicking through the possibilities until I remain as the most likely reality. I imagine her face processing the news of my arrival, the spectrum of expressions it will cast and recast – from disbelief to puzzlement to distrust. I sit down and fix my eyes on the swing doors leading to the heart of the facility.

'*You!*' Lily says as she blazes through the doors a few minutes later. She is just as beautiful at fifty-five but her face has more lines, perhaps from smiling at her daughter. 'Did you not hear? He gave up the Sun for you.'

'What do you mean?' I want her to spell it out so that I can savour it.

'He gave up his research,' she says. 'He's just teaching now.'

So Luke had been burned, too. In the aftermath of our break-up I hadn't allowed myself to think of how he might have been affected. The knowledge that he has abandoned his precious work makes me even more determined to find him and discover how else our trajectories might compare.

Lily looks at me suspiciously. I know that she is assessing how I have grown. I know that she is also dying to ask me what I want – even if it means hearing that I intend to steal away the father of her little girl for a while. Then something changes in her and she instinctively holds her left wrist, with a long pale hand.

'Aix-Marseille,' she says. 'The university.'

I wait for a cutting comment, but nothing. It must be so agonising for her to have to bite her tongue. I wonder if she has any kind of inkling of the pain she helped put me through.

'Thanks.'

'Why *are* you here?'

I think for a moment about what to say. 'I've realised that all the balls are still in the air.'

Lily laughs, and I see all her teeth.

I walk back to the road and wait for a bus back to Vinon. It's a long wait until the bus comes, almost an hour, but I have such a sense of purpose that I don't mind at all. I scuff up the dust with my shoes and wonder whether Luke has any idea whatsoever about my being in France, whether some wave of intuition has flown to him ahead of me, whether he still thinks about me every day, or just now and then. On the bus I read the names of the passing villages and wonder how often Luke must have read those very same signs.

As I board the bus for Marseilles at Vinon I ask the driver where I should alight for the university. He asks me whether I am a student and I shake my head. When we reach the stop for the university he calls to me in pidgin English down the bus: 'The English girl not a student, this is you!'

I drag my rucksack down the steps and onto the pavement, where I stand for a while to get my bearings. On either side of the wide city street the intricate front facades of some of France's oldest buildings taper down into paths through perfect green lawns. In the middle of one lawn is an ancient fountain, where seven silver cherubs are posed in a shallow pool, their chubby fingers following jets of purple water. Above the fountain is a sign for the university faculties, one, two and three, down past the fountain and away from the street.

I pick up my backpack and turn my body in the right direction, and then I trek like a pilgrim down the path opposite, past the fountain and through archways and courtyards, my eyes scouring the architecture for signs. I ask a student for directions to the physics department only to learn that the sciences are spread between all three faculties, and it takes me another hour to search them all, until only one lecture hall remains. Inside the hall I try each lecture theatre in turn, listening at each door, not wanting to burst in until I am sure. Eventually I hear Luke's voice ringing out from the far end of the corridor on the top floor and I stop in my tracks. It's a voice I haven't heard for so long and it is unequivocally his, but stronger and deeper; it shakes me to the root of my feet but I keep walking. I sneak in the hall and take a seat on the back row, keeping my head down.

I can't understand everything that Luke is saying in the lecture even though he speaks slowly, perhaps still not fluent himself yet, although I do pick up the word *gravité* once or twice.

I raise my head to look at him, my heart pounding with adrenaline. It strikes me as preposterous that he is there in the world, just a few metres from me, the same man but not the same. I look him up and down and measure him against the person I once knew, once held, once kissed every square centimetre of. His hair is longer, his stomach rounder, his shirt sleeves sliding over his hands as he rummages through his notes and draws diagrams in red, blue and green on the whiteboard. It is strange to see him in different clothes, in shoes I don't know. But there he is. He is still *awesome* to me. I steady myself.

Luke looks at his watch. The wall clock behind him says four fifty-eight. He concludes the lecture, asks whether there are any questions and then thanks the students.

As the theatre begins to clear, a female student makes her way down to the front to ask a question. I see the flirtatious dip of her head, the jiggle of her breasts, the way her blush spreads upwards when he answers. As more girls gather round, I see Luke toss his head and say something grand and dismissive, and the girls laugh as he collects up his papers, and he soaks up their attention as though he needs it, and I see the man there inside that little god of mine.

I stand up. When he sees me he drops his papers as though he has seen a ghost.

'Helen?' he says, and the room is silent apart from the resounding second syllable of my name.

The girls whisper and scatter. I pick up my rucksack and walk down the steps to the front of the theatre.

'What are you doing?'

His mouth makes spitless ticking sounds and I know that I have caught him off-guard, and his evident nervousness gives me confidence. I don't answer, only kiss him, simple and straight on the lips. I want him to wonder a little longer.

'Careful now,' he says, the old look in his eye. 'I'm a recovering egomaniac...'

I feel an ache of desire ricochet inside me, a secret pulse spring back into rhythm. He looks me up and down.

'Are you really here to see me?'

'Yes.'

He smiles but then his brow buckles. 'I sent you a letter. Did you not get it?'

'Yes.'

'I never heard...'

'I flushed it down the toilet.'

He steps backwards and looks down at the floor. 'I see.'

'I wasn't ready.'

He looks me up again and grins, his power returning.

'Like a bolt out of the blue.' I stay exactly where I am as he moves closer. I don't flinch as he touches my arm. 'But for how long?'

'I don't know that yet.'

It is the truth after all. I didn't know what I was going to find.

'Have you eaten today?'

'You know, I'm not sure I have.'

'There's this little place I know...'

'Imagine you,' I say, 'knowing a *little place*.'

He picks up his papers and puts on his jacket. As we walk to the bistro he tells me about his daughter.

'The day she was born, I looked into her eyes and felt the need to call my mother and make that peace.' He shakes his head and laughs. 'Ha!'

'But Astrid doesn't live with you?'

'Three nights a week. The rest of the time I live alone, in a flat by the river. With a balcony.'

'Are you not lonely?'

I am afraid that he will avoid the question, or say that he has a lover, but I need to know, because if I hide behind my pride, I may as well not have lived through the past six years, and those years *have* to mean something now.

'Sometimes.'

'And when you are lonely do you spend time with anyone in particular?'

He laughs but he doesn't look at me. 'Are you joking? There's been no one for me since you.'

He sounds so uncomfortable that it has to be the truth.

'I was living with a man,' I say, and I study his face for traces of jealousy.

'A *man*?' says Luke. 'Not good enough.'

I look away and I hear the wet click of his mouth as he smiles, and I know that he is relieved, too.

The evening is warm, so when we reach the bistro we decide to sit outside, on ageing wicker chairs with tired slats of foam for cushions. The table is set with a plastic serviette dispenser, two stubby glass tumblers and an ashtray. I look at these simple things and I think, *Yes, good, this is all we need.* We both order steak-frites and chocolate torte from the day's menu and a bottle of house wine.

A thousand things reveal the changes in Luke: the way he gently sweeps his fringe away with the back of his hand whenever it slides into his eyes, around which the beginnings of wrinkles are spoking out like sun rays. He makes encouraging hums as I talk. He has lost much of his aloofness; still questioning but not combatting. His shoulders are slightly rounded in his tank top, above the surprising curve of his biceps in his short-sleeved shirt. He looks as though he is taking care of himself, not making so many excuses. He stretches his muscles, sips his wine and smokes at a leisurely pace instead of furiously chaining cigarettes one after the other. He is almost, almost relaxed. When the waiter has finished taking our order, Luke says *Merci beaucoup* and smiles. These atomic actions, these tiny kindnesses, make all the difference.

'Sweetheart,' he says as I fill in the parts he has missed from my new *story-so-far*.

We sit there together, exactly where we are. When our steak-frites arrive I pick up a thin chip and take it towards his lips. He kisses my fingers as he eats it. And there, until darkness falls, we feed each other slowly in the shade.

About the Author

Emma Jane Unsworth's short fiction has been published by Prospect Magazine, Comma, Nightjar Press, Redbeck Press and Channel 4 Books. She has worked as a journalist for many years and currently writes a fortnightly column for the Big Issue in the North. She lives in Manchester with her partner, the musician Guy Garvey.